FATHERS AND SONS

Ivan Sergeivich Turgenev is one of the giants of Russian literature, and this is his greatest novel. Through the philosophy and character of Bazarov, the nihilist, we see the clash of the nobility with the peasants and the rising middle class—conflicts that grew in intensity during the nineteenth century and led to revolution in the second decade of the twentieth century.

The Reader's Supplement to this ENRICHED CLASSICS edition appears in the center insert. It has been prepared under the supervision of an editorial committee directed by Harry Shefter, Professor of English, New York University, and author of many books used extensively for the improvement of skills in the language arts. The contributing editor for this edition was Professor Aaron Traister, New York University. An introduction, written for the original edition of *Fathers and Sons* by Neal Burroughs, has been incorporated into the Reader's Supplement. Grateful acknowledgment is made to the Picture Collection Division of the New York Public Library, which provided much of the illustrative material.

Titles available in the

ENRICHED CLASSICS SERIES

The Adventures of Tom Sawyer • MARK TWAIN
And Then There Were None • AGATHA CHRISTIE
Anne Frank: The Diary of a Young Girl
Billy Budd • HERMAN MELVILLE
The Bridge of San Luis Rey • THORNTON WILDER
Crime and Punishment • FYODOR DOSTOEVSKY
Dr. Jekyll and Mr. Hyde • ROBERT LOUIS STEVENSON
Don Quixote • MIGUEL DE CERVANTES
Fathers and Sons • IVAN TURGENEV
The Good Earth • PEARL S. BUCK
Gulliver's Travels • JONATHAN SWIFT
Heart of Darkness • JOSEPH CONRAD
Jane Eyre • CHARLOTTE BRONTË
Life with Father • CLARENCE DAY
Lost Horizon • JAMES HILTON
Lust for Life • IRVING STONE
The Mayor of Casterbridge • THOMAS HARDY
Oedipus the King • SOPHOCLES
Of Human Bondage • W. SOMERSET MAUGHAM
Pride and Prejudice • JANE AUSTEN
Pygmalion • GEORGE BERNARD SHAW
The Red Badge of Courage • STEPHEN CRANE
The Return of the Native • THOMAS HARDY
The Scarlet Letter • NATHANIEL HAWTHORNE
Silas Marner • GEORGE ELIOT
Vanity Fair • WILLIAM MAKEPEACE THACKERAY
War and Peace • LEV TOLSTOY
Wuthering Heights • EMILY BRONTË

Fathers and Sons

by Ivan Turgenev

Translated from the Russian by
BERNARD ISAACS

Edited by
NEAL BURROUGHS

WASHINGTON SQUARE PRESS ENRICHED CLASSICS
POCKET BOOKS • NEW YORK

FATHERS AND SONS

ENRICHED CLASSICS edition published June, 1972

2nd printing.........................July, 1974

L

Published by

POCKET BOOKS, a division of Simon & Schuster, Inc.,
630 Fifth Avenue, New York, N.Y.

───────────────────────────────

WASHINGTON SQUARE PRESS editions are distributed
in the U.S. by Simon & Schuster, Inc., 630 Fifth Avenue,
New York, N.Y. 10020 and in Canada by Simon & Schuster of Canada, Ltd., Markham, Ontario, Canada.

───────────────────────────────

Standard Book Number: 671-47963-6.

To the memory of

Vissarion Grigorievich Belinsky

1

ON May 20, 1859, a hatless gentleman somewhat over forty years old, wearing a dusty coat and checked trousers, came out on to the doorstep of a little country inn on the X— Highway and inquired of his servant, "Well, Pyotr? No sign of them yet?"

The servant was a plump-faced youth with whitish down on his chin and lackluster eyes. Everything about him, including his pomaded motley-colored hair, the turquoise earring in one ear, and his polite manners, showed him to be a product of the modern progressive generation. The servant condescendingly glanced at the road and answered, "No sign yet, sir."

"No sign?" his master repeated.

"No, sir," the man reiterated.

The gentleman sighed and seated himself on a little bench. Let us introduce him to the reader, while he sits there with legs tucked under him, gazing around meditatively.

His name was Nikolai Petrovich Kirsanov. Within fifteen versts* of the inn he had a good estate of two hundred souls, or—as he preferred to call it, since he had granted his peasants the right of tenure and set up a "farm" of his own—a property of two thousand dessyatins.** His father, a general, who had seen active service in 1812, a coarse half-educated but not ill-natured Russian, had been in harness all his life, commanding

---

* Versta (sing.), a pre-1917 measure of length equal to 0.6629 mile, or 1.067 kilometers.
** Dessyatina (sing.), a measure of surface equal to 2.7 acres.

first a brigade, then a division, and had always lived in the
provinces, where, by virtue of his rank, he had been a person
of importance. Like his brother Pavel, of whom more anon,
Nikolai Petrovich was born in the south of Russia and was
educated at home until the age of fourteen, surrounded by
cheap tutors, swaggering but obsequious adjutants and other
regimental and staff gentlemen. His mother (*née* Kolyazina),
called Agatha as a girl and Agafokleya Kuzminishna Kirsanova
as a general's wife, was one of those "officer ladies" who wear
the breeches in both marital and military affairs; she affected
ornate caps and rustling silk gowns; in church, she was always
first to come up to the cross; she spoke loudly and volubly;
she permitted her children to kiss her hand in the morning
and gave them her blessing at night—in fine, she enjoyed life.
Being the son of a general, Nikolai Petrovich (who was far
from being distinguished for bravery and had even been
dubbed "craven-heart") was to have entered the military
service like his brother Pavel, but he broke a leg the very day
the news of his commission arrived, and after being laid up
for two months, he retained a slight limp for the rest of his
life. His father gave him up in disgust and launched him on a
civil career. As soon as the boy turned eighteen he took him
to St. Petersburg and placed him in the university. At about
that time his brother became an officer of the Guards. The
young men took up quarters together under the distant sur-
veillance of Ilya Kolyazin, a maternal uncle and a high government official. Their father returned to his division and his
wife, and once in a while, sent his sons large quartos of grey
paper scrawled over in a bold clerkish hand, graced at the
bottom with many a flourish and curlycue: "Pyotr Kirsanov,
Major General." Nikolai Petrovich graduated from the university in 1835 *cum laude*, with a master's degree, and the
same year General Kirsanov was placed on the retired list,
following an unfortunate review, and went to live in St. Petersburg with his wife. He had just rented a house in Tavrichesky
Gardens and become a member of the English Club when he
suddenly died of a stroke. Agafokleya Kuzminishna soon
followed him: she could not get used to the loneliness of

metropolitan life—the misery of a retired existence got the better of her. Meanwhile, Nikolai Petrovich had contrived to cause his parents no small chagrin by falling in love with the daughter of his former landlord, Prepolovensky, a man in the civil service. She was a pretty girl of what is called advanced views: she used to read the serious articles in the science columns. He married her as soon as the period of mourning was over following the death of his parents and, quitting the Ministry of Appanages, where he had procured a post through his father's influence, was blissfully happy with his Masha. First they lived in a summer villa near the Forestry Institute, then in a pretty little flat in town with a tidy staircase and a chilly parlor, and finally in the country, where he settled down for good and where a son, Arkady, was shortly born to him. The young couple lived very happily and quietly. They were practically inseparable; they read together, played together on the piano and sang duets. She planted flowers and looked after the poultry; he attended to the affairs of the estate and occasionally went out shooting, while Arkady grew and grew—in the same happy quiet way. Ten years passed like a dream. In 1847 Kirsanov's wife died and the blow all but crushed him. His hair turned grey in a few weeks: he was on the point of going abroad, for the sake of distraction, when the year 1848 intervened. He was obliged to return to the village and, after a rather prolonged period of idleness, devoted himself to improving his estate. In 1855 he took his son to the university in St. Petersburg, where he spent three winters with him, hardly ever going out and trying to make friends with Arkady's young chums. The last winter he had not been able to come—and so we find him in the month of May, 1859, already grey and chubby, with a slight stoop, waiting for his son, who had taken a master's degree as he had once done.

The servant, out of a sense of decorum, or perhaps to escape his master's eye, withdrew to the gateway and lit his pipe. Nikolai Petrovich, his head bent, studied the rickety steps of the porch: an overgrown, mottled chick strutted about on the steps, its big yellow feet pattering loudly; a grimy cat, perched demurely on the banister, watched it with a hostile look. The sun was scorching. From the dim shadows of the passageway came a smell of warm rye bread. Nikolai Petrovich fell into a reverie. "My son . . . a master . . . Arkasha . . ." kept revolving in his mind; he tried to think of something else, but would inevitably come back to the same thoughts. He recalled his dead wife. "She didn't live to see the day!" he whispered sadly. A fat pigeon alighted in the roadway and steered itself toward a puddle near the well to take a drink. Nikolai Petrovich was preoccupied with this scene when his ear caught the sound of approaching wheels.

"They're coming sir, I believe," the servant announced, popping out of the gateway.

Nikolai Petrovich jumped to his feet and started down the road. A tarantass,° drawn by three posting horses abreast, came into view; he caught a glimpse of the blue band of a university cap, the familiar lineaments of a dear face. . . .

"Arkasha! Arkasha!" Kirsanov shouted, breaking into a run and waving his arms. A few moments later his lips were pressed to the beardless, dusty, tanned cheek of the youthful graduate.

° A low four-wheeled road carriage, usually covered.

2

"LET me shake off the dust first, Dad," Arkady
said in a slightly travel-husky but fresh boyish voice, as he
gaily responded to his father's caresses. "I'll get you all
dusty."

"Never mind that, never mind," Nikolai Petrovich kept
repeating with a beatific smile, giving his son's coat collar,
and his own, a couple of slaps. "Let's have a look at you," he
added, stepping back, then hurried toward the inn, interject-
ing all the while, "this way, this way, we'll hurry those horses
up!"

Nikolai Petrovich seemed to be much more excited than
his son, who looked a bit bewildered and nervous. Arkady
checked him.

"I want to introduce to you a good friend of mine, Dad,"
he said. "Bazarov, the one I wrote you about so often. He
has been so kind as to consent to be our guest for a time."

Nikolai Petrovich turned around quickly, and going up to
a tall man in a long traveling coat with tassels who had just
stepped out of the tarantass, he warmly shook the red, un-
gloved hand, which the latter had slowly extended.

"I am delighted," he began, "and grateful to you for your
kind intention of paying us a visit; I hope. . . . May I ask
your name and patronymic?"

"Yevgeny Vasilich," Bazarov answered in a lazy but manly
voice and, turning back the collar of his coat, revealed to
Nikolai Petrovich his whole face. Long and lean, with a broad
forehead, a nose flat at the bridge and tapering towards the
tip, large greenish eyes and sandy drooping whiskers, his face

was enlivened by a calm smile and expressed self-confidence
and intelligence.

"I hope you will not find it dull with us, my dear Yevgeny
Vasilich," Nikolai Petrovich proceeded.

Bazarov's thin lips stirred slightly, but he made no reply
and merely raised his cap. His tawny hair, which was long
and thick, did not conceal the protuberances of his capacious
skull.

"What do you say, Arkady?" Nikolai Petrovich resumed,
turning to his son. "Shall we have the horses harnessed right
away—or would you like to have a rest?"

"We'll have a rest when we get home, Dad. Have the horses
harnessed."

"Very good, very good," his father assented. "Hey, Pyotr,
d'you hear? Look alive, my dear fellow. Hurry up."

Pyotr, being the model servant he was, had not kissed his
young master's hand and had merely bowed to him from a
distance, now disappeared once more through the gateway.

"I have my carriage here, but we can get a relay of three
horses for your tarantass, too," Nikolai Petrovich said in a
bustling manner, while Arkady was drinking water out of an
iron dipper, which the innkeeper's wife had brought him, and
Bazarov lit his pipe and went up to the driver, who was un-
harnessing the horses. "Only the carriage is a two-seater, and
I don't know how your friend. . . ."

"He'll go in the tarantass," Arkady interrupted him in an
undertone. "Don't stand on ceremony with him, please. He's
a wonderful chap, quite simple. You'll see."

Nikolai Petrovich's coachman led the horses out.

"Stir your stumps, Greatbeard!" Bazarov said to the driver
of the stage horses.

"D'you hear that, Mitya!" cried his mate, who was standing by with his hands thrust into the slits of his sheepskin
coat. "Hear what the gentleman called yer? Greatbeard—it's
what you are all right."

Mitya merely shook his head and pulled the reins off the
heated shaft horse.

"Look sharp, my lads, look sharp," Nikolai Petrovich cried. "There will be a tip coming!"

In a few minutes the horses were harnessed. The father and son got into the carriage; Pyotr clambered up on the box; Bazarov jumped into the tarantass, and sank back on the leather cushion, and both carriages rolled away.

3

"WELL, so you've got your degree and have come home at last," Nikolai Petrovich was saying touching Arkady now on the shoulder, now on the knee. "At last!"

"How is Uncle? Is he all right?" asked Arkady, who, despite the genuine, almost childish delight that filled his heart, was eager to turn the conversation from emotional to more matter-of-fact topics.

"He's quite well. He wanted to come with me to meet you, but changed his mind for some reason or other."

"Have you been waiting long?" asked Arkady.

"About five hours, I should say."

"Good old Dad!"

Arkady turned impulsively toward his father and gave him a hearty kiss on the cheek. Nikolai Petrovich laughed softly.

"What a splendid horse I've got for you!" he began. "You wait and see. And your room has been freshly papered."

"Is there a room for Bazarov?"

"We'll find one for him too."

"Please be nice to him, Dad. I can't tell you how I value his friendship."

"Have you known him long?"

"No, not very."

"Ah, I thought I didn't see him last winter. What does he go in for?"

"His chief subject is natural science. But he knows everything. He intends to take his doctor's degree next year."

"Ah! So he's studying medicine," observed Nikolai Petrovich and fell silent. "Pyotr," he said presently, pointing his hand, "aren't those our peasants?"

Pyotr looked in the direction his master was pointing. Several carts drawn by unbridled horses were bowling swiftly along a narrow country lane. In each cart there sat one or at the most two peasants, their sheepskin coats thrown open.

"They are, sir," replied Pyotr.

"Where are they going—to town?"

"I suppose so. To the tavern," he added scornfully, inclining his head towards the coachman, as though calling him to witness. But the latter did not stir; he was a man of the old school and did not accept the modern views.

"I'm having a lot of trouble with the peasants this year," Nikolai Petrovich went on, turning to his son. "They don't pay their quitrent. What's one to do?"

"Are you satisfied with your hired hands?"

"Yes," Nikolai Petrovich muttered. "The trouble is they're being tampered with; they haven't buckled down to the job properly yet; they spoil the harness. They ploughed fairly well, though. I suppose things will come right in the end. But you aren't interested in farming now, are you?"

"It's too bad you haven't got any shade here," Arkady said, leaving the question unanswered.

"I have had a big awning put up over the balcony on the north side," Nikolai Petrovich said. "Now we can dine in the open."

"Won't that be a bit in the bungalow style? But that doesn't matter. My, but the air here is wonderful! How delicious it smells! Really, I don't think it smells so sweet anywhere else in the world! And the sky here, too . . ."

Arkady suddenly broke off, stole a look behind him and said no more.

"Of course, you were born here," Nikolai Petrovich said, "and everything is bound to strike you as remarkable."

"Really, Dad, it makes no difference where a man is born."

"But. . ."

"No, it makes absolutely no difference."

Nikolai Petrovich cast a sidelong look at his son, and the carriage traveled on for half a mile before the conversation was resumed.

"I don't remember whether I wrote you or not," began Nikolai Petrovich, "but your old nurse, Yegorovna, is dead."

"Is that so? Poor old thing! But Prokofich is alive, isn't he?"

"Yes, and not a bit changed. Still the same old grumbler. In fact, you won't find many changes at Maryino."

"You still have the same steward?"

"Well, that's about the only change I have made. I decided not to keep any of the freed serfs in my employ—those I used to have in the household—or at any rate not to give them any jobs of responsibility." (Arkady motioned in Pyotr's direction.) *"Il est libre, en effet,"* Nikolai Petrovich remarked in an undertone. "But then he is only a valet. My new steward is a townsman; he seems to know his business. I am giving him two hundred and fifty rubles a year. But," he added, rubbing his forehead and eyebrows, which with him was always a sign of inward embarrassment, "I told you just now that you would not find any changes at Maryino. . . . That's not quite so. I ought to warn you, though. . ."

For an instant he faltered and then continued in French.

"A strict moralist would find my candor misplaced; but, firstly, the thing can't be concealed, and, secondly, you know I have always had my own ideas about what the relations between a father and a son should be. Still, you have every right to disapprove of me. At my age, you know. . . . In short, this . . . this girl, of whom you have probably heard already. . ."

"Fenichka?" Arkady asked carelessly.

Nikolai Petrovich reddened.

"Please don't speak her name out loud. Well, yes—she is living with me now. I have put her up in the house . . . there were two small rooms there. Of course, all that can be changed."

"Heavens, Dad, what for?"

"Your friend will be staying with us . . . it's rather awkward. . . ."

"As far as Bazarov's concerned, please don't worry. He's above all that."

"What about you though," Nikolai Petrovich continued.

"The little outbuilding is such a poor place—that's the trouble."

"For goodness sake, Dad!" Arkady interposed. "Anybody would think you were apologizing. You ought to be ashamed of yourself!"

"I really ought to be ashamed," Nikolai Petrovich said, turning redder than ever.

"Oh, come, Dad, what nonsense, really!" and Arkady smiled affectionately. "What a thing to be apologizing for!" he thought to himself, and a feeling of indulgent tenderness for his kind, softhearted father, tinged with a sort of secret superiority, filled his heart. "What nonsense," he repeated, involuntarily reveling in a sense of his own development and freedom.

Nikolai Petrovich glanced at him through the fingers of his hand with which he continued to rub his forehead, and felt a pang in his heart. But he instantly pulled himself up.

"This is where our fields start," he said after a long silence.

"And that is our forest in front, I believe?" Arkady said.

"Yes. Only I've sold it. It's coming down this year."

"What made you sell it?"

"I needed money; besides, that land is going to the peasants."

"Who don't pay you quitrent, by the way?"

"That's their lookout; still, they must pay sometime, surely."

"I'm sorry about the forest, though," Arkady said, and began to look around him.

The places through which they were passing could hardly be called picturesque. Field after field stretched away to the horizon, dipping, then rising again; here and there were patches of woods and winding ravines overgrown by low scanty brush, which put one in mind of those depicted on the old-fashioned maps of the time of Catherine the Great. They passed streams with overhanging banks eroded at the base; tiny ponds with rickety dams; and little villages of squat huts under dark roofs half denuded of thatching, and ramshackle little threshing barns with walls of wattled brushwood and gaping doorways opening on deserted threshing floors, and churches, some brick-built with the plaster peeling off in places, others built of wood with lurching crosses and moldering graveyards. Arkady's heart slowly contracted. As luck would have it the peasants they met were all a shabby lot on miserable nags. The roadside willows, with trunks stripped of bark and branches broken, stood like ragged beggars. Gaunt, scraggy, rawboned cows hungrily nibbled the grass growing along the ditches. They looked as though they had just wrenched themselves from the fell clutches of some death-dealing monster, and the dismal sight of these emaciated creatures in the midst of that lovely spring day evoked the pale specter of a cheerless, endless winter with its blizzards, its frosts and its snow. "No," thought Arkady, "this is not a fertile region; it certainly does not impress one as being prosperous or industrious. Things mustn't, they mustn't go on like this. Reforms are essential . . . but how are they to be brought about, how is one to begin?"

Thus Arkady mused . . . and while he mused, spring was coming into its own. Everything around was golden-green. Everything—the trees, the bushes, the grass—throbbed, and stirred, and shone under the warm breath of a soft breeze. Everywhere the larks trilled in gushing rivulets of song; the lapwings emitted their wailing cry as they flapped over the low-lying meadows or flitted noiselessly over the hillocks. The rooks made a pretty showing, strutting darkly among the tender green of the half-grown spring corn; they disappeared in the already whitening rye, their heads alone bobbing up at intervals amidst its misty waves. Arkady gazed long upon the scene, and his thoughts, relaxed, dimmed and faded. He flung off his coat and looked at his father with such a gay boyish glance that the latter gave him another hug.

"We haven't far to go now," Nikolai Petrovich said. "We'll see the house as soon as we get up that hill. We shall make a fine job of life together, Arkady; you'll help me about the farm, if you don't find it dull. We should become close friends, get to know each other better, shouldn't we?"

"Of course," said Arkady. "But what a marvelous day it is!"

"To welcome you, my dear. Yes, it's spring in all its glory. I agree with Pushkin though—you remember that bit from *Eugene Onegin:*

> *How sad to me thy coming is,*
> *Spring, spring, the time of love!*
> *What. . .*

"Arkady!" came Bazarov's voice from the tarantass. "Send me a match; I've nothing to light my pipe with."

Nikolai Petrovich broke off, while Arkady, who had begun to listen to him in some astonishment, though not without sympathy, hastily drew a silver matchbox out of his pocket and sent it to Bazarov by Pyotr.

"D'you want a cigar?" Bazarov cried again.

"I do," answered Arkady.

Pyotr came back with the matchbox and a thick black cigar which Arkady promptly lit, spreading around him such a strong acrid smell of rank tobacco that Nikolai Petrovich, who had never smoked in his life, was obliged to turn his nose away, albeit imperceptibly, so as not to hurt his son's feelings.

A quarter of an hour later both vehicles drew up before the steps of a new wooden house, painted grey, with a roof of red sheet iron. This was Maryino, also known as New Hamlet or, as the peasants called it, Lone Man's Farm.

4

NO crowd of house serfs poured out to the porch to greet the masters; the only one there was a girl of twelve, followed by a lad greatly resembling Pyotr and dressed in a grey livery jacket with white armorial buttons—the servant of Pavel Petrovich Kirsanov. He opened the door of the carriage and unfastened the apron of the tarantass in silence. Nikolai Petrovich, together with his son and Bazarov, entered a dark and almost empty hall, through the door of which they caught a glimpse of a young woman's face, and proceeded into the drawing room furnished in the latest style.

"Well, here we are at home," Nikolai Petrovich said, taking off his cap and tossing back his hair. "Now for supper and a rest."

"Not a bad idea, something to eat," Bazarov said, stretching himself and sinking into a sofa.

"That's right, supper, let's have supper," said Nikolai Petrovich, and for no apparent reason stamped his feet. "Ah, and here's Prokofich."

A man of about sixty entered, white-haired, lean and swarthy, in a brown swallowtail with brass buttons and a pink neckerchief. He grinned, went up and kissed Arkady's hand, then bowed to the guest, retreated to the door and placed his hands behind his back.

"Well, Prokofich, here he is," Nikolai Petrovich began. "He's come at last. Eh? How do you find him?"

"The young master is looking fine, sir," the old man said, and grinned again, only to cover it up promptly by drawing his bushy eyebrows together in a frown. "Do you wish to have the table laid, sir?" he added impressively.

"Yes, yes, please. But don't you want to go to your room first, Yevgeny Vasilich?"

"No, thanks, there's no need to. Just tell them to bring up that old suitcase of mine and these togs here," he added, taking off his traveling coat.

"Very good. Prokofich, take the gentleman's coat." (Prokofich with a kind of puzzled air took Bazarov's "togs" in both hands and, holding them aloft, went out on tiptoe.) "And what about you, Arkady, will you go up to your room for a moment?"

"Yes, I must get cleaned up," Arkady said, making for the door; but at the same moment a man of medium height, dressed in a dark English suit, a fashionable low cravat and patent leather shoes, entered the drawing room. This was Pavel Petrovich Kirsanov. He looked about forty-five; his close-cropped hair shone with a dark luster, like new silver; his face, saturnine but free from wrinkles, had remarkably clear-cut, finely chiseled features, and bore traces of unusual good looks; especially attractive were his clear, dark, almond-shaped eyes. The whole aspect of Arkady's uncle, so refined and well-bred, still retained a youthful shapeliness and that air of aspiring upwards, away from the earth, that usually disappears after a man's twenties.

Pavel Petrovich drew his hand out of his trouser pocket—a beautiful hand with long pink nails, looking all the more beautiful against the snow-white cuff fastened with a single large opal—and extended it to his nephew. After a preliminary handshake in the European manner, he kissed him in the Russian style, or rather brushed his cheek three times with his perfumed moustache and said, "Welcome."

Nikolai Petrovich introduced him to Bazarov, whom Pavel Petrovich greeted with a slight inclination of his supple body and a faint smile, but did not give him his hand, which he restored to his pocket.

"I was beginning to think you weren't coming today," he said in a pleasant voice, rocking on his toes, shrugging his shoulders and revealing beautiful white teeth. "Did anything happen on the way?"

"No, nothing happened," Arkady replied, "we were held

up a bit, that's all. But we're as hungry as wolves now. Tell
Prokofich to hurry up, Dad. I'll be back in a moment."

"Wait a minute, I'm coming with you," Bazarov exclaimed,
starting up from the sofa. The two young men went out.

"Who's that?" Pavel Petrovich asked.

"Arkady's chum, a very clever fellow, he says."

"Is he going to stay with us?"

"Yes."

"What, that hairy fellow?"

"Why, yes."

Pavel Petrovich drummed his finger tips on the table.

"I think Arkady—*s'est dégourdi*," he remarked. "I'm glad
he's come back."

Little was said at supper. Bazarov, especially, uttered few
words, but ate much. Nikolai Petrovich related various inci-
dents from what he called his farmer's life, dwelt on impend-
ing government measures, talked about committees, deputa-
tions, the necessity of introducing machines, and so on. Pavel
Petrovich paced slowly up and down the dining room (he
never had supper), taking an occasional sip from a glass of
red wine and, still more rarely, uttering a remark or rather an
exclamation, such as "Ah! aha! hm!" Arkady recounted several
items of St. Petersburg news, but was conscious of a slight
embarrassment such as usually comes over a young man when
he has just grown out of childhood and returns to a place
where he had always been looked upon as a child. He dragged
his speech out needlessly, avoided the word "Dad" and even
once used "Father" instead—true he mumbled rather than
said it—and with an ostentatious show of ease and freedom
poured himself out and drank much more wine than he really
wanted. Prokofich, his mouth working continuously, did not
take his eyes off him. As soon as supper was over they all
separated.

"Queer fellow, that uncle of yours," Bazarov said to Arkady,
sitting by his bedside in his dressing gown and sucking a short
pipe. "Fancy all that foppery out in the country! And talk
about fingernails—his could be placed on exhibition!"

"Of course, you don't know," answered Arkady, "he was a

society lion in his day. I'll tell you his story some day. He was awfully handsome, and the women were crazy about him."

"Oh, I see. So it's for old times' sake. There's nobody to charm down here though, more's the pity. I kept looking at that marvelous collar of his, stiff as a board, and that clean-shaven chin. Don't you think it's ridiculous, Arkady Niko-laich?"

"Well, I daresay! But he's a good sort, really."

"He's an archaism! But your father's a fine chap. He could do better than read poetry though, and I don't think he knows much about farming—but he's a good old soul."

"My father's a regular brick."

"Did you notice, he seemed a bit nervous?"

Arkady nodded as though he were not nervous himself.

"Funny thing, these romantic old fellows," Bazarov continued. "They work their nervous systems up to a state of excitation and, naturally, the balance is upset. However, good night! There's an English wash-stand in my room, but the door doesn't lock. Still, they should be encouraged—English wash-stands I mean. They stand for progress!"

Bazarov went away, and Arkady gave himself up to a feeling of joy. How sweet it was to fall asleep in your own home, in a familiar bed, under a quilt which fond hands had fashioned, perhaps the hands of his dear nurse—those kind, tender, tireless hands. Arkady thought of Yegorovna and sighed and blessed her. He said no prayer for himself.

Both he and Bazarov soon fell asleep, but there were others in the house who did not go to sleep for quite a while. His son's homecoming had excited Nikolai Petrovich. He went to bed but did not extinguish the candle, and, with his head propped up on his hand, lay thinking long thoughts. His brother sat in his study until well after midnight, in a roomy armchair before the fireplace, in which a coal fire had burnt itself down to smouldering embers. Pavel Petrovich had not undressed; only red Chinese bedroom slippers had replaced the patent leather shoes on his feet. He held in his hands the latest issue of *Galignani's Messenger*, but he was not reading. He stared into the grate where a bluish flame flickered on and off. Heaven knows where his thoughts strayed, but they did not stray into the past alone; his face looked grim and concentrated, unlike that of a man absorbed only in recollections. And in a small back room, sitting on a big chest, in a blue sleeveless jacket with a white kerchief thrown over her dark hair, was a young woman, Fenichka, now listening, now dozing, now glancing at the open door through which she could see a child's cot and hear the regular breathing of a sleeping baby.

5

THE next morning Bazarov woke up before any of the others and went out. "Hm!" he thought, looking around, "a pretty poor place this." When fixing the bounds between his own and his peasants' lands, Nikolai Petrovich had had to set apart four dessyatins of absolutely flat bare land as a site for the new manor house. He had built his house and outbuildings, laid out a garden, dug a pond and sunk two wells. But the saplings did not thrive, there was very little water in the pond, and that in the wells turned out to be brackish. Only one arbor of lilac bushes and acacia had done fairly well; here occasionally tea or dinner was served. It did not take Bazarov more than a few minutes to explore the garden, the cattle shed and the stable and to come upon two small boys, with whom he immediately made friends. He took them along with him to a small swamp, within a mile of the house, to hunt frogs.

"What do you want the frogs for, sir?" one of the boys asked.

"Well, I'll tell you," answered Bazarov, who possessed a peculiar knack of inspiring confidence in the common folk, though he was never ingratiating and treated them off-handedly. "I cut the frog open and have a look to see what's going on inside of him. And as you and I are just the same as frogs, except that we walk on two legs, I'll get to know what's going on in our insides, too."

"What do you want to know that for?"

"So as not to make a mistake if you fall ill, and I have to treat you."

"Why, are you a doctor?"

"Yes."

"Vaska, d'ye hear that, the gentleman says you and me's the same as frogs. Ain't that funny!"

"I'm scared of frogs," observed Vaska, a barefooted boy of seven with a flaxen head, dressed in a grey coat with a stand-up collar.

"What's there to be scared of? They don't bite!"

"Well, into the water with you, philosophers," Bazarov said.

Meanwhile Nikolai Petrovich awoke too and went to see Arkady, whom he found up and dressed. Father and son went out on the terrace under the awning; the samovar was already boiling on a table near the balustrade, among great bunches of lilac. A little girl appeared—the one who had been the first to meet them when they arrived—and said in a shrill voice:

"Fedosya Nikolayevna ain't well and she can't come and she told me to ask you to pour the tea yourself or should she send Dunyasha?"

"That's all right, I'll pour it myself," Nikolai Petrovich put in hurriedly. "What do you want in your tea, Arkady—cream or lemon?"

"Cream," replied Arkady; after a short silence, he asked, "Dad?"

Nikolai Petrovich looked up in some embarrassment.

"What is it?"

Arkady dropped his eyes.

"Excuse me, Dad, if my question strikes you as being out of place," he began. "But your own frankness yesterday seems to call for equal frankness on my part. . . . You won't be angry, will you?"

"Say what you wanted."

"You give me the courage to ask. . . . Isn't the reason Fen . . . Isn't it because of my being here that she doesn't want to come to pour the tea?"

Nikolai Petrovich turned his head away slightly.

"Perhaps," he said presently. "She thinks . . . she's ashamed. . . ."

Arkady raised his eyes quickly to his father's face.

"She has nothing to be ashamed of. In the first place you know what my ideas are on that score," (Arkady relished the words he spoke) "and, secondly, I wouldn't interfere in your way of living and your habits for anything in the world. Besides, I'm sure you couldn't have made an improper choice. If you let her live with you under one roof she must be worthy of it. In any case a son can't be his father's judge, and particularly I, and particularly a father like you, who has never restricted my liberty in any way."

Arkady had started with a tremor in his voice; he felt magnanimous, while at the same time realizing that he was reading his father something in the nature of a lecture. The sound of his own speeches, however, has a strong effect upon a man, and Arkady uttered the last words firmly and even strikingly.

"Thanks, Arkady," Nikolai Petrovich said in a low voice, and his fingers strayed once more to his eyebrows and forehead. "What you say is quite right. Certainly, if the girl was unworthy . . . This is no frivolous whim of mine. It's awkward for me to talk to you about it; but, you understand, she feels shy in your presence, especially on the first day of your coming here."

"If that's so, then I'll go to her myself!" cried Arkady, with a fresh surge of magnanimity, and jumped up from his chair. "I'll make it clear to her that she has no reason to be shy of me."

Nikolai Petrovich also rose to his feet.

"Arkady," he began, "please don't . . . really . . . there is . . . I should have told you that . . ."

But Arkady was no longer listening and ran out. Nikolai Petrovich looked after him and sank back into his chair in confusion. His heart throbbed. Did he at that moment realize how singular his future relations with his son would necessarily become? Did he realize that Arkady would perhaps be showing him greater respect by keeping out of this business? Did he reproach himself for being too weak? It is hard to say. He was experiencing all of these emotions, but merely in the form of sensations, and even these were vague. The flush was still on his face; his heart still palpitated.

There was a sound of hurrying footsteps, and Arkady came onto the terrace.

"We've become acquainted, Father!" he exclaimed with an expression of tender and benign triumph on his face. "Fedosya Nikolayevna is really not quite well today and will come out later. But why didn't you tell me I've got a brother? I'd have kissed him last night, as I did just now."

Nikolai Petrovich wanted to say something—wanted to get up, to open his arms. Arkady flung himself on his neck.

"Hullo! Cuddling again?" they heard the voice of Pavel Petrovich behind them.

Father and son were equally relieved at his entrance at that moment. There are touching situations from which one is, nevertheless, glad to escape.

"Does it surprise you?" Nikolai Petrovich cried gaily. "I've been dreaming of Arkady's homecoming for ages, and I haven't had a really good look at him since he arrived."

"I am not surprised at all," observed Pavel Petrovich. "I wouldn't mind giving him a hug myself."

Arkady went up to his uncle, and again felt the touch of his perfumed moustache on his cheeks. Pavel Petrovich sat down to the table. He wore a smart morning suit of English cut, with a small fez on his head. The fez and a carelessly tied small cravat suggested the untrammeled ways of country life; but the stiff collar of his shirt—a colored one this time, which was the proper apparel for that time of day—propped up the clean-shaven chin as inexorably as ever.

"Where's that new friend of yours?" he asked Arkady.

"He's gone out; he's usually up and about early. The main thing is not to pay any attention to him; he doesn't like ceremony."

"Yes, that's obvious." Pavel Petrovich began, slowly, to butter his bread. "Will he be staying here long?"

"It all depends. He's stopping over on his way to his father's."

"And where does his father live?"

"In our *gubernia,** about eighty versts from here. He has a little estate there. He used to be an army surgeon."

"Tut, tut, tut! And I've been wondering all the time where I'd heard that name—Bazarov! Nikolai, if I am not mistaken, there was a medical chap in our father's division by the name of Bazarov, wasn't there?"

"I think there was."

"Why, of course. So that medical fellow is his father. Hm!" Pavel Petrovich twitched his moustache. "Well, and what about Mr. Bazarov, himself, what is he?" he said slowly.

"What is Bazarov?" Arkady looked amused. "Shall I tell you what he really is, Uncle?"

"Please do, nephew."

"He is a nihilist."

"A what?" Nikolai Petrovich asked, while Pavel Petrovich stopped dead, his knife with a dab of butter on the tip arrested in mid-air.

"He is a nihilist," Arkady repeated.

"A nihilist," Nikolai Petrovich said. "That's from the Latin *nihil*—nothing, as far as I can judge. Does that mean a person who . . . who believes in nothing?"

"Say, 'Who respects nothing,'" put in Pavel Petrovich, applying himself to the butter again.

"Who regards everything critically," Arkady observed.

"Isn't that the same thing?" asked Pavel Petrovich.

"No, it isn't. A nihilist is a person who does not look up to any authorities, who does not accept a single principle on faith, no matter how highly that principle may be esteemed."

"Well, and is that a good thing?" Pavel Petrovich broke in.

"It all depends, Uncle. It may be good for some people and very bad for others."

"I see. Well, this, I see, is not in our line. We are men of the old school—we believe that without principles," (he pronounced the word softly, in the French manner, whereas Arkady clipped the word and accentuated the first syllable)

---

* In Russia, the basic administrative and territorial unit (the gubernatorial) from the early eighteenth century up to the time when district division was introduced after 1917.

"—principles taken on faith, as you put it, one cannot stir a step or draw a breath. *Vous avez changé tout cela*, God grant you good health and a generalship, but we'll be content to look on and admire, *Messieurs les . . .* what do you call them?"

"Nihilists," Arkady said distinctly.

"Yes. We used to have *Hegelists*, now we have nihilists. We shall see how you manage to live in a void, in a vacuum. And now please ring the bell, brother Nikolai Petrovich. It's time for my cocoa."

Nikolai Petrovich rang the bell and called, "Dunyasha!" But instead of Dunyasha, Fenichka herself appeared on the terrace. She was a young woman of about twenty-three, daintily soft and fair-skinned, with dark hair and eyes, child-ishly full red lips and delicate little hands. She wore a neat print dress and a new blue kerchief lay lightly upon her rounded shoulders. She carried a large cup of cocoa and, hav-ing placed it before Pavel Petrovich, stood overcome with bashfulness, the hot blood spread in a deep blush under the delicate skin of her pretty face. She dropped her eyes and stood there by the table, leaning lightly on her finger tips. She seemed to be ashamed of having come, yet looked as though she felt she was within her rights to have done so.

Pavel Petrovich knit his brows sternly, while Nikolai Petro-vich felt embarrassed.

"Good morning, Fenichka," he mumbled.

"Good morning, sir." she answered in a clear but quiet voice, and with a sidelong glance at Arkady, who gave her a friendly smile, she quietly withdrew. She walked with a slightly waddling gait, but even that was becoming to her.

For awhile all was silent on the terrace. Pavel Petrovich sipped his cocoa, then suddenly looked up.

"Here comes Mr. Nihilist," he murmured.

Indeed, Bazarov was striding down the garden, stepping over the flowerbeds. His duck coat and trousers were muddy; a clinging marsh weed was twined round the crown of his old round hat; in his right hand he held a small bag with something alive squirming in it. He quickly approached the terrace and said with a nod, "Good morning, gentlemen; sorry

I'm late for tea; I'll be back in a moment—must fix up a place for these captives."

"What have you got there, leeches?" asked Pavel Petrovich.

"No, frogs."

"Do you eat them or breed them?"

"I use them for experiments," Bazarov said indifferently and went into the house.

"He's going to dissect them," Pavel Petrovich said. "He doesn't believe in principles, but he believes in frogs."

Arkady glanced regretfully at his uncle, and Nikolai Petrovich furtively shrugged his shoulders. Pavel Petrovich perceived that his joke had fallen flat and began to talk about the farm and the new steward, who had recently come to him complaining that Foma, one of the hired laborers, was a "rowdy customer" and had got completely out of hand. "That's the kind of Aesop he is," the steward had said, among other things. "He's earned himself a disgraceful reputation. He'll come to a bad end. He will—you mark my words."

6

BAZAROV reappeared, sat down at the table and began, hurriedly, to drink his tea. The two brothers regarded him in silence, while Arkady's eyes traveled stealthily from uncle to father.

"Did you go far?" Nikolai Petrovich presently asked Bazarov.

"You've got a little swamp here, close to the aspen wood. I flushed five snipe. You can shoot them, Arkady."

"Don't you go in for shooting?"

"No."

"You're studying physics, I understand?" Pavel Petrovich asked in his turn.

"Yes, physics; the natural sciences generally."

"The *Deutschländer* are said to have made considerable progress in this field."

"Yes, the Germans are our teachers in that subject," Bazarov answered casually.

Pavel Petrovich had used the word *Deutschländer* instead of Germans for the sake of irony, but this had passed unnoticed.

"Do you have as high an opinion of the Germans as all that?" inquired Pavel Petrovich with studied suavity. He was beginning to feel a secret irritation. His aristocratic nature was up in arms at Bazarov's sheer insouciance. This son of an army sawbones, far from being diffident, answered bluntly and truculently, and there was something rude, almost insolent, in the tone of his voice:

"Their men of science are a practical lot."

"So they are. Well, I suppose you have no such flattering opinion about Russian scientists, have you?"

"I suppose so."

"That's very praiseworthy selflessness," retorted Pavel Petrovich, drawing himself up erect and throwing his head back. "But Arkady Nikolaich has just been telling us that you recognize no authorities. Don't you believe them?"

"Why should I recognize them? And what am I to believe in? When anyone talks sense, I agree—that's all."

"Do the Germans all talk sense?" Pavel Petrovich murmured, and his face assumed an expression as impassive and detached as though his thoughts had gone woolgathering.

"Not all of them," Bazarov said, stifling a yawn. He was obviously unwilling to continue the word play.

Pavel Petrovich glanced at Arkady as much as to say, "A polite fellow, this friend of yours, I must say."

"For my part," he went on, not without some effort, "I must plead guilty to disliking the Germans. I say nothing of the Russian Germans; we know that type. But I can't even stomach the German Germans. Those of the old days, well— one could put up with them in a pinch; then they had their— well, Schiller, Goethe, you know. . . . My brother, for instance, thinks a lot of them. Now they've all become chemists and materialists. . . ."

"A decent chemist is twenty times more useful than any poet," broke in Bazarov.

"Is that so?" commented Pavel Petrovich with a slight lift of his eyebrows, looking as if he were going to doze off. "You don't believe in art then, I suppose?"

"The Art of Making Money, or No More Piles!" Bazarov said with a sneer.

"So, so. You are having your joke, I see. You repudiate everything then, is that it? All right. Does that mean you believe only in science?"

"I've already told you that I believe in nothing. And what is science, science in general? There are sciences, as there are trades and callings; but science in general does not exist at all."

"Very good, sir. But what about the other conventions, those accepted in human society; do you maintain the same negative attitude there as well?"

"What's this, a cross-examination?" Bazarov said.

Pavel Petrovich paled slightly. Nikolai Petrovich deemed it necessary to intervene.

"We shall discuss this matter more fully with you some day, my dear Yevgeny Vasilich; we shall learn your views and let you know our own. For my part, I'm very glad to know you are studying natural science. I hear that Liebig has made some surprising discoveries in soil fertilization. You might help me in my agricultural pursuits; you might be able to give me some useful advice."

"I am at your service, Nikolai Petrovich; but it's a far cry to Liebig! A person has to learn his *a b c* first before he can begin to read, whereas we haven't set eyes on our alphabet yet."

"Well, you certainly are a nihilist, I see," thought Nikolai Petrovich.

"Still, I hope you won't mind me bothering you, in case of need," he added aloud. "And now, brother, I think it's time for us to be seeing the steward."

Pavel Petrovich stood up.

"Yes," he said, looking at nobody in particular. "It's a sad thing to live five years in the country, as we do, enjoying no intercourse with the great minds of the age! You become a silly ass before you know it. Here you are, trying not to forget what you've been taught, when—lo and behold!—it turns out to be all tommyrot, and you're told that sensible people no longer waste time on such trifles, and that you yourself are an old dunderhead, if you please. Ah, well! The young people are cleverer than we, it seems."

Pavel Petrovich turned slowly on his heel and slowly walked out. Nikolai Petrovich followed him.

"Is he always like that?" Bazarov asked coolly, as soon as the door had closed behind the two brothers.

"Look here, Yevgeny, you handled him rather roughly, you know," Arkady said. "You've insulted him."

"I'm damned if I'm going to humor these rustic aristocrats! It's nothing but conceit, high-handedness and foppery! Why didn't he stay in St. Petersburg, if that's the way he's made? Well, enough of him! I've found a water beetle, a rather rare specimen—*Dytiscus marginatus*—do you know it? I'll show it to you."

"I promised to tell you his story—" began Arkady.

"The beetle's?"

"Come, come, Yevgeny. My uncle's story. You'll see he's not at all the man you think he is. He deserves sympathy rather than sneers."

"I'm not denying it, but what makes you harp on him?"

"One must be fair, Yevgeny."

"What's the implication?"

"No, just listen. . . ."

And Arkady told him his uncle's story. The reader will find it in the next chapter.

7

PAVEL Petrovich Kirsanov received his early education at home, like his younger brother Nikolai, and afterward, in the Corps of Pages. He was extremely handsome from childhood on, and in addition, he was self-confident and had a droll sarcastic sense of humor. He could not fail to please. As soon as he received his officer's commission he began to appear in society. He was made a fuss of, and indulged his every whim, even to the extent of playing the fool and posing—but even this was becoming to him. Women lost their heads over him; men called him a fop and secretly envied him. As has already been said, he shared lodgings with his brother, whom he loved sincerely, though he in no way resembled him. Nikolai Petrovich had a slight limp; his features were small, and pleasing, but somewhat melancholic; his eyes were small and black, his hair soft and thin. He liked to take things easy, but he was fond of reading and shunned society. Pavel Petrovich never spent an evening at home, was famed for his daring and agility (he set the fashion for gymnastics among the society youth), and had not read more than five or six French books. At twenty-eight he was already a captain; a brilliant career was before him. Suddenly everything changed.

At that time a woman used to appear on rare occasions in St. Petersburg society, a Princess R—, whom many still remember. She had a well-bred, respectable (but rather stupid) husband, and no children. She had a way of suddenly going abroad and suddenly returning to Russia and, in general, led a queer life. She had the reputation of being a frivolous coquette who plunged avidly into the whirl of pleasure, danced to exhaustion, and laughed and joked with young men, whom she entertained, before dinner, in her dimly lit drawing room. But at night she would weep and pray, unable to find peace, and she often feverishly paced her room until morning, wringing her hands in anguish, or sat, pale and cold, over a psalmbook. Day would come, and she would be the lady of fashion once more, making her round of calls, laughing, chatting and throwing herself headlong into anything that could afford her the slightest distraction. She had a magnificent figure; her heavy braids were like spun gold and reached below her knees. But no one would have called her beautiful. Her one good feature was her eyes, and not so much the eyes (they were grey, and not large) as their look, which was swift and deep, with an almost devil-may-care defiance, and wistful to the verge of despondency—an enigmatic look. They had a strange light in them, those eyes of hers, even when her tongue was babbling inanities. She dressed exquisitely.

Pavel Petrovich met her at a ball and danced a mazurka with her, in the course of which she did not utter a single sensible word. He fell passionately in love. He was accustomed to easy conquests, and soon attained his object here, too; but the ease of his success did not cool his ardor. On the contrary, he became still more strongly and agonizingly attached to this woman, in whom, even at moments of complete surrender, there still remained something sacrosanct and inaccessible—something no one could reach. What lay hidden in that soul was a mystery to all save God alone. She seemed to be a prey to some occult forces, unfathomable even to herself, that worked their will upon her, and for whose whims her poor mind was no match. Her conduct was a chain of incongruities; the only letters that might have aroused her husband's legitimate suspicions she wrote to a man who was practically a stranger to her.

Her love was freighted with sorrow. She never laughed or joked with the person upon whom her choice had fallen, but she would listen and gaze upon him in perplexity. Sometimes, and for the most part suddenly, this perplexity would give way to chill horror; her face would become deathlike and wild; she would shut herself up in her bedroom, and her maid, putting an ear to the keyhole, would catch the sound of her smothered sobbing.

Time and again, when returning to his rooms after a tender rendezvous, Kirsanov would suffer the bitter pangs of mortification, which wring the heart with a sense of utter failure. "What more do I want?" he would ask himself, and his heart was numb with pain. He once gave her a ring, with a sphinx engraved on the stone.

"What is this?" she asked. "A sphinx?"

"Yes," he replied, "and that sphinx is you."

"Me?" she queried, and slowly gave him that inscrutable look of hers. "That is very flattering, you know!" she added, with faint mockery, while her eyes still held the same odd look.

Pavel Petrovich suffered torment even while Princess R— loved him, but when she cooled towards him—and that happened fairly soon—he nearly went mad. He was distraught with love and jealousy. He gave her no peace and trailed after her everywhere. She grew tired of his importunities and went abroad. Despite the pleadings of his friends and the remonstrances of his superiors, he resigned his commission and followed the Princess. He spent four years abroad, sometimes following her about, at other times intentionally losing sight of her. He felt ashamed of himself, despised his own weakness—but it was no use. Her image, that baffling, almost senseless, but fascinating image, had become too deeply embedded in his heart. At Baden chance threw them together again on the old footing. Never, it seemed, had she loved him so passionately. . . . But a month had hardly elapsed when it was all over. The flame had flared up for the last time, and was then extinguished for ever.

Realizing that separation was inevitable, he wanted at least to remain her friend, as though friendship with such a woman were possible. She gave him the slip at Baden and, henceforth, steadily avoided him.

Kirsanov went back to Russia and tried to resume his former life, but he could not get back into the old groove. He roamed from place to place, like one stricken. He still went out in society, still retained his man-of-the-world habits and could even boast two or three new conquests; but he no longer expected anything from himself or from others, and did nothing. He grew older; his hair turned grey. To sit in the club of an evening, bitterly bored or listlessly arguing with bachelor cronies, had become a necessity for him—and that, as we know, is a bad sign. Of course, nothing was further from his mind than matrimony. Ten years passed in this way—colorless, barren, swift, terribly swift years. Nowhere does time fly so quickly as it does in Russia. (In prison they say, it flies still more quickly.) One day, during dinner at the club, Pavel Petrovich heard of Princess R—'s death. She had died in Paris in a state bordering on insanity. He left the table, and for a long time he paced up and down the club rooms. He came to a stop near the cardplayers and remained standing there as if rooted to the spot. It was no earlier than usual when he went home.

After awhile he received a small parcel containing the ring which he had given the Princess. She had drawn a cross over the sphinx and had asked that he be told that the answer to the riddle was the cross.

This took place at the beginning of 1848, just when Nikolai Petrovich came to St. Petersburg, after the death of his wife. Pavel Petrovich had seen practically nothing of his brother since the latter had settled down in the country. Nikolai Petrovich's marriage had coincided with the early days of Pavel Petrovich's acquaintance with the Princess. After his wanderings abroad, he had gone to his brother's place with the intention of spending a few months there, in enjoyment of his brother's domestic bliss, but he had not been able to stand more than a week of it. The difference in the positions of the two brothers had been too great. In 1848 this difference was less marked: Nikolai Petrovich had lost his wife; Pavel Petrovich had lost his memories. After the death of the Princess, Pavel Petrovich tried hard to banish her from his thoughts. But whereas Nikolai enjoyed the sense of a life well spent, with his son growing up before his eyes, Pavel, on the contrary, was a lonely bachelor, entering upon that dim twilight of life when youth has gone and old age has not yet come, filled with regrets akin to hopes and hopes akin to regrets.

This period of life was more trying to Pavel Petrovich than to other men; in losing his past, he had lost everything.

"I'm not inviting you to Maryino," Nikolai Petrovich had once said to him. (He had given his estate that name in honor of his wife.) "You found it dull there when my dear wife was alive, and now, I am afraid, you'll be bored to death."

"I was silly and restless then," answered Pavel Petrovich. "I have now grown sober, if not wiser. Now, on the contrary, I'd like to stay with you for good, if you don't mind."

By way of reply Nikolai Petrovich embraced him. After this conversation a year and a half passed, however, before Pavel Petrovich carried out his resolve. But, once he was settled in the country, he did not leave it, not even during those three winters which Nikolai Petrovich had spent with his son in St. Petersburg. He took to reading, mostly in English (his whole life in the past had been built on English ways). He seldom saw his neighbors and only went out at election time, when he hardly opened his mouth, except to tease and startle the landed gentry of the old school with his liberal sallies—but he held himself aloof from the younger generation. Both sets considered him proud; but both respected him for his air of distinction and aristocratic manners, for the fame of his conquests, for the exquisite way he dressed, and for the fact that he always stopped in the best room at the best hotels, for the fact that he dined well and had once dined with Wellington at Louis-Philippe's table—for always carrying about with him a real silver dressing case and a portable bathtub—for the wonderful "gentlemanly" scent he used—for his excellent game of whist and the fact that he always lost. Lastly, they respected him for his scrupulous integrity. The ladies considered him a charmingly melancholic person, but he did not cultivate their society. . . .

"So, there you are, Yevgeny," Arkady said, as he finished

his narration. "Now you see how unfairly you judged my uncle! To say nothing of how many times he has helped my father out of difficulties, given him all his money—you may not know it, but the estate is not divided up—yet he is always ready to help anybody, and always takes the part of the peasants. True, when he speaks to them, he grimaces and sniffs Eau de Cologne. . . ."

"To be sure—nerves," Bazarov interposed.

"Perhaps, but his heart's in the right place. He's by no means a fool, either. He's given me no end of good advice . . . especially . . . especially as regards women."

"Aha! Blowing on somebody else's cold water after scalding himself on his own milk. We know all about that!"

"In short," Arkady went on, "he's terribly unhappy, believe me. It's a shame to despise him."

"But who despises him?" Bazarov protested. "I must say, though, that a man who has staked his whole life on the card of a woman's love and who, when that card is trumped, falls to pieces and lets himself go to the dogs—a fellow like that is not a man, not a male. You say he's unhappy—you know best. But all the nonsense hasn't been taken out of him yet. I'm sure he really believes he's a smart fellow just because he reads that rag *Galignani* and saves a muzhik from a flogging once a month."

"But remember the kind of education he's had, and the time he lived in," Arkady said.

"Education?" Bazarov broke in. "Every man must educate himself—like me, for instance. As for the time, why should I be affected by it? Better let it be affected by me. No, my dear chap, that's just sheer lack of discipline and futility. And what, I'd like to know, are these mysterious relations between man and woman? We physiologists know all about these relations. You just study the anatomy of the eye: where's the enigmatic look you talk about? It's all romanticism, piffle, rot. Let's, rather, go and have a look at the beetle."

And they both went off to Bazarov's room, which was already permeated with a peculiar medico-surgical odor, mingled with the smell of cheap tobacco.

8

PAVEL Petrovich did not stay long at his brother's interview with the steward of the estate, a tall skinny man with a sweetish consumptive voice and roguish eyes who replied to all his master's remarks, "Why, certainly, sir, to be sure, sir," and tried to represent all the peasants as drunkards and thieves. The farm, which had recently been remodeled on new lines, creaked like an unoiled cart wheel and cracked like homemade furniture of unseasoned wood. Nikolai Petrovich was not disheartened, but he frequently sighed and brooded. He realized that he could not go on without money, but nearly all his money was gone. Arkady had spoken the truth: Pavel Petrovich had helped his brother out more than once. Very often, when he saw him floundering and racking his brains to find a way out of his difficulties, Pavel Petrovich would walk slowly up to the window, thrust his hands into his pockets, mutter, *"Mais je puis vous donner de l'argent,"* and give him some money. But that day he had none, and so preferred to withdraw. Business worries bored him to death; moreover, he had a constant suspicion that Nikolai Petrovich, for all his zeal and activity, was not handling things the right way, though he could never himself suggest where he erred. "My brother's not practical enough," he would say to himself, "he's being cheated."

Nikolai Petrovich, on the other hand, had a high opinion of his brother's acumen and always sought his advice. "I'm a soft, weak-willed fellow. I've spent all my life in the backwoods," he would say, "whereas you've been around and know people well: you have the eye of an eagle." Pavel Petrovich, by way of reply, would merely turn away, but he did not disabuse his brother's mind.

Leaving Nikolai Petrovich in his study, he went down the passage which separated the front part of the house from the back, stopped deep in thought before a low door, plucked at his moustache and knocked.

"Who's there? Come in," sounded Fenichka's voice.

"It's me," Pavel Petrovich said, opening the door.

Fenichka jumped up from the chair on which she had been sitting with her baby boy. She placed the baby in the arms of a girl, who promptly carried him out of the room, and hastily adjusted her kerchief.

"Pardon me if I have disturbed you," Pavel Petrovich began, without looking at her, "I just wanted to ask you. . . . I believe somebody is going to town today . . . would you order some green tea for me, please."

"Yes, sir," Fenichka answered. "How much do you want?"

"Oh, half a pound will do, I think. You've made a change here, I see," he added with a quick look around, a look which glided over Fenichka's face in passing. "Those curtains," he murmured, seeing she had not understood him.

"Ah, yes, the curtains. Nikolai Petrovich gave them to me—but they have been up a long time."

"Yes, and it's a long time since I've been in your room. It's very nice here now."

"Thanks to Nikolai Petrovich's kindness," Fenichka murmured.

"Are you more comfortable here than in your old room?" Pavel Petrovich inquired politely, without the trace of a smile.

"Oh yes, sir."

"Who is in your old room now?"

"The laundry maids."

"Ah!"

Pavel Petrovich fell silent. "He's going now," Fenichka thought. But he did not go, and she stood before him as if rooted to the spot, nervously fiddling with her fingers.

"What made you send the baby away?" Pavel Petrovich said at length. "I'm fond of children. Let me see him."

Fenichka blushed with confusion and delight. She was afraid of Pavel Petrovich: he hardly ever spoke to her.

"Dunyasha," she cried, "will you bring Mitya in here" (she never used the familiar "thou" to anybody in the house). "No, wait a minute; get him dressed first."

Fenichka started for the door.

"It doesn't matter," observed Pavel Petrovich.

"I won't be long," Fenichka said, and was gone.

Left by himself, Pavel Petrovich made a careful survey of the room. The small, low-ceilinged chamber was very cosy and clean. It smelt of freshly painted floor boards, camomile and melissa. Chairs with lyre-shaped backs were ranged against the walls; they had been purchased by the late general in Poland during the campaign. In one corner a bed stood under a muslin canopy, next to a clamped chest with an arched lid. In the opposite corner, a little image-lamp was burning before a large dark icon representing St. Nicholas: a tiny porcelain egg, suspended by a red ribbon attached to the nimbus, hung down over the saint's breast. Glinting greenly on the windowsills stood jars of last year's preserves, on the carefully tied paper lids of which was inscribed, in Fenichka's own sprawling hand, "*goozberry.*" (Nikolai Petrovich was particularly fond of that preserve.) Suspended from the ceiling by a long cord hung a cage containing a bobtailed siskin which chirped and hopped about incessantly. The cage constantly shook and swayed, and the hemp seeds drooped to the floor with a patter. On the wall between the windows, over a small chest of drawers, hung some poor photographs of Nikolai Petrovich, in various poses, taken by an itinerant photographer; next to them was a bad photograph of Fenichka herself—a sightless face with an unnatural smile looked out of a dark little frame—the rest was simply a smudge. And above Fenichka, General Yermolov (in a Circassian felt cloak) scowled at the Caucasian Mountains looming in the distance from under a silk pincushion, in the shape of a boot, dangling over his eyebrows.

Five minutes went by. There was a rustling and a whispering in the next room. Pavel Petrovich picked up a well-thumbed book from the chest of drawers, an odd volume of Massalsky's *Royal Streltsi,* and turned over several pages. The door opened, and Fenichka came in, with Mitya in her arms. She had dressed him in a little red shirt with an embroidered collar and had combed his hair and wiped his face. He was breathing hard, wriggling his body and waving his little arms the way all healthy babies do; the fresh shirt obviously pleased him: delight was written all over his plump little person. Fenichka had put her hair in order, too, and changed her kerchief, but she could have spared herself the trouble. For what in the world can be more fascinating than a pretty young mother with a healthy baby in her arms?

"What a chubby little fellow," Pavel Petrovich said indulgently, and tickled Mitya's twin chins with the tip of his long fingernail. The child stared at the siskin and began to chuckle.

"It's Uncle," Fenichka said, bending her face down to him and giving him a little shake. Dunyasha quietly placed a lighted pastille on a copper disc on the windowsill.

"How old is he?" asked Pavel Petrovich.

"Six months, going on seven, come the eleventh."

"Won't it be eight, Fedosya Nikolayevna?" Dunyasha put in, timidly.

"No, seven, to be sure!" The baby chuckled again, fixed his eyes on the chest, and suddenly clutched his mother's nose and lips with all five fingers. "Naughty, naughty," Fenichka said, without drawing her face away.

"He looks like my brother," Pavel Petrovich remarked.

"Who else should he look like?" Fenichka thought.

"Yes," Pavel Petrovich went on, as though talking to himself, "a decided resemblance."

He regarded Fenichka attentively, almost sadly.

"It's Uncle," she repeated, this time in a whisper.

"Ah! Pavel! So this is where you are!" Nikolai Petrovich's voice sounded suddenly.

Pavel Petrovich spun around with a frown, but his brother was looking at him with such unfeigned delight and gratitude that he could not help responding with a smile.

"It's a fine little fellow you have," he said and glanced at his watch. "I dropped in about some tea for myself."

And, assuming a matter-of-fact air, Pavel Petrovich immediately left the room.

"Did he come in on his own?" Nikolai Petrovich asked Fenichka.

"Yes. He just knocked and came in."

"Well. . . . And has Arkady been in to see you again?"

"No. Hadn't I better move back to the wing, Nikolai Petrovich?"

"What for?"

"I was thinking it would be best for the time being."

"N-no. . . ." Nikolai Petrovich said hesitatingly, fingering his forehead. "We should have thought of it before. Hullo, dumpling," he said with sudden animation, and going up to the baby, kissed him on the cheek, after which, bending slightly, he put his lips to Fenichka's hand which lay creamily white against the baby's red shirt.

"Nikolai Petrovich! What are you doing?" she faltered. She dropped her eyes, then slowly looked up again. The look in her eyes was charming as she gazed up from under her lowered lids, smiling tenderly and a little foolishly.

Nikolai Petrovich had met Fenichka under the following circumstances. One day some three years before, he had had occasion to spend the night at an inn in a remote provincial town. He had been agreeably impressed by the cleanliness of his room and the freshness of the linen. "The mistress must be a German," he had thought. But she proved to be a Russian, a woman of about fifty, well-spoken and neatly dressed, with a pleasant, intelligent face. He had a talk with her over his tea—she took his fancy.

Nikolai Petrovich had, at that time, just moved into his new house, and, as he did not want to keep serfs about the place, he was on the lookout for hired servants. The landlady of the inn, for her part, complained about the scarcity of travelers and the hard times. He offered her a position as his housekeeper and she accepted. Her husband had died a long time before, leaving her an only daughter, Fenichka. Within a fortnight, Arina Savishna (that was the new housekeeper's name) had arrived with her daughter at Maryino and moved into the small wing of the house. Nikolai Petrovich's choice had proved a happy one. Arina soon had everything in the house shipshape. Fenichka, who was seventeen at the time, was rarely seen and never mentioned: she lived unobtrusively and quietly. On Sundays only, Nikolai Petrovich might catch a glimpse of the delicate profile of her milk-white face in some corner of the parish church. A little over a year passed in this way.

One morning Arina had come into his study and, with her usual low bow, asked whether he could help her daughter, who had got a spark from the stove in her eye. Like all stay-at-homes, Nikolai Petrovich practised domestic doctoring and had even acquired a homoeopathic medicine chest. He ordered the patient to be brought to him at once. On hearing that the master had sent for her, Fenichka was terrified, but went with her mother nevertheless. Nikolai Petrovich drew her to the window and took her head in both his hands. Having carefully examined her inflamed eye, he prescribed a lotion, which he made up himself then and there, and, tearing his handkerchief into strips, showed her how to apply it. Fenichka heard him out and turned to go away. "Kiss the master's hand, silly child," Arina said. Nikolai Petrovich did not hold out his hand, and, thrown into confusion himself, he implanted a kiss on the top of her bent head. Fenichka's eye soon got well, but the impression which she had made on Nikolai Petrovich did not pass so quickly. That pure, sweet, timorously upturned face haunted him; he felt the touch of her soft hair on his palms; saw those innocent, slightly parted lips through which the pearly teeth glistened moistly in the sun. He began to watch her more closely in church and tried to draw her into conversation. At first she had been very shy, and one evening when she met him on a narrow footpath running through a rye field, she had stepped into the tall dense rye, overgrown with wormwood and cornflowers, to avoid meeting him face to face. He had seen her head through the golden lattice work of rye, peeping out at him like some wild little creature, and had called to her kindly:

"Good evening, Fenichka! I don't bite, you know."

"Good evening," she had whispered, without coming out of her hiding place.

Gradually she grew accustomed to him, but was still shy in his presence. Then suddenly her mother, Arina, died of cholera. What was she to do? From her mother, she had inherited a love of order, common sense, and correctness: but she was so young, so lonely, and Nikolai Petrovich was so kind and modest. . . . The rest requires no telling. . . .

"So my brother actually came in to see you?" Nikolai Petrovich asked her. "Just knocked and came in?"

"Yes."

"Well, that's fine. Let me play with Mitya."

And Nikolai Petrovich began tossing him up almost to the ceiling, to the huge delight of the infant and the no little anxiety of the mother who, every time he flew up, reached out her arms to his exposed little feet.

Pavel Petrovich returned to his luxurious study, papered in elegant grey, hung with weapons against a colorful Persian rug, with walnut furniture upholstered in dark green mock velvet, a Renaissance bookcase of old black oak, bronze statuettes on a magnificent desk, and a cosy fireplace. He threw himself on the sofa, his hands clasped behind his head, and lay motionless, gazing at the ceiling with a look almost of despair. Whether to conceal from the very walls what his face betrayed, or for some other reason, he got up, drew the heavy window curtains, and flung himself on the sofa again.

9

THAT day Bazarov, too, made Fenichka's acquaintance. He was strolling about in the garden with Arkady, trying to explain to him why some of the trees, particularly the young oaks, had not taken root.

"You should plant more white poplars and fir trees, and perhaps some limes, and give them some loam. That arbor has done well," he added, "because acacia and lilac are adaptable fellows and don't need much tending. I say! There's somebody in here."

Fenichka, with Dunyasha and Mitya, were sitting in the arbor. Bazarov stopped, and Arkady nodded to Fenichka, as to an old acquaintance.

"Who's that?" Bazarov asked him, when they had passed by. "What a pretty girl!"

"Who?"

"It's plain enough; only one pretty girl was there."

Arkady, not without embarrassment, told him briefly who Fenichka was.

"Aha!" Bazarov said. "Your father knows a good thing when he sees it. I like him, by Jove! He's all there. However, we must get acquainted," he added, and retraced his steps to the arbor.

"Yevgeny!" Arkady cried out in dismay, "for God's sake be careful!"

"Don't you worry," Bazarov said. "We're no greenhorns, we city folk."

Coming up to Fenichka, he took off his cap.

"Allow me to introduce myself," he began, with a polite bow, "Arkady Nikolayevich's chum, and a harmless person."

Fenichka got up from the bench and looked at him in silence.

"What a fine baby!" Bazarov went on. "Don't worry, I haven't got an evil eye. Why are his cheeks so red? Is he cutting his teeth?"

"Yes, sir," Fenichka murmured. "He's cut four teeth already, and now his gums are swollen again."

"Let me have a look . . . don't be afraid, I'm a doctor."

Bazarov took the baby in his arms. To the amazement of both Fenichka and Dunyasha, the baby did not show the slightest resistance or fear.

"I see, I see. . . . Everything's all right. He's going to have a fine set of teeth. If anything happens, let me know. And how do you feel?"

"Quite well, thank God."

"Thank God—that's the great thing. And you?" he added, turning to Dunyasha.

Dunyasha, who was a very proper maid indoors, but a very mischievous one outdoors, merely giggled by way of reply.

"Splendid. Here, take this strapping fellow of yours."

Fenichka took the baby from him.

"How quiet he was in your arms," she murmured.

"All children are quiet with me," Bazarov answered. "A little bird told me the secret."

"Children have a feeling for those who love them," remarked Dunyasha.

"That is so," confirmed Fenichka. "Now Mitya won't go to some people, not for anything."

"Will he go to me?" Arkady said. He had been standing at a distance for awhile, and now joined them.

He held his hands out invitingly, but Mitya threw his head back with a wail, much to Fenichka's distress.

"Next time—when he gets to know me better," Arkady said indulgently, and the friends walked away.

"What's her name did you say?" asked Bazarov.

"Fenichka . . . Fedosya," Arkady said.

"And her patronymic? One must know that, too."

"Nikolayevna."

"*Bene.* What I like about her is that she is not too ashamed of it. I suppose some people would find that reprehensible. But that's nonsense! Why should she be ashamed? She's a mother—well, that makes her right."

"*She's* right enough," observed Arkady, "but my father . . ."

"And he's right, too," Bazarov broke in.

"I shouldn't say so."

"I don't suppose you like the idea of there being another heir in the family?"

"You ought to be ashamed of yourself, thinking me capable of such thoughts," Arkady retorted hotly. "That's not the reason why I consider my father wrong. I believe he should have married her."

"Oho-ho!" Bazarov said calmly. "So that's how magnanimous we are! You still attach importance to marriage. You ought to know better."

The friends walked on a few paces in silence.

"I've looked over your father's place," resumed Bazarov. "The farm cattle are poor, the horses are just nags, the buildings have seen better days, and the hands look like a bunch of downright loafers. As for the steward—he's either a knave or a fool, I can't quite make out which."

"You're very critical today, Yevgeny Vasilich."

"And those goody-goody peasants will cheat your father, as sure as eggs are eggs. You know the saying, 'The Russian muzhik will gobble up God himself.'"

"I begin to agree with my uncle," Arkady said. "You have a downright bad opinion of Russians."

"Nonsense! The one good thing about the Russian is the rotten opinion he has of himself. What really matters is that two and two make four; the rest is all nonsense."

"And is nature nonsense too?" Arkady said, gazing thoughtfully into the distance at the variegated fields which were bathed in the mellow light of the sun, now low in the sky.

"Yes, nature is nonsense too, in the way you understand

it. Nature's not a temple but a workshop, and man is a work-man in it."

The lingering notes of a violoncello drifted across to them from the house. Somebody was playing with feeling, if inex-pertly, Schubert's *Expectations,* and the sweet, silver-toned, melody floated on the air.

"What's that?" Bazarov said in amazement.

"It's my father."

"Your father plays the 'cello?"

"Yes."

"Why, how old is he?"

"Forty-four."

Bazarov suddenly burst into a laugh.

"What are you laughing at?"

"Upon my word! A man at the age of forty-four, a *pater familias,* living in the country, playing the 'cello!"

Bazarov was still laughing. But Arkady, however much he stood in awe of his mentor, did not even smile this time.

10

ABOUT a fortnight passed. Life at Maryino ran its usual course. Arkady led the life of a sybarite. Bazarov worked. Everyone in the house had become used to him, to his casual ways and his terse, abrupt manner of speech. Indeed, Fenichka herself had so far accepted him that she had him wakened one night when Mitya was seized with convulsions. He had answered the call, sitting up with her for nearly two hours, half-bantering, half-yawning, as was his wont, and had relieved the baby. Pavel Petrovich, however, hated him with all the intensity of his being: he thought him proud, insolent, cynical and plebeian. He suspected that Bazarov did not respect him—as good as despised him—him, Pavel Kirsanov! Nikolai Petrovich was a bit afraid of the young "nihilist" and doubted whether his influence on Arkady was a good one; yet he willingly listened to him and willingly attended his physical and chemical experiments. Bazarov had brought a microscope with him and spent hours over it. The servants, too, grew fond of him, though he liked to chaff them: they felt that he was really one of them, not of the gentry. Dunyasha was not averse to giggling with him and casting sidelong glances, full of meaning, as she passed by him. Pyotr, a very stupid and conceited fellow, with tensely wrinkled brows, whose only merits were courteous manners, an ability to read by syllables and a habit of frequently cleaning his little coat with a clothes brush—even Pyotr would grin and brighten up whenever Bazarov took notice of him. The farm urchins trailed after "the doctor gent" like so many puppies. Old Prokofich was the only one who did not like him; he served him at table with a sullen face, called him a "miscreant" and "rapscallion" and likened him and his whiskers to a pig in a bush. Prokofich was, in his own way, an aristocrat—no less so than Pavel Petrovich.

The best time of the year set in—early June. The weather was exceptionally fine. True, there was a remote possibility of another outbreak of cholera, but the inhabitants of that gubernia were already accustomed to its visitations. Bazarov usually got up very early and walked two or three versts, not for a stroll—he was no lover of aimless walks—but to collect herbs and insects. Sometimes he took Arkady with him. On the way back they would often start an argument. Arkady usually got the worst of it, although he generally talked the most.

One day they were rather late getting back. Nikolai Petrovich went out into the garden to meet them, and, drawing level with the arbor, he suddenly caught the sound of quick footsteps and the voices of the two young men. They were coming down the other side of the arbor and could not see him.

"You don't know my father well enough," Arkady was saying.

Nikolai Petrovich stood stock-still.

"Your father's a good fellow," Bazarov said, "but he's a back number; his singing days are over."

Nikolai Petrovich strained his ears. . . . Arkady said nothing. The "back number" stood for a minute or two without stirring, then slowly went back to the house.

"The other day I found him reading Pushkin," Bazarov resumed. "That's the limit, really. You ought to explain things to him. After all he's not a boy. It's time he dropped that nonsense. Fancy being romantic in our times! Give him something worth-while to read."

"What would you advise?" Arkady asked.

"Well, I should say Büchner's *Stoff und Kraft,* to begin with."

"I think so, too," Arkady assented. "*Stoff und Kraft* is written in a popular style."

"So there you are," Nikolai Petrovich was saying to his brother that day after dinner, sitting in the latter's study.

"You and I have become back numbers; our singing days are over. Ah, well! Perhaps Bazarov is right. But frankly, there's one thing I'm very sorry for. This was just the time when I hoped that Arkady and I would become close friends, but it seems that I've dropped behind while he has gone ahead, and we can't understand each other."

"What makes you think he has gone ahead? And in what way does he differ so strikingly from us?" Pavel Petrovich said impatiently. "That *signore*, the nihilist fellow, has crammed all that into his head. I detest that wretched medico; if you ask me, he's just a charlatan. I'm sure that, for all his frogs, he isn't much up in physiology either."

"No brother, you are wrong. Bazarov is a clever and well-informed man."

"And disgustingly conceited," Pavel Petrovich interrupted again.

"Yes," Nikolai Petrovich said, "he's conceited, but I suppose that's as it should be. One thing I can't make out though. I seem to be doing everything to keep up with the times: I have settled the peasants and started a farm—the whole gubernia calls me a *Red*. I read, I study, and in general I try to keep an open mind for everything modern—and yet they say my singing days are over. Why, brother, I am really beginning to think they are!"

"How is that?"

"Well, judge for yourself. Today I was sitting reading Pushkin. I remember, it was *The Gypsies*. All of a sudden Arkady comes up to me and, without saying a word, with a look—you know—of kindly commiseration, gently takes the book away from me as if I were a child, puts another one in front of me, a German one . . . smiles, and goes away carrying Pushkin off with him."

"You don't say! And what was the book he gave you?"

"Here it is."

Nikolai Petrovich drew out of his back pocket Büchner's notorious booklet, ninth edition.

Pavel Petrovich turned the booklet over in his hands.

"Humph!" he grunted. "Arkady Nikolaich is solicitous about your education. Well, did you try to read it?"

"I did."

"Well?"

"Either I'm stupid, or it's all twaddle. I suppose I must be stupid."

"You haven't forgotten your German, have you?" asked Pavel Petrovich.

"No, I understand German."

Pavel Petrovich turned the book over in his hands again and threw his brother a glance from under his brows. Neither said anything.

"By the way," Nikolai Petrovich broke the silence, clearly anxious to change the subject. "I have received a letter from Kolyazin."

"Matvei Ilyich?"

"Yes. He's come down to make an official inspection of the gubernia. He's a bigwig now and writes to say that he has a kinsman's desire to see us, and invites the two of us, and Arkady, to call on him in town."

"Are you going?" asked Pavel Petrovich.

"No. And you?"

"I won't go either. Damned if I'm going to drag myself fifty versts for nothing. *Mathieu* wants to show himself off to us in all his glory, that's all! He'll have plenty of local incense without our burning any to him. A great man, indeed—a privy councilor! If I had continued in the service and stayed in that silly harness, I'd have been an adjutant general by now. Then, don't forget, you and I are back numbers."

"Yes, brother; it's about time to call in the undertaker and let him take our measure," Nikolai Petrovich said, heaving a sigh.

"You won't catch me giving in so soon," his brother muttered. "I have a feeling that we'll come to grips with that medical fellow yet."

And come to grips they did, that very evening at tea. Pavel Petrovich came down to the drawing room ready for battle, irritated and determined. He was only waiting for an excuse to hurl himself at the enemy, but an excuse was long in coming. Bazarov was generally not talkative in the presence of the "old Kirsanov boys" (as he called the brothers), and that evening he felt out of sorts and drank cup after cup of tea in silence. Pavel Petrovich chafed with impatience, but at last he saw his chance.

The name of a neighboring landowner cropped up during the conversation. "A rotter, a wretched aristocrat." Bazarov said airily—he had met the man in St. Petersburg.

"Allow me to ask," Pavel Petrovich began, his lips quivering, "if according to you, the words 'rotter' and 'aristocrat' are synonymous?"

"I said 'wretched aristocrat,'" Bazarov retorted, lazily taking a sip of his tea.

"Exactly. I presume you hold the same opinion of 'aristocrats' as you do of 'wretched aristocrats.' I consider it my duty to inform you that I do not share that opinion. I venture to say that everyone knows me for a man of liberal views and a champion of progress. But, precisely for that reason, I respect aristocrats—the real ones. Remember, my dear sir," (at these words Bazarov raised his eyes to Pavel Petrovich's face) "remember, my dear sir," he repeated vehemently, "the English aristocrats. They will not yield an iota of their rights, and that is why they respect the rights of others. They demand that people fulfil their obligations to them and for that very reason they fulfil *their own* obligations to others. The aristocracy has given England her freedom and it upholds that freedom."

"We've heard that tune before," Bazarov said. "But what are you trying to prove?"

"What I'm a-trying to prove, my dear sir, is this. . . ." (When angry Pavel Petrovich intentionally lapsed into bad grammar. The whim was a survival of Alexandrian traditions. The bigwigs of the day, on the rare occasions when they used their mother tongue, affected a slovenliness of speech, as much as to say, "We are native Russians, but we are also grandees, who are permitted to disregard the rules of grammar.") "What I'm a-trying to prove is that unless a person has self-respect and a sense of personal dignity—and those instincts are well-developed in the aristocrat—there can be no secure foundation for the social . . . *bien public* . . . social structure. Individuality, my dear sir—that's the main thing. Individuality must stand as firm as a rock, for it is the foundation upon which everything is built. I am well aware, for instance, that you find my habits, my dress, even my personal fastidiousness an object of amusement, but I assure you that these things are a matter of self-respect, a matter of duty, yes, sir, duty. I live in the country, in the backwoods, but I will not lose my self-esteem, my sense of personal dignity."

"By your leave, Pavel Petrovich," Bazarov said, "you talk about self-respect, yet you sit doing nothing. Just how does that benefit the *bien public?* You could be doing that without self-respect."

Pavel Petrovich paled.

"That's quite a different thing. I am not obliged to explain to you just now why I sit and do nothing, as you are pleased to put it. I merely want to say that aristocratism is a principle, and only immoral or shallow people can live nowadays without principles. I told Arkady that the day after he arrived, and I am telling it to you now. Don't you agree, Nikolai?"

Nikolai Petrovich nodded.

"Aristocratism, liberalism, progress, principles," Bazarov was saying, meantime, "goodness, how many foreign . . . and useless words! A Russian has no need for them."

"What *does* he need then? According to you, we are outside humanity, outside its laws. Why, the logic of history demands. . . ."

"Who wants that logic? We get along without it."

"What do you mean?"

"What I say. You, I trust, don't need logic to put a piece of bread into your mouth when you are hungry. Of what use are these abstract ideas?"

Pavel Petrovich threw up his hands.

"I don't understand you. You insult the Russian people. I

don't understand how one can deny principles, maxims! What do you believe in?"

"I've already told you, Uncle, that we don't recognize authorities," interposed Arkady.

"We believe in whatever we consider useful," Bazarov said. "These days negation is more useful than anything else— so we negate."

"Everything?"

"Yes, everything."

"What? Not only art, poetry, but even . . . it's too shocking to utter. . . ."

"Everything," Bazarov repeated with indescribable coolness.

Pavel Petrovich stared at him. He had not expected this. Arkady, on the other hand, flushed with pleasure.

"But, look here," Nikolai Petrovich broke in. "You negate everything or, to be more exact, you destroy everything. But who is going to do the building?"

"That's not our affair. The ground has to be cleared first."

"The present state of the nation demands it," Arkady added, importantly. "We must meet these demands. We have no right to indulge our personal egoism."

The last remark was obviously not to Bazarov's taste; it smacked of philosophy, that is to say, romanticism. But he did not want to contradict his young disciple.

"No, no!" Pavel Petrovich exclaimed with sudden vehemence. "I am not going to believe that you gentlemen really know the Russian people, that you are representative of its needs, or its aspirations! No, the Russian people is not what you imagine it to be. It has a sacred regard for tradition; it is patriarchal; it cannot live without faith. . . ."

"I'll not dispute that," Bazarov interrupted. "I am even prepared to agree with you there."

"If so, then. . . ."

"It still doesn't prove anything."

"Exactly, it doesn't prove anything," Arkady chimed in, with the assurance of an experienced chess player who has

anticipated a possibly dangerous move on the part of his opponent and is, therefore, unperturbed.

"What do you mean, it doesn't prove anything?" Pavel
Petrovich muttered in astonishment. "Then you are going
against your own people?"

"What if we are?" Bazarov cried. "When the people hear
the noise of thunder, they believe that it's the prophet Elijah
riding his chariot across the skies. What then? Would you have
me agree with them? Yes, they're Russians—but am I not a
Russian, too?"

"No, you are not a Russian, after what you've been saying!
I cannot own you as a Russian."

"My grandfather ploughed the land," Bazarov said with
arrogant pride. "Ask any of your muzhiks which of us he'd
more readily acknowledge as his fellow-countryman, you or I.
Why, you don't even know how to talk to him."

"Yet you talk to him and despise him at the same time."

"What if he deserves to be despised! You criticize my outlook, but what makes you think that it is something accidental
in me, that it's not an outcome of that national spirit which
you so zealously defend?"

"To be sure! Of what use to anyone are nihilists?"

"As to whether they are of any use or not is not for us to
decide. I daresay even you consider yourself useful in a way,
too."

"Now, gentlemen, don't let us become personal, please,"
cried Nikolai Petrovich, rising from his seat.

Pavel Petrovich smiled and, placing a hand on his brother's
shoulder, pressed him back into his seat.

"You needn't worry," he said. "I won't forget myself—precisely because of that feeling of self-respect at which our
friend . . . our friend, the doctor, pokes such cruel fun. Excuse
me," he resumed, turning once more to Bazarov. "Do you by
any chance believe your doctrines to be new? If so, you are
deluding yourself. The materialism you preach has appeared
here many a time before and has never had a leg to stand
on. . . ."

"Another foreign word," Bazarov interjected. He was be-

ginning to lose his temper, and his complexion had assumed
a coarse coppery hue. "In the first place we do not preach anything; that is not our custom. . . ."

"What *do* you do?"

"I'll tell you. Until quite recently, we talked about our
officials taking bribes, about the lack of roads, the poor state
of commerce and the courts of justice. . . ."

"Ah yes, of course, you are denouncers—that's what it's
called, I believe. I myself agree with many of your accusa-
tions, but. . . ."

"Then it dawned on us that just talking about our sores
was a waste of breath, that it merely led to banality and
dogmatism. We saw that those clever fellows of ours, the
so-called progressive men and denouncers, were of no earthly
use—that we were wasting our time, talking nonsense about
art, unconscious creativity, parliamentarianism, the bar and
the devil knows what else—when it was simply a question of
men's daily bread, when we were suffocating from crass su-
perstitions, when all our stock companies were going bank-
rupt simply because there's a dearth of honest men, when the
very emancipation the government was fussing over would
hardly do us any good—because the muzhik would be only
too glad to rob himself so he could get drunk in the pothouses."

"I see," Pavel Petrovich interrupted. "So you have convinced yourself of all this and have made up your mind not
to tackle anything seriously?"

"And have made up our mind not to tackle anything,"
Bazarov echoed grimly. He was suddenly annoyed with himself for having loosened his tongue before this aristocrat.

"And do nothing but damn?"

"Do nothing but damn."

"And that's called nihilism?"

"That's called nihilism," Bazarov repeated, this time wtih
pointed insolence.

Pavel Petrovich narrowed his eyes slightly.

"I see!" he said in a singularly calm voice. "Nihilism is to
cure all our ills—and you, *you* are our deliverers and heroes.
So. But what makes you take the others to task, the denoun-

cers, for instance? Don't you go about ranting like the rest of them?"

"Whatever our faults, that is not one of them," Bazarov muttered.

"What then? Do you act? Do you intend to act?"

Bazarov did not answer. Pavel Petrovich controlled himself with an effort.

"Hm! To act, to demolish. . . ." he went on. "But how do you set about the business of demolishing without even knowing the why or wherefore?"

"We demolish because we are a force," Arkady remarked.

Pavel Petrovich surveyed his nephew and smiled ironically.

"Yes, a force—an unleashed power," Arkady said, drawing himself up.

"You wretched boy," Pavel Petrovich cried, no longer able to contain himself. "At least *you* might stop to think what you are supporting in Russia with that hackneyed maxim of yours! Really, it's enough to try the patience of an angel! Force! There's force in the savage Kalmyk and the Mongol, too, but who wants it? We cherish civilization—yes, sir—and the fruits of civilization. Don't tell me these fruits are paltry. The worst kind of dauber, *un barbouilleur,* even a piano thumper, hired for five kopeks a night at dance parties, is more useful than you are, because he is a representative of civilization and not of brute Mongolian force! You fancy yourselves to be progressive men, but all you are good for is to squat in a Kalmyk tent! Force! Don't forget, you strong gentlemen, that there are just four and a half of your fraternity against the millions of others who will not allow you to trample their sacred creeds, and who will crush you!"

"If we're crushed, it serves us right," Bazarov said. "But that's easier said than done. We're not so few as you imagine."

"What? Do you seriously think you can stand up against a whole nation?"

"Moscow was burned by a penny candle, you know," Bazarov replied.

"I see. First we're as proud as Lucifer; then we start mocking at everything. So that's the latest fad among the young;

so that's what captures the imagination of inexperienced youngsters! There, if you please, sits one of them, right beside you. He all but worships you. Look at him!" (Arkady turned away with a frown.) "And this contagion is already widespread. I have been told that our painters in Rome never set foot inside the Vatican. Raphael is considered almost a fool, because, don't you see, he's an authority; but they themselves are disgustingly impotent and barren, with an imagination that does not carry them beyond the *Girl at a Fountain*—and even that is painted execrably. According to you they are the right sort, are they not?"

"According to me," Bazarov answered, "Raphael is not worth a nickel, and they're no better either."

"Bravo, bravo! Do you hear that, Arkady . . . that's how modern young men should speak! Come to think of it, why shouldn't they follow you? Formerly young men had to study; they didn't want to be thought ignoramuses, so they had to work hard willy-nilly. But now they merely have to say, 'Everything in the world is nonsense!' and, aha! the trick is done. The young men are delighted. Really, before, they were simply fatheads, and, now, they've suddenly become nihilists."

"Well, there goes your vaunted sense of self-respect," Bazarov observed phlegmatically, while Arkady flared up, his eyes flashing. "Our argument has gone a bit too far. I think we had better drop it. I'll be prepared to agree with you," he added, getting up, "when you can show me a single institution in our national life, whether domestic or social, which does not merit utter and ruthless denunciation."

"I'll show you millions of such institutions," cried Pavel Petrovich, "millions. Take our village community, for example."

Bazarov's lips curled in a sneer. "As for the village community," he said, "you'd better talk to your brother about that. He now has first-hand knowledge, I believe, of the village community—mutual guarantee, temperance and all that eyewash."

"The family—what about the family as it exists among our peasants?" shouted Pavel Petrovich.

"That's another question I would advise you not to go into too deeply. I suppose you know about the practice of adultery with one's daughter-in-law? Take my advice, Pavel Petrovich, give yourself a couple of days; you will hardly find anything in less. Go over all our classes, examine each one closely; and Arkady and I will meanwhile. . . ."

"Go ahead jeering at everything," Pavel Petrovich interjected.

"No, dissect frogs. Come on, Arkady. Good day, gentlemen!"

The two friends went out. The brothers were left alone, and, at first, they merely looked at one another in silence.

"Well," Pavel Petrovich began at length, "there you have our young generation! There they are—our successors!"

"Successors," Nikolai Petrovich echoed, with a sad sigh. He had been on tenterhooks all through the dispute, now and again stealing pained glances at Arkady. "Do you know what I have been thinking, brother? Once I had a quarrel with our dear mother; she shouted and wouldn't listen to me. At last I told her that she couldn't understand me, that we belonged to different generations. She was terribly offended, and I thought, 'It can't be helped. It's a bitter pill, but it's got to be swallowed.' Well, now it's our turn, and our successors can say to us, 'You are not of our generation, swallow the pill.'"

"You're much too benign and modest," Pavel Petrovich said. "I'm convinced, on the contrary, that you and I are much more in the right than those young gentlemen, though we do, perhaps, express ourselves in an old-fashioned way, *vieilli,* and have none of their cocksureness. But how smug the young people are today! You ask a fellow, 'What wine will you have, red or white?' 'I'm in the habit of taking red,' says he in a bass voice, with a face as solemn as if all the world were looking at him at that moment."

"Will you have any more tea?" Fenichka asked, putting her head in at the door. She did not have the temerity to come into the drawing room while there were sounds of dispute there.

"No, you can tell them to take the samovar away," replied Nikolai Petrovich, and rose to meet her. Pavel Petrovich wished him a curt *bon soir* and retired to his study.

11

HALF an hour later Nikolai Petrovich went into the garden to his favorite arbor. Sad thoughts preyed on him. He now saw clearly, for the first time, that he and his son were drifting apart, and that the rift would grow wider as time went on. It was in vain then that he had sat for days on end in the winter out there in St. Petersburg, poring over new books; in vain that he had lent an eager ear to the talk of the young men; in vain that he had felt so elated at being able to slip in a word of his own during their discussions. "My brother says that we are right," he thought. "Vanity aside, I really think they are farther from the truth than we are, and yet I feel they have something that we haven't—they have an advantage over us. Youth? No, it isn't only that. Isn't it because they have less of the grand manner than we have?"

Nikolai Petrovich's head sank on his chest, and he passed a hand over his face.

"But to reject poetry?" he mused anew. "To have no feeling for art, nature. . . ."

He looked round him, as if trying to understand how one could have no feelings for nature. Evening was closing in. The sun was hidden behind an aspen wood which stood within half a verst of the garden; the shadow of the aspen wood stretched endlessly across the motionless fields. A peasant was driving a little white horse down a dark strip of road along the wood, his whole figure clearly visible, even to a patch on his shoulder, though he rode in the shade. The legs of the trotting horse made a clear, pretty picture. The sunbeams filtered through the wood, shedding such a warm glow on the aspen trunks that they looked like pines, and their foliage appeared almost blue. Above, the pale blue of the sky was faintly roseate with the flush of sunset. The wind had dropped. The swallows winged their way high up in the sky; belated bees buzzed lazily and drowsily among the lilac blossoms; midges swarmed in a column over a solitary, far-stretching bough. "God, how beautiful!" thought Nikolai Petrovich, and his favorite verse came to his lips; but he remembered Arkady and *Stoff und Kraft* and fell silent. And he lingered there, giving himself up to the melancholy solace of lonely thoughts.

He liked daydreaming; country life had developed that trait in him. Not so long ago he had sat thus, daydreaming, while waiting for his son at the little inn, but a change had since come about, the relations which had then been vague had now taken shape—and definite shape! He recalled once more his dead wife, not as he had known her for many years, a housewifely matron, but as a young girl, with a slender waist, an innocent, questioning gaze and tightly coiled hair over a childlike neck. He recollected their first meeting: he was a student at the time. He met her on the staircase of his lodgings and, accidentally brushing against her, had turned around to apologize; but he only managed to stammer, "Pardon, monsieur." She had lowered her head and smiled, and, suddenly taking fright, had run away. Then, at a bend in the stairs, she had glanced at him shyly, assumed a serious air and blushed. Then the first timid visits, the half-words and half-smiles, the perplexity, the sadness and the yearnings, and finally the breathless rapture. . . . Where had it all gone? She had become his wife—he had been happy as few men were happy in this world. "Those first sweet moments of bliss," he mused. . . . "Why could they not live on forever?"

He did not try to analyze his thoughts, but he yearned to go back to those halcyon days with something stronger than memory; he longed to feel his Marie near him again, to sense the warmth of her, the touch of her breath. He could almost feel her hovering presence. . . .

"Nikolai Petrovich." Fenichka's voice sounded near him. "Where are you?"

He was startled. He felt neither distress nor shame; he

never even admitted the possibility of comparison between his wife and Fenichka, but he was sorry that she had sought him out. Her voice immediately brought him back to reality, to his grey hair, his advancing age.

The dream world which he had been about to enter, which had already risen from the dim waves of the past, shifted and vanished.

"I'm here," he answered, "I'll come soon; you go along." "There it is—the grand manner," flashed through his mind. Fenichka peered in at him without speaking and disappeared. He was astonished to find that night had crept in while he had been dreaming. Everything around him was dark and hushed, and Fenichka's face flashed past looking pale and small. He half rose to go home, but his melting heart was too full, and he slowly began to pace the garden, now gazing wistfully at the ground, now looking up at the sky which was already bright with clustering stars. He walked until he was almost exhausted, but the uneasiness within him—a kind of yearning, a vague anxiety—would not be allayed. Oh, how Bazarov would have mocked him had he known what was then passing in his soul! And Arkady, too, would disapprove. Tears came to his eyes, unbidden tears—he, a man of forty-four, a farm owner, an employer; this was a hundred times worse than the violoncello.

Nikolai Petrovich continued to pace the garden, and could not bring himself to go into the house, that peaceful, snug abode which smiled at him with all its lighted windows; he could not tear himself away from the darkness, the garden, the caressing touch of the fresh air on his face, the heartache and the yearning. . . .

At a bend in the path he came upon Pavel Petrovich.

"What's the matter?" he asked Nikolai Petrovich. "You're as pale as a ghost. You're not well. Why don't you lie down?"

Nikolai Petrovich told him in a few words about the state of mind he was in and left him. Pavel Petrovich walked to the end of the garden, and he, too, became lost in thought. He, too, raised his eyes skyward. But his fine dark eyes reflected nothing but the light of the stars. He was not born a romanticist, and that fastidious, dry but passionate soul of his, so misanthropically French, was not given to dreaming. . . .

"Do you know what?" Bazarov was saying to Arkady that night. "I've had a brain storm. Today your father was talking about an invitation received from that distinguished relative of yours. Your father's not going. What do you say to taking a run up to town—that gentleman has invited you, too. Look at the weather we're having. Let's go and look the town over. We'll knock around for five or six days and have a good time!"

"Will you come back here?"

"No, I'll have to be going to my father's. He lives thirty versts from town, you know. I haven't seen him for ages, or Mother, either. Must let the old folks have their bit of fun. They're good souls, especially Father—an amusing old boy. I'm the only child, you know."

"Do you intend to stay there long?"

"I don't think so. It will probably be dull."

"Will you drop in here on your way back?"

"I don't know . . . I'll see. Well, what do you say? Let's go!"

"Just as you like," Arkady said without enthusiasm.

Inwardly he was overjoyed at his friend's proposition, but thought it his duty not to show his true feelings. Was he not a nihilist after all?

The next day he and Bazarov left for town. The young members of the Maryino household were sorry about their going; Dunyasha, in fact, shed a few tears . . . but the old folks felt relieved.

12

THE town which our friends were visiting was under the jurisdiction of a young governor who was both a progressive and a despot, as is often the case in this old Russia of ours. During the first year of his administration he managed to disagree with the gubernia Marshal of the Nobility—a retired cavalry captain of the Guards, the owner of a stud farm and a convivial host—and with his own subordinates. The resultant dissensions reached such a pitch that the Ministry at St. Petersburg eventually decided to send a commissioner to investigate the matter.

The choice fell on Matvei Ilyich Kolyazin, son of the Kolyazin under whose guardianship the Kirsanov brothers had lived in St. Petersburg. He too was of the "younger school," that is to say, he had recently turned forty; but he aimed at becoming a statesman and wore a star on either side of his chest, one of them a foreign decoration and nothing much to boast of. Like the governor upon whom he had come to pass his verdict, he was considered a progressive, and though he was a bigwig he did not act like the majority of bigwigs. Although he had a very exalted opinion of himself and his vanity knew no bounds, he bore himself simply, looked kindly, listened indulgently, and laughed so good-humoredly that one might have taken him on sight for a "regular guy." When occasion demanded, however, he could put on airs, as the saying goes. "What's wanted is energy," he would assert at such times, *"l'énergie est la première qualité d'un homme d'état."* Nevertheless there was no official of any experience who could not lead him by the nose and it was easy to see that he was a fool. Matvei Ilyich professed a deep regard for Guizot and

tried to impress all the sundry that he himself did not belong
to the conservative bureaucrats, the *routiniers,* and that not
a single manifestation of public life passed him unnoticed.
He followed the trend of modern literature, with an air of
careless majesty, the air of a grown-up, who meets a procession of small boys in the street and might condescend to
join it. Actually Matvei Ilyich had not advanced much beyond
those officers of state of Alexandrian days, who prepared
for an evening reception at Madame Svechina's St. Petersburg salon by perusing a page of Condillac in the morning,
but his methods were different and more up-to-date. He was
a smart courtier, a cunning blade, and nothing more; in business matters he was incompetent, in sagacity poor. But he
knew how to look out for his own interests: nobody could lead
him by the nose *there,* which, after all, is the important thing.

Matvei Ilyich received Arkady with the geniality of an
enlightened dignitary. He was astonished, however, when he
heard that his kinsmen, to whom he had extended his invitation, had stayed behind in the country. "Your Dad always was a queer fellow," he said, swinging the tassels of
his gorgeous velvet dressing gown; then turning suddenly
to a young official in a close-buttoned uniform who looked like
the last word in respectability, he sharply inquired, with a
preoccupied air, "What is it?" The young man, whose lips
had stuck together through prolonged disuse, rose to his feet
and looked at his superior with a puzzled air. Having thus
nonplused his subordinate, Matvei Ilyich paid no further
attention to him.

Our dignitaries generally like to puzzle their subordinates,
and the methods they use to attain that end are varied. With
one device, a very popular one, or, as the English say, "quite
a favorite," the high official suddenly ceases to understand
the simplest words and makes out that he is deaf. He will
ask, for example: "What day is it?"

He will be told with the utmost deference:

"It is Friday today, Your Exc . . . c . . . c . . . lency."

"Eh? What? What's that? What did you say?" the high
functionary will ask with a strained look.

"It is Friday, Your Exc . . . ccc . . . lency."

"How? What? What's Friday? What about Friday?"

"Friday, Your Exc . . . ccc . . . lency, a day of the week."

"The deuce it is, what will you be teaching me next!"

Matvei Ilyich was, after all, a dignitary, even though he was considered a liberal.

"I advise you, my friend, to make a call on the Governor," he said to Arkady. "You understand, I'm giving you this advice not because I entertain old-fashioned ideas about having to kowtow to those in authority, but simply because the Governor is a decent fellow. Besides, you would probably like to make the acquaintance of local society. You're not a bear, I hope? He's giving a grand ball the day after tomorrow."

"Will you be at the ball?" asked Arkady.

"He's giving it for me," Matvei Ilyich replied, almost in a tone of regret. "Do you dance?"

"I do, but rather poorly."

"That's a pity. There are some pretty girls around here, and besides it's a shame for a young man not to be able to dance. Mind you, I have no old-fashioned notions on that score. I don't for a minute believe that a man's wit should be in his feet; but Byronism is absurd, *il a fait son temps.*"

"It's not a question of Byronism at all, Uncle."

"I'll introduce you to the ladies here; I'm taking you under my wing," Matvei Ilyich said and laughed self-complacently. "You'll find it warm there, eh?"

A servant came in and announced the President of the Administrative Chamber, a sweet-eyed old man with a puckered mouth who was a great nature-lover, especially on a summer day when, he said, "Every little bee takes a little bribe from every little flower. . . ." Arkady withdrew.

He found Bazarov at the inn where they were staying and was a long time persuading him to visit the Governor's. "Ah, well," Bazarov gave in at last. "In for a penny, in for a pound. Let's take a look at the landed gentry—that's what we came for anyway!"

The Governor received the young men affably, but did not

offer them a seat and did not sit down himself. He was always busy and bustling. The first thing in the morning he would get into a tight-fitting uniform and an exceedingly tight cravat; and all day he missed his meals and went without sleep in the eternal bustle and excitement of issuing orders. He had been nicknamed Bourdaloue in the gubernia, and this was an allusion not to the famous French preacher, but to the Russian word *bourda*—meaning slop. He invited Kirsanov and Bazarov to the ball at his house and, two minutes later, reinvited them, taking them to be brothers and calling them Kaisarov.

As they were going home from the Governor's a man suddenly jumped out of a passing droshky,* a short man, wearing a tunic of the Pan-Slavist mode.** With a shout of Yevgeny Vasilich!" he ran up to Bazarov.

"Oh! It's you, Herr Sitnikov," Bazarov said, continuing to stride along the pavement. "What wind brings you here?"

"Would you believe it, just sheer accident," the man replied. Turning to the cab, he waved his hand half a dozen times and sang out, "Follow us, cabman, follow us! My father has some business here," he went on, skipping over the gutter, "and asked me to attend to it. I heard today that you had arrived and looked you up immediately." (Indeed, on returning to their rooms, the friends found a visiting card with the corners turned down and with the name of Sitnikov inscribed on one side in French and on the other in Slavonic script.) "I hope you're not coming from the Governor's?"

"You can stop hoping; we're coming straight from him."

"Ah! In that case I'll call on him, too. Yevgeny Vasilich, introduce me to your . . . to the. . . ."

"Sitnikov, Kirsanov," Bazarov muttered without stopping.

"Very flattered, I'm sure," began Sitnikov, sidling along and smirking and hastily peeling off his much too elegant gloves. "I've heard a lot about . . . I'm an old acquaintance

---

* A light horse-drawn carriage.
** A heavily braided jacket of Hungarian origin affected by adherents of Pan-Slavism in Russia in the middle of the nineteenth century.—*Tr.*

of Yevgeny Vasilich's—his disciple, I might say. I'm indebted to him for my conversion. . . ."

Arkady looked at Bazarov's disciple. There was an air of dull anxious tensity about the small but not disagreeable features of his sleek-looking face; his small, deep-sunk eyes had an intent uneasy stare and his laugh, too, was uneasy—a short, wooden laugh.

"Would you believe it," he went on, "when I first heard Yevgeny Vasilich say we shouldn't recognize any authorities, I was simply delighted . . . it was like a revelation! Here, I thought, at last I have found a man! By the way, Yevgeny Vasilich, you must meet a certain lady here who is entirely capable of understanding you and for whom your visit will be a genuine treat; I believe you've heard of her."

"Who is she?" Bazarov asked, without enthusiasm.

"Kukshina, Eudoxie—Yevdoxia Kukshina. A remarkable personality, *émancipée* in the true sense of the word, an advanced woman. Do you know what? Let's call on her right now, all of us. She lives nearby. We'll have lunch there. I don't suppose you've had your lunch yet?"

"Not yet."

"Well, that's fine. She is not living with her husband, you know—quite independent."

"Is she pretty?" Bazarov said.

"Well . . . I wouldn't say so."

"Then what the devil are you making us go there for?"

"Ha, ha, that's a good one. She'll stand us a bottle of champagne."

"Go on! You can always tell the practical man. By the way, what's your old man doing, still tax-farming?"

"Yes," Sitnikov said hastily, with a squeaky laugh. "Well, let's go there, shall we?"

"I don't know, really."

"You wanted to see people. Go ahead," Arkady said, in an undertone.

"What about yourself, Mr. Kirsanov?" put in Sitnikov. "You've got to come, too."

"How can we all suddenly descend on her like that?"

"That's all right. You don't know Kukshina. She's tops!"

"Will there be a bottle of champagne?" Bazarov asked.

"Three bottles!" Sitnikov cried. "I vouch for that!"

"What with?"

"My head."

"Or your father's moneybags. All right, let's go."

13

THE small Moscow-style mansion where Avdotya Nikitishna (or *Yevdoxia*) Kukshina lived, stood in a street that had recently been destroyed by fire. Our provincial towns, as everyone knows, catch fire once every five years. Over a visiting card nailed askew on the door was a bellpull, and in the hall the visitors were met by a housemaid—or was it a lady's companion?—in a lace cap, an unmistakable sign of the mistress' progressive tendencies. Sitnikov inquired whether Avdotya Nikitishna was at home.

"Is that you, Victor?" cried a shrill voice from an adjoining room. "Come in."

The woman in the cap vanished.

"I am not alone," Sitnikov said, and, throwing a jaunty look at Arkady and Bazarov, he adroitly slipped out of his symbolical tunic and emerged in a nondescript sleeveless garment of peasant fashion.

"Never mind," replied the voice. *"Entrez."*

The young men went in. The room in which they found themselves was more like a study than a drawing room. Papers, letters, thick Russian magazines, for the most part uncut, lay scattered about on dusty tables; cigarette-ends were littered all over the place. On a leather sofa reclined a lady, still young, blonde, and somewhat disheveled, in a none too immaculate silk gown, with large bracelets on her stubby arms and a lace kerchief on her head. She got up from the sofa and, carelessly drawing about her shoulders a velvet pelisse lined with yellow ermine, murmured languidly, "Good morning, Victor," and shook Sitnikov's hand.

"Bazarov, Kirsanov," he said, imitating Bazarov's abrupt manner of speech.

"Delighted," said Kukshina, staring at Bazarov's round eyes, between which was perched a pink blob of a turned-up nose. She added, "I've heard about you," and shook hands with him.

Bazarov made a wry face. There was nothing repulsive about the dowdy little figure of the emancipated woman, but the expression of her face had an unpleasant effect. One almost felt like asking; "What's the matter, are you hungry? Or are you bored? Or are you nervous? Why are you acting so oddly?" Like Sitnikov she did not seem to be at all happy in her mind. She spoke and moved about in a manner that was at once over-free and awkward. She evidently considered herself a good-natured simple creature, and yet, whatever she did, one always had the impression that she was doing the very thing she did not want to do. She seemed to be doing everything, as children say, on purpose—that is to say, not simply, not naturally.

"Yes, I've heard about you, Bazarov," she repeated. (She had the habit, peculiar to many provincial and Moscow ladies, of addressing men by their surnames from the very first day of their acquaintance.) "Would you like a cigar?"

"Cigars are all right," said Sitnikov who, by this time, was lolling in an armchair with one leg perched on his other knee, "but let's have some lunch; we're terribly hungry. And what do you say to a bottle of champagne?"

"Sybarite," Yevdoxia said, laughing. (When she laughed she bared her upper gums.) "He is a sybarite, Bazarov, isn't he?"

"I like the comforts of life," Sitnikov declared pompously. "That does not prevent me from being a liberal."

"But it does, it does!" Yevdoxia murmured and ordered her maid to attend to the lunch and the champagne. "What do you think about it?" she asked, addressing Bazarov. "I'm sure you share my opinion."

"Certainly not," Bazarov retorted. "A piece of meat is better than a piece of bread, even from the chemical standpoint."

"Do you go in for chemistry? I'm crazy about it. I've even invented a mastic of my own."

"A mastic? You?"

"Yes, I. Do you know what for? To make doll's heads so that they won't break. I am a practical person, too, you know. But it's not ready yet. I must look up Liebig. By the way, have you read Kislyakov's article on female labor in the *Moskovskiye Vedomosti?* You must read it. You're interested in the problem of women's rights, aren't you? And the schools, too? What does your friend do? What's his name?"

Madame Kukshina let her questions fall, one after the other, with languid carelessness and without waiting for a reply—spoiled children speak like that to their nurses.

"My name is Arkady Nikolaich Kirsanov," Arkady said, "and I don't do anything."

Yevdoxia laughed.

"Isn't that charming! Why don't you smoke? Do you know, Victor, I'm cross with you."

"Why?"

"I hear you've been praising George Sand again. An unenlightened woman, that's all she is! You can't compare her to Emerson! She has no ideas about education, or physiology, or anything. I'm sure she never heard of embryology—a pretty thing not to know these days!" (Yevdoxia threw up her hands.) "Ah, what a splendid article Yelisevich has written on that subject! He's a gentleman of genius!" (Yevdoxia constantly used the word "gentleman" instead of "man.") "Bazarov, sit down on the sofa next to me. You may not know it, but I'm terribly afraid of you."

"And why—if I may ask?"

"You are a dangerous gentleman—you're so critical. Goodness gracious! It's funny, my talking like a country lady from the backwoods. But I really am a landlady. I manage the estate myself, and would you believe it, my steward, Yerofei, is a remarkable type—just like Cooper's Pathfinder. There's a kind of natural simplicity about him! I've settled here for good. Dreadful town—don't you think so? But what can you do!"

"It's as good as any other," Bazarov said coolly.

"Such petty interests, that's the worst about it! I used to spend the winter in Moscow . . . but my husband, M'sieu' Kukshin, has now set up house there. Besides, Moscow nowadays . . . somehow, it's not what it used to be. I was thinking of going abroad; I very nearly went last year."

"To Paris, of course?" Bazarov said.

"To Paris and Heidelberg."

"Why Heidelberg?"

"Oh, but Bunsen's there!"

Here Bazarov found himself at a loss.

"Pierre Sapozhnikov . . . do you know him?"

"No, I don't."

"Oh, Pierre Sapozhnikov—he's always at Lydia Khostatova's."

"I don't know her either."

"Well, he offered to accompany me. Thank God, I'm independent, I have no children. . . . What's that I said?— *Thank God!* On second thought, that doesn't matter."

Yevdoxia rolled a cigarette with tobacco-stained fingers, licked it down, sucked it, and lit up. The maid came in with a tray.

"Ah, here's lunch! Will you have a snack? Victor, uncork the bottle. That's in your line."

"Yes, so it is," Sitnikov mumbled and laughed again shrilly.

"Are there any pretty women here?" Bazarov asked, draining his third glass.

"Yes," answered Yevdoxia, "but they're all so empty-headed. Take *mon amie* Odintsova, for instance—she's not bad looking. It's a pity her reputation is not quite. . . . But that's not so bad—the thing is she has no breadth of outlook, no independent views, nothing. Our entire system of education should be changed. I've been thinking of that: our women are very badly brought up."

"It's a hopeless case," put in Sitnikov. "They deserve nothing but contempt, and that's what I feel for them—absolute and utter contempt!" (To be able to feel contempt and to vent that feeling was a pleasure Sitnikov reveled in; he criticized women, especially, but a few months later he would grovel before his own wife for no other reason than that she was *née* Princess Durdoleosova.) "Not one of them would be able to understand our conversation; not one of them is worth the breath we serious men waste on them!"

"But there is no need for them to understand our conversation at all," Bazarov said.

"What are you talking about?" queried Yevdoxia.

"Pretty women."

"What? Then you are of the same opinion as Proudhon?" Bazarov drew himself up haughtily.

"I share no one's opinions. I have my own."

"To hell with authorities!" Sitnikov shouted, glad of the opportunity to say something brave in the presence of a man to whom he played the sycophant.

"But even Macaulay . . ." Kukshina began.

"To hell with Macaulay!" Sitnikov yelled. "Are you defending those petticoats?"

"Not petticoats, but the rights of women, which I have sworn to defend to the last drop of my blood."

"To hell!" but here Sitnikov broke off. "I'm not disputing that," he muttered.

"No, I can see you are a Pan-Slavist!"

"No, I'm not a Pan-Slavist, though, of course . . ."

"No! no! no! You are a Pan-Slavist. You're an advocate of the Domostroi.* All you need is a horsewhip to lay about you!"

"A horsewhip's not a bad thing," Bazarov interposed, "but we've come to the last drop. . . ."

"Of what?" broke in Yevdoxia.

"Of champagne, my dear Avdotya Nikitishna, of champagne—not of your blood."

"I can't stand it when women are attacked," Yevdoxia went on. "It's terrible, terrible. Instead of attacking them you'd do better to read Michelet's *De l'amour*. It's wonderful! Gentlemen, let's talk about love," Yevdoxia added, letting her arm drop languidly on a rumpled sofa cushion.

* An ancient Russian code of worldly wisdom.—*Tr.*

A sudden silence fell.

"No, why talk about love," Bazarov said. "You just mentioned Odintsova. . . . That's what you called her, I believe? Who's that lady?"

"Oh, she's charming! Just sweet!" squealed Sitnikov. "I'll introduce you to her. Very clever girl, awfully rich, and a widow. Unfortunately, she's not quite developed yet: she should become more closely acquainted with our Yevdoxia. Here's to your health, *Eudoxie!* Let's clink *Et toc, et toc, et tin-tin-tin! Et toc, et toc, et tin-tin-tin!* . . ."

"Victor, you're a naughty boy."

The lunch was a protracted affair. The first bottle of champagne was followed by a second, then a third and even a fourth. Yevdoxia chattered away without pause, and Sitnikov echoed whatever she said. They talked a good deal about marriage—as to whether it was a prejudice or a crime, and whether people were born alike or not, and what was individuality. Matters eventually reached a point when Yevdoxia, flushed with wine and thumping the keys of a discordant piano with a click of her flat-nailed fingers, started to sing in a raucous voice. First she sang some Gypsy songs and then Seymour-Schiff's romanza, "Granada Slumbers On," while Sitnikov wrapped a scarf round his head and imitated a languishing lover at the words:

> *"Let thy lips, dear, with mine*
> *In fiery kiss be sealed. . . ."*

Arkady could stand it no longer.

"Gentlemen, this is beginning to look like Bedlam," he remarked aloud.

Bazarov, who had occasionally thrown in an ironical remark—being more engrossed with the champagne than anything else—yawned outright, rose, and, without taking leave of the hostess, left the room followed by Arkady. Sitnikov dashed out after them.

"Well, what do you say, what do you say?" he asked, hopping fawningly from side to side. "Didn't I tell you? A remarkable woman! We could do with more like her. She is in a way an example of the highest morality."

"And is that establishment of *thy* father's also a sample of the highest morality?" asked Bazarov, pointing to a pothouse which they happened to be passing.

Sitnikov laughed his squealing laugh again. He was terribly ashamed of his origin, and was not sure whether he should feel flattered or offended at Bazarov's unexpected familiarity.

14

SEVERAL days later the ball was held at the Governor's house. Kolyazin was the "hero of the day." The Marshal of the Nobility made known to all and sundry that, strictly speaking, he had come only out of respect, while the Governor contrived (even at the ball, and even when he was sitting still) to "issue orders." Kolyazin's geniality was equalled only by his majestic mien. He beamed on everybody, on some with a shade of loathing, on others with a shade of respect; he acted the gallant *"en vrai chevalier français"* with the ladies and laughed all the time—a loud, hearty, monotonous laugh, as behooves a statesman. He patted Arkady on the back and called him "dear nephew" for all to hear, bestowed on Bazarov, who was rigged out in an old dress suit, a fleeting, absent-minded but indulgent glance, and a vague but affable grunt, in which one could only make out an "I" and an "ever so"; he extended a finger to Sitnikov and smiled on him, though with his head averted. Even for Kukshina, who showed up without a crinoline and in soiled gloves, but with a bird of paradise in her hair, he had a mumured *enchanté*.

The place was crowded, and there were plenty of dancing partners; the civilians were mostly "wallflowers," but the military danced assiduously, particularly one of them who had spent six weeks in Paris where he had picked up some racy ejaculations such as *"Zut," "Ah fichtre," "pst, pst, mon bibi,"* and so forth. He pronounced them to perfection, with real Parisian *chic*, yet he would say *"si j'aurais"* when he meant *"si j'avais,"* used the word *"absolument"* in the sense of *certainly*. In short, he spoke that Russian corruption of French which so amuses Frenchmen when they are not obliged to

assure our fellow-countrymen that we speak their language
like angels, *"comme des anges."*

Arkady, as we know, was a poor dancer, and Bazarov did
not dance at all; they both seated themselves in a corner
where they were joined by Sitnikov. With a sneer on his face
and passing sarcastic remarks, he looked insolently round
the room and seemed to be enjoying himself immensely. Suddenly his face changed and, turning to Arkady, he muttered
in seeming confusion, "Odintsova is here."

Arkady turned and saw a tall woman in a black gown standing in the doorway of the hall. He was struck by the stateli-
ness of her carriage. Her bare arms hung gracefully down
the sides of her slender body; a sprig of fuchsia drooped
prettily from her gleaming hair on to her sloping shoulders;
a pair of limpid eyes looked out intelligently and placidly—
yes placidly, not pensively—from under a slightly overhanging
clear brow, and her lips were touched by an almost imperceptible smile. Her face seemed to emanate a soft and gentle
force.

"Do you know her?" Arkady asked Sitnikov.

"Yes. Would you like to be introduced?"

"I don't mind . . . after this quadrille."

Bazarov's attention was also drawn to Odintsova.

"Who's that?" he asked. "She looks out of the common
run."

After the quadrille was over Sitnikov led Arkady up to
Odintsova; obviously, he did not know her as well as he had
intimated: his speech was confused and she regarded him in
some surprise. But her face assumed an expression of warm
interest when Arkady's name was mentioned. She asked
whether he was not the son of Nikolai Petrovich.

"Yes, I am."

"I met your father twice and have heard a lot about him,"
she went on. "I am very glad to meet you."

An adjutant cut in at that instant and invited her to a
quadrille. She consented.

"Do you dance?" Arkady asked respectfully.

"Yes. What makes you think I don't? Do I look as old as all that?"

"Oh, no . . . but in that case, will you give me the mazurka?"

Odintsova smiled indulgently.

"Very well," she said, looking at Arkady not exactly patronizingly, but as married sisters look upon very young brothers.

Odintsova was not much older than Arkady—she was twenty-nine—but in her presence he felt like a schoolboy, a callow student, as though the difference in their ages was much greater. Matvei Ilyich came up to her with stately mien and honeyed speeches. Arkady fell back but kept his eyes on her all the time, and followed her throughout the quadrille. She spoke with the same ease to her dancing partner as she had to the statesman. Gently she nodded her head and turned her eyes and laughed softly once or twice. Her nose was somewhat fleshy, like most Russian noses, and her complexion was not perfectly clear; yet Arkady decided that he had never met a more fascinating woman. The music of her voice kept sounding in his ears; the very folds of her gown hung somehow differently, not as on other women, but more gracefully and flowingly, and her movements were smooth and unaffected.

A feeling of timidity overcame Arkady when, at the first sounds of the mazurka, he took a seat beside the lady, and tried to make conversation; all he could do was pat his hair in tongue-tied embarrassment. But his timidity and agitation did not last long; Odintsova's calmness communicated itself to him: in less than a quarter of an hour he was chatting with her easily about his father, about his uncle, about life in St. Petersburg and in the country. Odintsova listened with an air of polite sympathy, slightly opening and closing her fan; his conversation was interrupted when she was invited now and again to dance. Sitnikov, among others, invited her twice. She would come back to her seat again, pick up her fan without any visible sign of quickened breathing, and Arkady would resume the conversation, filled with a sense of elation at being near her, speaking to her, looking into her eyes, gazing at her beautiful brow and the whole of her sweet, grave and intelligent face. She spoke little herself, but her words showed a knowledge of the world; from some of her remarks Arkady inferred that this young woman had lived through and thought over a good deal.

"Who was that standing with you when Mr. Sitnikov led you up to me?" she asked him.

"Why, did you notice him?" Arkady asked in his turn. "He has a fine face, hasn't he? His name's Bazarov; he's a friend of mine."

And Arkady began talking about "his friend."

He spoke of him in such detail and with so much enthusiasm, that Odintsova turned round and regarded him closely. Meanwhile the mazurka was drawing to a close. Arkady was sorry to lose his partner: he had spent such a pleasant hour with her! During all that time, he had been aware of an undercurrent of condescension on her part, as of something he should be grateful for—but the hearts of the young are not oppressed by such sensations.

The music stopped.

"*Merci,*" Odintsova said, rising. "You have promised to come and see me. Bring your friend along with you. I'm very curious to meet a man who has the courage to believe in nothing."

The Governor came up to Odintsova, announced that supper was ready, and offered her his arm with a preoccupied air. She looked back at Arkady with a parting smile and a nod as she moved away. He made her a low bow, gazed at her retreating figure (how shapely it looked in the clinging black silk with its greyish sheen) and thought to himself, "She has already forgotten my existence." He experienced a feeling of gentle resignation. . . .

"Well?" Bazarov asked Arkady as soon as the latter had joined him in their corner. "Did you have a good time? A gentleman has just been telling me that this lady is—oh-ho-ho! He looked like a fool to me, though. What's your opinion—is she really oh-ho-ho?"

"I don't quite understand that definition," Arkady said.

"Don't be such an innocent!"

"Well then, I don't understand that gentleman of yours. Odintsova is very charming, to be sure, but she's so cold and reserved, that . . ."

"Still waters run deep, you know!" Bazarov threw in. "You say she's cold. That just suits your taste. You are fond of ice cream, aren't you?"

"Perhaps," Arkady muttered. "I'm no judge of that. She wants to meet you and asked me to bring you down to see her."

"I can imagine the colors you painted me in! You did the right thing, though. Take me down. Whatever she is, a provincial lioness, or an *émancipée* of the Kukshina type, she certainly has shoulders the likes of which I haven't set eyes on for a long time."

Bazarov's cynicism jarred on Arkady, but—as often happens—he rebuked his friend for something entirely different from what he actually disliked in him.

"Why don't you want to admit freedom of thought in women?" he said in a low tone.

"Because, my dear chap, as far as I can see, only scarecrows go in for free thought among women."

With that the conversation ended. The two young men left immediately after supper. Kukshina said good-bye to them with a nervously spiteful though half-timid kind of laugh: her vanity had been deeply wounded by the fact that neither of them had paid her any attention. She was last to leave the ball, and after three in the morning danced a polka-mazurka with Sitnikov in the Parisian style, with which edifying spectacle the Governor's gala ball came to an end.

15

"LET'S see what species of mammal this person belongs to," Bazarov said to Arkady the next day, as they mounted the stairs of Odintsova's hotel. "My nose tells me there's something wrong here."

"I'm surprised at you!" Arkady cried. "Do you mean to say, that you, Bazarov, are so narrow-minded as to believe . . ."

"Don't be so funny!" Bazarov broke in carelessly. "It's time you knew that in our idiom 'wrong' means 'right.' It's all grist to the mill. You were telling me yourself today about the odd circumstances of her marriage, though, to my way of thinking, there's nothing odd about marrying a rich old man. On the contrary, it's a sensible thing to do. I don't believe town gossip; but there's something in it."

Arkady said nothing and knocked at the door. A young servant in livery showed the two friends into a large room, furnished, like all rooms in Russian hotels, in bad taste, but full of flowers. Presently Odintsova came in, wearing a simple morning dress. She looked even younger in the light of the spring sun. Arkady introduced Bazarov and noted, with secret surprise, that he seemed to feel embarrassed, while Odintsova was perfectly at her ease, just as she had been the night before. Bazarov, conscious of his embarrassment, felt annoyed. "Well, I never—overawed by a petticoat!" he thought, and, lolling in an armchair like Sitnikov, he began to talk with exaggerated nonchalance. Odintsova regarded him steadily with her clear eyes.

Anna Sergeyevna Odintsova was the daughter of Sergei Nikolayevich Loktev, a notorious beau, adventurer and

gambler, who, after living it up and cutting a figure for fifteen
years in St. Petersburg and Moscow, ended by losing his last
kopek. He was obliged to retire to the country, where he
shortly died, leaving a very scant property to his two daughters,
Anna, aged twenty, and Katerina, aged twelve. Their mother,
who came of an impoverished family of princes, died in St.
Petersburg when her husband was still in his prime. On the
death of her father, Anna's plight was a difficult one. The brilliant education which she had received in St. Petersburg had
not equipped her for housekeeping, estate management, and
all the cares of life in rustic obscurity. She knew no one in
the whole parish from whom to seek advice. Her father
had shunned his neighbors, whom he had despised and
who had despised him, each in his own way. She did not
lose her head, however, and promptly invited her mother's
sister, Princess Avdotya Stepanovna X, to live with them.
The latter was a spiteful, snobbish old lady, who, on taking
up her abode in her niece's house, took all the best rooms for
herself. She grumbled and complained from morning till
night, and never took a walk in the garden unattended by
her only serf, a dour-faced lackey in a shabby pea-green
livery with sky-blue galloons and a cocked hat. Anna patiently bore all her aunt's whims, and quietly set about her
sister's upbringing, seemingly reconciled to the idea of wasting her youth in retirement.

But fate decreed otherwise. She happened to catch the eye
of a certain Odintsov, a very rich man of about six and forty,
an eccentric hypochondriac, stout, heavy and sour, though
neither stupid nor ill-natured. He fell in love with her and
proposed; she consented to become his wife. He lived with
her for about six years, and on his death bequeathed to her
his whole fortune. Anna Sergeyevna stayed on in the country
for about a year after his death, then went abroad with her
sister, but visited only Germany; feeling homesick, she came
back to live at her beloved Nikolskoye, within forty versts of
the town of N—. There she had a fine, richly appointed
house with a beautiful garden and greenhouses: the late
Odintsov had never denied himself anything. Anna Serge-

yevna rarely made an appearance in town, going there usually on business and then only for a short time. She was not popular in the gubernia. Her marriage with Odintsov had created quite a stir, and many cock-and-bull stories were spun about her; she was said to have abetted her father in his sharp practices, and had been induced to go abroad, it was insinuated, in order to hush up a scandal. "Draw your own conclusions!" shocked gossipmongers would wind up. "She's been through fire and water," it was said of her, and the provincial wag was known to have added, "and boiling oil." All this gossip reached her ears, but she ignored it: hers was an independent and rather determined character.

Odintsova sat back in her chair with her hands folded, listening to Bazarov. He was rather unusually talkative and was patently putting himself out to entertain, which gave Arkady more cause for wonder. He could not decide whether Bazarov was succeeding in his purpose or not. Anna Sergeyevna's face betrayed nothing of what was passing in her mind: she preserved throughout the same unchanged subtle expression of friendliness; her lovely eyes were alight with attention, but it was a placid attention. Bazarov's affected manner during the first few minutes of his visit had struck her unpleasantly, like a bad odor or a strident sound; but she was quick to perceive that he was embarrassed, a fact which she even found flattering. Vulgarity alone she shrank from, and vulgarity was not one of Bazarov's faults.

This was a day of surprises for Arkady. He had expected Bazarov to talk with such a clever woman as Odintsova about his convictions and opinions; indeed, she had herself expressed a wish to meet a man "who has the courage to believe in nothing"; instead of which here was Bazarov discussing medicine, homeopathy and botany. Odintsova, it appeared, had not been wasting her time in seclusion: she had read some good books and her Russian was excellent. She began speaking about music, but finding that Bazarov rejected art, she gently led the way back to botany, though Arkady had started talking about the significance of folk melodies. Odintsova still treated him like a younger brother: it was as though she merely appreciated in him the kindliness and artlessness of youth, nothing more. The conversation, unhurried, diverse and animated, lasted over three hours.

Our friends at length got up to take their leave. Anna Sergeyevna regarded them with a friendly look, held out to both of them her beautiful white hand and, after a moment's thought, said with a hesitant, but kindly smile:

"If you're not afraid of being bored, gentlemen, come and see me at Nikolskoye."

"Oh, I say, Anna Sergeyevna," Arkady cried, "I'd consider it one of the greatest joys. . . ."

"And you, M'sieu' Bazarov?"

Bazarov merely bowed, and Arkady, as a last surprise, saw that his friend was blushing.

"Well," he said to him out in the street, "do you still believe that she's 'oh-ho-ho'?"

"I don't know what to make of her! She's all frozen up!" retorted Bazarov, adding, after a pause, "Milady, the grand duchess. All she needs is a train behind her and a coronet on her head."

"Our grand duchesses don't speak Russian like that," Arkady said.

"She's been through the mill, my dear chap, she's had a taste of our bread."

"Say what you like, but she's sweet," Arkady said.

"A gorgeous body!" Bazarov continued. "What a study for the dissecting-room."

"Stop that, Yevgeny, for God's sake! There's a limit, you know."

"All right, don't get the wind up, mollycoddle. Anyway, she's first rate. Must go down and see her."

"When?"

"What about the day after tomorrow? What's the use of hanging around here? To drink champagne with Kukshina? Or to flap our ears at that Liberal dignitary, the relative of yours? The day after tomorrow then let it be. By the way, my father's bit of a farmstead is not far from there. It's the Nikolskoye on the N— road, isn't it?"

"Yes."

"*Optime*. Don't let's dawdle; only fools dawdle—and wise birds. A gorgeous body, by God!"

Three days later the two friends were on their way to Nikolskoye. It was a bright day, not too hot, and the sleek little stage horses trotted along at a brisk pace, swinging their plaited tails. Arkady gazed down the road and smiled, he knew not why.

"Congratulate me," Bazarov suddenly exclaimed. "It's the 22nd of June today, my Saint's Day. We'll see what luck he'll bring me. They're waiting for me at home today," he added, dropping his voice. "Never mind, let them wait!"

16

THE country house in which Anna Sergeyevna lived stood on an open hillside close to a yellow brick church with a green roof, white columns and fresco paintings over the portal representing the resurrection of Christ in the "Italian" manner. In the foreground was the prone figure of a swarthy helmeted warrior, remarkable for the rotundity of his contours. Beyond the church a long straggling village stretched in two rows with here and there a chimney pot projecting above the thatched roofs. The manor house was built in the same style as the church, a style commonly known to us as Alexandrian; the house, too, was painted yellow and had a green roof, white columns and a façade with a coat-of-arms on it. The provincial architect had designed both buildings with the approval of the late Odintsov, who tolerated no silly and fanciful innovations, as he expressed it. The house was flanked on both sides by the dark trees of an old garden, while a drive, lined by trimmed fir trees led up to the entrance.

Our friends were met in the hallway by two stalwart footmen in livery, one of whom immediately ran off in search of the butler. The butler, a fat man in a black frock coat, promptly answered the call and conducted the guests up a carpeted staircase to their room containing two bedsteads and all the necessary toilet articles. This was apparently a well regulated house: everything was spick and span, everything discreetly fragrant, like the waiting rooms of a ministry.

"Anna Sergeyevna requests you to join her in half an hour," announced the butler. "Is there anything you wish in the meantime?"

"No, nothing, my dear man," Bazarov answered, "unless you'd be good enough to fetch a glass of vodka."

"Yes, sir," the butler said, somewhat surprised, his boots creaking as he withdrew.

"What *grand genre!*" Bazarov said. "I believe that's what its called in your set? Grand duchess is about right."

"A fine grand duchess," Arkady retorted, "who straightaway invites a couple of priceless aristocrats like you and me."

"Especially me, a coming bonesetter, son of a bonesetter and a deacon's grandson. You know that I'm the grandson of a deacon, I suppose?" And he added after a brief pause with curling lip, "Like Speransky.* She certainly indulges herself that lady, I must say! Aren't we expected to appear in dress suits?"

Arkady merely shrugged, but he, too, felt a bit uncomfortable.

Half an hour later Bazarov and Arkady went down into the drawing room. This was a spacious, airy room, rather luxuriously, but none too tastefully furnished. The massive, expensive furniture was ranged in the conventional prim manner along the walls, which were papered in brown with a gold pattern; the late Odintsov had ordered it in Moscow through a friend and agent of his, a wine merchant. Over the central divan hung a portrait of a fat, fair-haired gentleman who seemed to be looking down at the visitors with displeasure.

"The old boy, I suppose," Bazarov whispered to Arkady and, wrinkling his nose added, "Shouldn't we beat a retreat?"

At this moment the hostess entered. She was wearing a light barége dress; her hair, brushed smoothly back from the ears, imparted a girlish look to her clear, fresh face.

"Thank you for having kept your word to stay as my guests," she began. "It's not bad here, really. I'll introduce you to my sister; she plays the piano well. That doesn't interest you, M'sieu' Bazarov, but M'sieu' Kirsanov, I believe, is fond of music; besides my sister I have an old aunt living with me, and one of the neighbors sometimes drops in for

* M. M. Speransky (1772-1839), an official in the government of Alexander I, author of a political reform project.

a game of cards; there you have all our company. And now let us sit down."

Odintsova made this little speech with peculiar distinctness, as though she had learned it by heart; then she turned to Arkady. Her mother, it appeared, had known Arkady's mother and had been her confidante during Nikolai Petrovich's courtship. Arkady began speaking warmly about his mother, while Bazarov proceeded to examine the albums. "What a meek lamb I've become," he said to himself.

A beautiful borzoi in a blue collar ran into the drawing room, its claws pattering on the floor, followed by a girl of about eighteen, dark-haired and warm-skinned, with a somewhat round but attractive face and small dark eyes. She carried a basket filled with flowers.

"Here's my sister, Katya," Odintsova said with a nod in her direction.

Katya curtsied, sat down beside her sister, and began to sort out the flowers. The borzoi, whose name was Fifi, went up to each of the guests in turn, wagging its tail and thrusting its cold muzzle into their hands.

"Did you pick all those flowers yourself?" Odintsova asked.

"Yes," replied Katya.

"Is Auntie coming down to tea?"

"Yes, she is."

When Katya spoke, she smiled with a charming, shy candor and had a habit of looking upward in an amusing, stern way. Everything about her was delightfully fresh and unsophisticated: her voice, the tender down on her face, her pink hands with the pale rings on the palms, and the slightly contracted shoulders. She was constantly changing color and taking breath.

Odintsova turned to Bazarov.

"You're looking at those pictures out of politeness, Yevgeny Vasilich," she began. "It doesn't amuse you. You'd better draw closer to us and let's discuss something."

Bazarov drew his chair closer.

"What would you like to discuss?" he asked.

"Whatever you like. I warn you that I love an argument."

"You?"

"Yes, I. You seem surprised. Why is that?"

"Because, as far as I can judge, you are of a calm, cold disposition, and one has to let himself be carried away in an argument."

"You have gotten to know me rather quickly, haven't you? For one thing, I am impatient and insistent—ask Katya; secondly, I am easily carried away."

Bazarov looked at her.

"Perhaps, you know best. So you want to argue. All right. I've been looking at the views of Saxonian Switzerland in your album; you said that they couldn't amuse me. You said that because you don't credit me with artistic feeling. It's true I don't possess any; but those views might interest me geologically, as a study of mountain structure, for instance."

"Excuse me; as a geologist, you'd sooner refer to a book, to some special work on the subject, but not to a drawing."

"A drawing would show me graphically what a book would take ten pages to tell me.

Anna Sergeyevna said nothing for a while.

"Haven't you really any sense of the artistic at all?" she asked, resting her elbows on the table, thereby bringing her face closer to Bazarov's. "How do you manage without?"

"What's the use of it, I'd like to know?"

"Well, if only to study and know people."

Bazarov smiled ironically.

"For one thing, experience can do that for me; and in the second place, let me tell you, the study of personalities is a waste of time. All people are alike, both in body and soul; every one of us has a brain, a spleen, a heart, and lungs similarly arranged; and the so-called cardinal virtues are the same in all of us: slight modifications do not count. One human specimen is sufficient to judge the rest by. People are like trees in a forest; no botanist is going to bother over each individual birch tree."

Katya, who was leisurely selecting flowers for a nosegay, looked up at Bazarov with a perplexed expression, and encountering his swift, careless glance, blushed to the roots of her hair. Anna Sergeyevna shook her head.

"Trees in a forest," she repeated. "In your opinion then, there's no difference between a foolish person and a clever one, between a good and a bad person?"

"Yes, there is: as between a sick person and a healthy one. A consumptive's lungs are not in the condition that yours or mine are, although they are made the same way. We know approximately what causes bodily ailments; moral disease is merely the result of bad education and all the nonsense that people's heads are crammed with from childhood; in short, the outrageous state of society is at the bottom of it all. Improve society, and there will be no disease."

Bazarov said all this with an air of "I don't care whether you believe me or not!" He smoothed his whiskers with a slow movement of his long fingers, while his eyes moved restlessly about the room.

"And you believe," said Anna Sergeyevna, "that when society is improved there will no longer be any foolish or wicked people?"

"In any case, under a sensible arrangement of society it is immaterial whether a person is foolish or clever, wicked or good."

"Yes, I understand; we shall all have the same kind of spleens."

"Exactly, madam."

Odintsova turned to Arkady.

"And what is your opinion, Arkady Nikolayevich?"

"I agree with Yevgeny," he replied.

Katya regarded him from under knitted brows.

"You astonish me, gentlemen," Odintsova said, "but we shall discuss that another time. I hear Auntie coming down for tea; we must spare her ears."

Princess X—, Anna Sergeyevna's aunt, a slight, frail woman with a grey scratch wig, a wizened little face and staring malicious eyes, entered the room, and with barely a nod to the guests, lowered herself into a wide velvet-covered armchair which no one else dared sit in. Katya put a stool under her feet. The old lady did not thank her, did not even glance up, her hands merely stirred under the yellow shawl, which almost enveloped her puny body. The princess was fond of yellow; even the ribbons on her cap were a vivid yellow.

"How did you sleep, Auntie?" Odintsova said, raising her voice.

"That dog is here again," the old woman grumbled, and seeing Fifi make several uncertain steps in her direction, she exclaimed, "Shoo, shoo!"

Katya called Fifi and opened the door.

Fifi bounded out joyously, anticipating a stroll, but finding herself outside alone began to scratch at the door and whine. The princess scowled, and Katya had half a mind to go out.

"Tea is ready, I should imagine," Odintsova said. "Let us go, gentlemen; Auntie, come and have tea."

The princess rose without a word and was first to leave the room. The rest followed her into the dining room. A liveried servant boy noisily pulled out another sacred and cushioned armchair into which the princess deposited herself; Katya, who was pouring out the tea, served her first, in a teacup decorated with a coat-of-arms. The old lady put some honey in her tea (she considered it wasteful to have sugar with her tea, although she never spent a kopek on anything) and suddenly asked in a hoarse voice:

"And what does *P'ince* Ivan write?"

Nobody answered her. Bazarov and Arkady soon perceived that nobody paid any attention to her, though they treated her with respect. "They keep her for swank, because she's princely spawn," Bazarov thought. After tea Anna Sergeyevna suggested a stroll; but it began to drizzle, and the company, with the exeception of the princess, returned to the drawing room. The neighbor who was fond of a game of cards dropped in. He was a stout, grey-haired little man by the name of Porfiry Platonich, very polite and easily amused, with short legs, which looked as if they had been carved out for him. Anna Sergeyevna, who was most of the time in conversation with Bazarov, asked him whether he would care to join them in an old-fashioned game of *preference*. Bazarov

consented, saying it was necessary to prepare himself for the
duties of a country practitioner.

"Take care," observed Anna Sergeyevna, "Porfiry Platonich
and I will beat you. And you, Katya," she added, "play something for Arkady Nikolayevich; he is fond of music, and we'll
listen, too."

Katya reluctantly crossed over to the piano; and Arkady,
who was really fond of music, reluctantly followed her: he
had a suspicion that Odintsova was dismissing him, and his
heart, as is every young man's at his age, had been stirring with
a vague languorous feeling, like a presentiment of love. Katya
opened the piano, and without looking at Arkady asked in a
low voice:

"What would you like me to play for you?"

"Whatever you wish," Arkady answered indifferently.

"What kind of music do you like?" Katya asked again,
without changing her position.

"Classical," Arkady answered in the same tone.

"Do you like Mozart?"

"Yes."

Katya took out Mozart's Sonata-Fantasia in C Minor. She
played very well, though rather primly and unemotionally.
With eyes fixed on the music and teeth clenched hard, she
sat rigidly erect, and only towards the end of the sonata her
face grew flushed and a wisp of hair uncurled over her dark
eyebrow.

Arkady was particularly struck by the finale of the sonata,
where the delightful vivacity of the carefree melody is suddenly invaded by a surge of such poignant, almost tragic grief.
But the thoughts roused in him by the strains of Mozart's
music had nothing to do with Katya. Looking at her, he
simply thought: "This young lady doesn't play at all badly,
and she's not bad-looking either."

Having finished the sonata, her hands still on the keys,
Katya asked, "Enough?" Arkady said he did not dare trouble
her further, and started talking to her about Mozart, asking whether she had chosen that sonata herself or whether
somebody had recommended it to her. But Katya answered

him in monosyllables: she withdrew into herself. Once she had withdrawn into her shell she was generally long in coming out again; her face on such occasions would wear a dogged, almost dull look. She could not exactly be called shy; she was only mistrustful and slightly cowed by her sister's tutelage, a fact which the latter, of course, never suspected. Arkady bridged an awkward pause by calling Fifi, who had come back into the room, and patting her head with a benevolent smile. Katya busied herself again with her flowers.

Meanwhile, Bazarov was piling up forfeits. Anna Sergeyevna played a skillful hand, and Porfiry Platonich was well able to stand up for himself too. Bazarov's loss, insignificant though it was, was not altogether pleasant. Over supper Anna Sergeyevna once more broached the subject of botany.

"Let us go for a walk tomorrow morning," she said to him, "I want you to tell me the Latin names of wild plants and their properties."

"What do you want the Latin names for?" Bazarov asked.

"There must be order in everything," she replied.

"What a wonderful woman Anna Sergeyevna is!" Arkady exclaimed, alone with his friend in their room.

"Yes," Bazarov answered, "she's a brainy woman. She's seen a thing or two, let me tell you."

"In what sense do you say that, Yevgeny Vasilich?"

"In a good sense, my dear fellow, in a good sense, Arkady Nikolaich! I'm sure she manages her estate splendidly, too. But it's not she who is wonderful, it's her sister."

"What? That dark little thing?"

"Yes, that dark little thing. There's where you have all the freshness, and innocence, and timidity, and reticence and everything else. She's worth taking up. You could mould her into anything you want; but the other one knows all the tricks of the trade."

Arkady said nothing, and each went to bed with his own thoughts.

Anna Sergeyevna, too, was thinking of her guests that evening. She liked Bazarov, liked him for his absence of affectation and his very bluntness. She found in him something new, something she had never come across before, and she was habitually curious.

Anna Sergeyevna was a rather queer creature. While she had no prejudices or even strong beliefs, she neither gave ground nor covered it. She saw many things clearly; many things interested her, but nothing satisfied her completely; she scarcely desired complete satisfaction. Her mind was at once inquisitive and apathetic; her doubts were never allayed to the point of forgetfulness and never grew to the point of anxiety. Had she not been rich and independent she might, perhaps, have thrown herself into the fray and known passion. But she lived an easy life, though at times she felt bored, and her days passed in unhurried procession with only an occasional ripple of excitement. Roseate visions sometimes sprang up before her mind's eye, but she relaxed when they had gone and felt no regrets at their passing. Imagination sometimes carried her away beyond the pale which the decrees of conventional morality permit; but even then her blood coursed unquickened through her calm lovely body. Sometimes, on coming out of a fragrant bath, all warm and languorous, she would fall to musing on life's paltriness, its sorrows, its toil and evils. Her heart would suddenly swell with daring impulses and noble aspirations; but let a current of air blow from the half-opened window and Anna Sergeyevna would shrink and complain and very nearly lose her temper, and all she wanted at that moment was to stop that horrid draught from blowing on her.

Like all women cheated of love, she longed for something, she knew not what. Actually she wanted nothing, although it seemed to her she wanted everything. She could barely stand the late Odintsov (it had been a marriage of convenience on her part, though she would not, perhaps, have consented to become his wife unless she had considered him a good man), and had conceived a secret loathing for all men, whom she always thought of as a messy, heavy, limp lot of helplessly tiresome creatures. Somewhere abroad she had once met a handsome chivalrous-looking young Swede with frank blue eyes beneath an open brow; he had made a powerful impression on her, but this had not prevented her from returning to Russia.

"A queer man, that medico!" she mused, as she lay in her luxurious bed under a light silk coverlet, her head resting on lace-covered pillows. Anna Sergeyevna had inherited some of her father's love of luxury. She had been very fond of her sinful but kindhearted parent, and he had adored her, joking with her as an equal and confiding in her without restraint. She hardly remembered her mother.

"He's a queer fellow!" she repeated to herself. She stretched, smiled, clasped her hands behind her head, then ran her eyes over a page or two of a silly French novel, dropped the book and fell asleep, cool and clean in her fresh fragrant lingerie.

Soon after breakfast the next morning, Anna Sergeyevna went botanizing with Bazarov and did not return until dinner time; Arkady did not go anywhere and spent nearly an hour with Katya. He had not found her company boring, and she herself had proposed repeating yesterday's sonata; but when Odintsova returned at last and he caught sight of her, his heart felt a momentary pang. She came down the garden, and her eyes under her round straw hat were shining more brightly than usual. She was toying with the slender stalk of a wild flower; her light mantle had slipped to her elbows, and the broad grey ribbons of her bonnet clung on her breast. Bazarov walked behind, self-assured and careless as usual, but Arkady did not like the expression on his face, cheerful and even gentle though it was. Muttering, "Morning!" through his teeth, Bazarov went to his room, while Odintsova absently shook Arkady's hand, and passed on her way.

"Good morning," Arkady thought. . . . "As if we hadn't seen each other today."

17

TIME (we all know) sometimes flies like a bird, sometimes crawls like a snail; but a man is happiest when he does not even notice whether it passes swiftly or slowly. It was in such a state of mind that Arkady and Bazarov spent fifteen days at Odintsova's. This was partly due to the well-ordered regimen Odintsova had introduced in her home. She strictly adhered to this regulated mode of life and made others do the same. Everything in the course of the day was done at its appointed time. In the morning, punctually at eight, the household assembled for breakfast; between breakfast and lunch everybody did as he pleased, while the mistress discussed business with her steward (her estate worked on the quitrent basis), the butler and the housekeeper. Before dinner the company gathered once more for a chat or to do some reading; the evening was devoted to walks, cards and music; at half past ten Anna Sergeyevna retired to her room, issued her orders for the morrow, and went to bed.

Bazarov did not like this monotonous and rather solemn regularity of the daily life. "It's like moving on rails," he said. The liveried footmen and dignified butlers offended his democratic tastes. He believed that they might as well go the whole hog and dine in the English manner, in full dress and white tie. He once broached the subject with Anna Sergeyevna. She had such a way with her that no one hesitated to speak his mind plainly before her. She heard him out and said, "From your point of view perhaps you are right—in that respect I suppose I am the grand lady; but if you dared to live an unordered life in the country you'd be bored to death," and she went on doing things her own way. Baza-

rov grumbled; but both he and Arkady found the life in
Odintsova's house so pleasantly easy precisely because things
"moved on rails."

Indeed, a change had taken place in both young men from
the very first days of their sojourn at Nikolskoye. Bazarov,
who was obviously in Anna Sergeyevna's good graces, though
she rarely agreed with him, began to reveal signs of uneasiness
hitherto foreign to him: he was irritable, untalkative, sulky,
and restless; while Arkady, who had entirely made up his
mind that he was in love with Odintsova, abandoned himself to a quiet melancholy. This melancholy, however, did
not prevent him from cultivating Katya's friendship; it even
helped him to establish very pleasant, friendly relations
with her. "*She* doesn't appreciate me? Oh, all right! But
here's a gentle creature who doesn't reject me," Arkady
thought, and his heart once more knew the sweetness of
generous impulses. Katya was dimly aware that he sought
comfort in her society, and she did not deny either to him or to
herself the innocent pleasure of a half-shy, half-trusting friendship. When Anna Sergeyevna was present they avoided talking
to each other; Katya always seemed to shrink under her
sister's keen eye, while Arkady, as befits a man in love, had no
attentions for anybody when his beloved was near at hand; he
really felt at home, however, only with Katya. He realized that
entertaining Odintsova was a thing he was not equal to; he
was shy and tongue-tied when alone with her, and she did not
know what to say to him: he was too young for her. With
Katya, on the contrary, Arkady was quite at ease; he was indulgent, and gave her free rein to voice her impressions inspired by music, by the reading of a book of poetry and similar trifles, himself unaware that these *trifles* attracted him too.
Katya, on her part, did not interfere with his moping moods.
Arkady enjoyed Katya's company, and Odintsova Bazarov's,
and it usually happened that both couples, after being together for a while, would presently drift apart, especially
when out strolling. Katya *adored* nature, and Arkady loved
it, too, though he never dared admit it; Odintsova was indifferent to it, and so was Bazarov. The fact that our friends

were almost constantly separated was not without its conse-
quences: their relations underwent a gradual change. Bazarov no longer spoke to Arkady about Odintsova and even
stopped criticizing her "aristocratic airs"; he still spoke highly
of Katya, but advised his friend to restrain her sentimental
inclinations; his praise, however, was hurried, his counsels
dry, and altogether he talked much less with Arkady than
before. He seemed to be avoiding him, seemed to be ashamed.

Arkady noticed all this, but kept his opinion to himself.

The actual reason for this "new turn" was the feeling which
Odintsova had inspired in Bazarov, a feeling which tormented
and maddened him, but which he would have promptly
denied with a sneering laugh and a cynical remark had anybody even remotely hinted at the possibility of what was
actually happening to him. Bazarov was a great admirer of
women, but love in the ideal or, as he expressed it, romantic
sense, he called tommyrot, unpardonable folly; chivalry he
looked upon as something in the nature of a monstrosity or
a disease, and on more than one occasion expressed his surprise that Toggenburg with all the Minnesingers and troubadours had not been put in a madhouse. "If you like a woman,"
he said, "try to get down to brass tacks; if it doesn't come off,
never mind, snap your fingers, there are plenty of others."
Odintsova had caught his fancy; the rumors concerning her,
the freedom and independence of her ideas, her obvious lik-
ing for him—all this, one would think, was grist to his mill;
but he soon became aware that he would not be able to "get
down to brass tacks" with her, and as for snapping his fingers,
he found to his dismay that he could not do it. His pulse
quickened at the mere thought of her; he could easily have
come to terms with his pulse, but something else had happened to him, something he never would have admitted,
something he had always jeered at, and against which all his
pride rose up in arms. When talking with Anna Sergeyevna
he went out of his way to show his careless scorn for everything romantic, but when left alone he was shocked to dis-
cover the romanticist within himself. He would then go off
into the woods, and stride about there aimlessly, breaking

branches as he went along and cursing both her and himself under his breath; or else he would creep into the hayloft and, stubbornly shutting his eyes, try to force himself to sleep, which, of course, he did not always succeed in doing. Suddenly he would imagine those chaste arms entwining his neck, those proud lips responding to his kisses, and those profound eyes gazing tenderly—yes, tenderly, into his, and his head would reel, he would forget himself for a moment until indignation would get the better of him. He caught himself at all kinds of "shameful" thoughts, as though the devil were teasing him. At times he thought he noticed a change in Odintsova too, something peculiar in the expression of her face, as if. . . . At this point he would stamp his foot or gnash his teeth and shake his fist in his own face.

As a matter of fact, Bazarov was not wholly mistaken. He had caught Odintsova's fancy; he interested her and she thought of him a great deal. In his absence she was not bored and did not miss him; but she became animated as soon as he appeared upon the scene; she willingly remained alone with him and willingly talked to him, even when he made her angry or offended her good taste and refined habits. It seemed as if she wanted to test him, and herself while she was at it.

One day while walking with her in the garden, he suddenly announced gloomily that he intended to leave soon for his father's place in the country. The color fled from her cheeks, and a pang shot through her heart; so strong a pang that it surprised her and long afterwards she wondered what it could have meant. Bazarov had announced his departure not with the idea of testing her, of seeing what would come of it: he never "made things up." That morning he had seen his father's steward, Timofeich, who had had charge of him when he was a child. This Timofeich, a spry seedy-looking little old man with bleached yellow hair, a red weather-beaten face and tiny drops of moisture in his shrunken eyes, unexpectedly appeared before Bazarov in his short peasant coat of stout grey-blue pilot cloth girdled by a bit of old belt and tarred high boots.

"Hullo, old man!" Bazarov had exclaimed.

"Good morning, master Yevgeny Vasilich," the old man had said, and his face suddenly wreathed in wrinkles and lit up with a happy smile.

"What brings you here? You've come for me, I suppose?"

"Goodness gracious, sir, no!" Timofeich mumbled (he bore in mind the strict injunction his master had given him when he set out). "I was going to town on the master's business when I heard about Your Honor being here, so I dropped in on the way—to have a look at Your Honor . . . but as for bothering you, I'd never think of it!"

"Tell me another one," Bazarov had interrupted him. "Is this the way to town?"

Timofeich had shifted from one foot to the other and said nothing.

"Is Father all right?"

"Yes, sir, thank God."

"And Mother?"

"And Arina Vlasyevna, too, thank God."

"They're waiting for me, I suppose?"

The little fellow cocked his tiny head.

"Ah Yevgeny Vasilich, how could it be otherwise! As sure as there's a God above, it makes one's heart bleed to look at your parents."

"Well, all right, all right! Don't lay it on. Tell them I'll be coming soon."

"Very good, sir," Timofeich had said with a sigh.

As he left the house he jammed his cap on his head with the help of both hands, clambered into a ramshackle racing sulky, which he had left standing by the gates, and trotted off, but not in the direction of the town.

That evening Odintsova was sitting in her room with Bazarov, while Arkady paced up and down the drawing room listening to Katya playing. The princess had retired to her room upstairs; she disliked all visitors, and these "wild ones," as she called them, in particular. In the common rooms she merely sulked; but in the privacy of her own chamber, before her maid, she would break out into such violent abuse that the cap on her head together with the wig would start dancing. Odintsova knew this.

"What is this about your going away," she began, "and what about your promise?"

Bazarov started.

"What promise?"

"Have you forgotten? You wanted to give me some lessons in chemistry."

"I'm sorry. My father is expecting me. I can't dally any longer. But you can read Pelouse *et* Frémy, *Notions générales de Chimie;* it's a good book and written in simple language. You'll find everything you need there."

"Do you remember telling me that no book was as good as. . . . I have forgotten how you expressed it, but you know what I mean . . . do you remember?"

"I'm sorry!" Bazarov repeated.

"Must you go?" Odintsova said, lowering her voice.

He glanced at her. She had thrown her head back against the armchair with her arms, bared to the elbow, folded on her breast. She looked paler in the light of a solitary lamp screened by a perforated paper shade. The soft folds of her loose white gown enveloped her; the tips of her feet, likewise crossed, were barely visible.

"Why should I stay?" Bazarov said.

Odintsova turned her head slightly.

"What do you mean—why? Aren't you enjoying yourself here? Or do you think nobody will be sorry you're gone?"

"I'm sure of it."

Odintsova was silent for a while.

"You are wrong there. Anyway I don't believe you. You couldn't have meant that seriously." Bazarov had not stirred. "Yevgeny Vasilich, why don't you say something?"

"What can I say? I don't think people are worth being sorry about—I more than others."

"Why so?"

"I'm a serious, uninteresting man. I'm no good at making conversation."

"You're fishing for compliments, Yevgeny Vasilich."

"It's not my habit. You ought to know that the refinements of life which you cherish so much are beyond me."

Odintsova bit the corner of her handkerchief.

"You may think whatever you like, but I shall find it dull when you go away."

"Arkady will remain," Bazarov said.

Odintsova gave a little shrug.

"I'll find it dull," she repeated.

"Really? At any rate you won't find it dull long."

"What makes you think so?"

"You told me yourself that you are bored only when your routine is upset. You have arranged your life with such impeccable regularity that there can be no room for boredom in it, or yearnings . . . no painful feelings of any kind."

"So you think I'm impeccable . . . I mean, that I have arranged my life so well?"

"Rather! For example: in a few minutes it will strike ten, and I know beforehand that you will drive me away."

"No, I won't, Yevgeny Vasilich. You may remain. Open that window. . . . I feel hot."

Bazarov got up and pushed the window. It flew open with a bang. He had not expected it to open so easily; and besides his hands shook. The dark, soft night with its almost black sky, its murmuring trees and the fresh smell of the cool sweet air peeped into the room.

"Pull the blind and sit down," Odintsova said. "I want to have a chat with you before you go away. Tell me something about yourself; you never talk about yourself."

"I try to talk to you about useful things, Anna Sergeyevna."

"You are very modest. But I'd like to know something about you and your family, about your father, for whom you are deserting us."

"Why is she saying all this?" Bazarov wondered.

"It's not in the least interesting," he said, "especially for you; we are lowly folk."

"And I am an aristocrat, I suppose?"

Bazarov looked up at her.

"Yes," he said with exaggerated harshness.

She smiled.

"I see you don't know me well enough, though you claim that all people are alike and not worth studying. I shall tell you my story some day . . . but first tell me about yourself."

"I don't know you well enough," Bazarov repeated. "Perhaps you are right; perhaps every person is really a riddle. Take yourself, for example; you shun society, you dislike it, yet you invite two students down to stay with you. Why do you, with your intellect and your beauty, live in the country?"

"What? What did you say?" Odintsova said quickly. "With my . . . beauty?"

Bazarov frowned.

"Never mind," he muttered, "I want to say that I can't make out why you live in the country?"

"You can't understand it, you say. But you have tried to explain it to yourself I suppose?"

"Yes. . . . I suppose you stay permanently in one place because you like to pamper yourself, you are fond of comfort and ease and indifferent to everything else."

Odintsova smiled again.

"You simply refuse to believe that I am capable of letting myself go, don't you?"

Bazarov threw her a look from under his brows.

"Out of curiosity, perhaps; nothing else."

"Indeed? Well, now I understand why you and I have become friends; you're like me, you know."

"You and I have become friends . . ." Bazarov murmured huskily.

"Yes! . . . But I'd forgotten that you wanted to go."

Bazarov rose to his feet. The lamp shone dimly in the middle of the darkened, fragrant, secluded room; through the fluttering blind the night poured in its tantalizing freshness and mysterious whisperings. Odintsova did not stir a limb, but a secret excitement was gradually taking possession of her. It communicated itself to Bazarov. He suddenly realized that he was alone with a beautiful young woman.

"Where are you going?" she said slowly.

He answered nothing and sank back into his chair.

"And so you consider me a cold, pampered, spoiled thing," she went on in the same tone, without removing her eyes from the window. "I always thought I was unhappy."

"You unhappy! Why? Surely you don't attach any importance to foul gossip?"

Odintsova frowned. She was annoyed at his having interpreted her in *this* way.

"That gossip does not even amuse me, Yevgeny Vasilich, and I'm too proud to let it annoy me. I'm unhappy because . . . I have no desire, no zest for living. You look at me incredulously and are probably thinking: there speaks the 'aristocrat.' I don't deny that I love what you call comfort, and yet I have little zest for life. Try and reconcile those inconsistencies if you can. In any case it's all romanticism to you."

Bazarov shook his head.

"You enjoy good health, independence, wealth; what more do you need? What do you want?"

"What do I want?" Odintsova repeated, and sighed. "I am very tired, I am old; it seems as if I have been living for ever so long. Yes, I'm old," she added, gently drawing the ends of her mantle over her bare arms. Her eyes met Bazarov's, and she blushed slightly. "I have so many memories behind me: life in St. Petersburg, wealth, then poverty, then my father's death, my marriage, then a trip abroad, as it should be . . . lots of memories, but nothing to remember, and ahead of me a long, long road and no goal. . . . I don't feel like going on."

"Are you so disillusioned?" asked Bazarov.

"No," Odintsova said slowly, "but I am unsatisfied. I think that if I could form a strong attachment for something. . . ."

"You want to fall in love," Bazarov interrupted her, "but you cannot—that's your misfortune."

Odintsova contemplated the sleeves of her mantle.

"You think I am not capable of falling in love?" she murmured.

"Hardly. Only I shouldn't have called it a misfortune. On the contrary, the person who has had that thing happen to him is the one to be pitied."

"What thing?"

"Falling in love."

"How do you know that?"

"By hearsay," Bazarov said moodily.

"You're flirting," he thought; "you're bored and so you are teasing me for want of anything better to do, while I. . . ." Indeed, his heart contracted with pain.

"And then I suppose you are too demanding," he said, leaning his whole body forward and toying with the fringe of his armchair.

"Perhaps. I believe in everything or nothing. A life for a life. Take mine and give me yours, but there must be no regrets, no drawing back. Otherwise, better not."

"Well," observed Bazarov, "those are fair conditions, and I'm surprised that you haven't yet . . . found what you want."

"Do you think it's so easy to give yourself up utterly?"

"Not if you stop to reflect, and bide your time, and put too high a value upon yourself; but it's quite easy to give yourself up without thinking."

"How do you expect a person not to prize himself? If I am not worth anything, of what use is my devotion to anybody?"

"That's not my concern; let the other person decide whether I'm worth anything or not. The main thing is to be capable of surrender."

Odintsova leaned forward in her chair.

"You speak as though you have been through it yourself," she said.

"I just passed an opinion, Anna Sergeyevna; all this, you know, is not in my line."

"But would you be capable of giving yourself up?"

"I don't know—I shouldn't like to boast."

Odintsova made no reply and Bazarov fell silent. The sounds of the piano floated across to them from the drawing room.

"Katya is playing rather late today," Odintsova observed.

Bazarov got up.

"Yes, it is rather late and time for you to retire."

"Wait a minute, what is the hurry? I have something to tell you."

"What is it?"

"Wait a minute," Odintsova whispered.

Her gaze rested on Bazarov; she seemed to be studying him closely.

He took a turn about the room, then suddenly went up to her, hurriedly said, "Good-bye," squeezed her hand so that she nearly cried out, and strode out. She lifted her crushed fingers to her lips and blew on them; obeying a sudden impulse she jumped up from the armchair and ran swiftly to the door, as if to call Bazarov back. A maid came in with a decanter on a silver tray. Odintsova stopped, dismissed her, then returned to her seat and her thoughts. Her plait had come undone and fell snakelike on her shoulder. The lamp burned for a long time in Anna Sergeyevna's room, and for a long time she sat motionless, only now and then stroking her arms nipped by the cold air of night.

Bazarov came into his bedroom two hours later, disheveled and gloomy, his boots wet with dew. He found Arkady at the writing table with a book in his hand, his coat buttoned right up.

"Haven't you gone to bed yet?" he said with a shade of annoyance.

"You were sitting with Anna Sergeyevna a long time tonight," said Arkady, ignoring his question.

"Yes, I was with her all the time you and Katya were playing the piano."

"I wasn't playing," Arkady began, then fell silent. He felt the tears welling up to his eyes, and he did not want to cry in front of his sarcastic friend.

Reader's Supplement

to

FATHERS AND SONS

IVAN SERGEIVICH TURGENEV (TURGENIEF), (1818–1883)

BIOGRAPHICAL AND HISTORICAL
BACKGROUND

Among the writers of the Russian realistic school, Turgenev is chronologically the fourth great master after Pushkin, Lermontov and Gogol. His literary activity extended through almost five decades, from the 1830's to the 1870's.

As an artist Turgenev possessed a diverse and brilliant talent. He was a poet, a dramatist, a novelist, a critic. His poetry, drama and critical works are unfortunately little known outside Russia.

Turgenev's name is inseparable from that period of Russian history which marked the transition from feudalism to private enterprise. Those were contradictory times, filled with philosophical and literary debate, charged with fierce political and economic struggle.

Ivan Sergeivich Turgenev was born on October 28, 1818, into a wealthy landed family in the city of Orel. Raised at his family estate (Spasskoe-Lutovinovo) north of that city, he received his early schooling at home—a usual practice with the wealthy nobility in those days. He was endowed with keen intelligence and a great capacity for learning, and entered Moscow University at fifteen. Later, he transferred to the University of St. Petersburg, from which he was graduated in 1836. He then went to Berlin to study Hegel, Goethe and ancient languages, after which he returned to Moscow to continue his studies. When he received his master's degree in philosophy in 1842, Turgenev was one of the best educated young men of his day.

How he was to use this knowledge was not quite clear to him. He had begun writing poetry while still a student, but he thought little of entering upon a literary career. Full of Hegelianism, he wished to teach this philosophy in Russia. However, the departments of philosophy had been closed by Emperor Nicholas I, and Turgenev had to enter the civil service, the last thing he desired. But there he was—an extremely gifted, broadly educated young Russian noble, with a mind equipped with the most up-to-date philosophy—serving as a mere cog in the bureaucratic machinery of a regressive, serf-owning state which he loathed. Turgenev became one of what were then called the "unwanted young men"—the restless, predominantly aimless, young nobles of the early nineteenth century.

Early in his short career as a civil servant, Turgenev wrote a report entitled *A Few Thoughts Concerning the Russian Economy and the Russian Peasant.* It was, by and large, cautious and mild, slavo-philistic in tone. But it also reflected the author's Western orientation. He wrote, in essence, that the Russian patriarchal way of life was a good thing, that Russia owed to it its moral purity and deep religiosity. On the other hand, Turgenev maintained that this ancient Russian patriarchism was "hindering civil progress in Russia," "it could not remain unchanged," and "all the outdated institutions passed down to us by the former patriarchal way of life" were "now outmoded and burdensome."

Russian literature in the 1840's was experiencing its "second birth." The age of Pushkin had just ended. Preceding that age, Russian literature had had no national foundation and no dynamism of its own. It was now quickly finding itself. Romanticism and poetry, which had dominated the first quarter of the century, gradually began to give way to realism and prose in the 1830's, as it did throughout Europe. In Russia, however, this process had been slowed for several reasons. One was that a laborious task had to be performed, the recreating of the national language, which had stagnated, partly due to the nobility's long use of French, and partly because of the heavy stamp of eighteenth-century classicism.

After the War of 1812, Russia had experienced a great spiritual rejuvenation. One of the results was a realization that the slumbering nation possessed truly fantastic but tightly shackled potentialities. Russia's best sons took a good look at her and were horrified at their country's backwardness. They came to the conclusion that Russia's monarchy and the system of serfdom were responsible for their country's plight. A secret movement was started by groups of officers and civilians. On December 14, 1825, they made an attempt at overthrowing the monarchy and establishing a constitutional republic. This failed. Monarchy was still too strong, and its challengers were too few and too weak, both ideologically and numerically.

The development of literature met with strong monarcho-aristocratic resistance. Young Pushkin led the way. He first threw off the burdensome weight of classicism that pressed like a tombstone on poetic form, and wrote free and vibrantly romantic verse. At the same time, braving aristocratic derision, he turned his back on French, unclogged the wellsprings of the dormant national tongue and tapped folklore.

Pushkin's conscientious probing into Russian life changed the substance of his art. A pure romanticist, he soon felt the influence of Byron, but then he began to look beyond himself. Thus he discovered realism and, during the 1830's, his realistic prose laid a new foundation for Russian literature. Before his death, Pushkin planted the seed of the first great realistic novel by suggesting the plot of *Dead Souls* to his *protégé,* Gogol.

The appearance of *Dead Souls,* although many places in it had been cut by censorship, amounted to nothing short of a revolution in Russian literature. For the first time, a novel showed Russian society as it really was, and so poignant was the bitter indictment of serfdom and the landlord society that people gasped in horror.

Dead Souls indicated the main lines along which Russian realistic prose was to develop. First, it was to be socially oriented; second, it was to be critical of society as it then existed. *Dead Souls* had those qualities: it was keenly social and it was sharply critical. What was true of Gogol and his work became equally true of the great authors and the great works that followed, of Goncharov and Hertzen, of Dostoevsky and Nekrasov, of Saltikov-Shchedrin and Tolstoi.

The critical and social character of Russian realism were determined precisely by the nature of life as it then existed in Russia. The country had been brought to virtual ruin by one thing—serfdom. For the early realistic prose writers, serfdom was the determining factor of Russian life, and its eradication their prime objective.

Although Turgenev had strong feelings about serfdom and regarded it as a socio-economic evil, he did not at once grasp the full meaning of it. This was one of the main reasons for the failure of his early prose, a failure that by 1847 had led him to some very sad conclusions.

"There was no need to continue such exercises," he later wrote concerning that period. "I firmly decided to quit them altogether. . . ."

Then one day, by accident, everything changed. But let Turgenev tell it: ". . . only because of I. I. Panaev who lacked material to fill the odd section of the first issue of *Sovremennik* [a literary magazine founded by Pushkin], and asked for something. I left with him a story entitled 'Khor' and Kalinich.' The words *From a Hunter's Sketches* were thought up and added by the same I. I. Panaev with the intention of getting the readers' indulgence. The story's success led me to write others and I returned to literature."

Turgenev's success was instantaneous. After having read several stories, critic V. G. Belinsky, the brilliant exponent of realism, wrote to the author: "If I am not mistaken your calling is to observe the phenomenon of life and describe it, having passed it through your imagination, but without relying on your imagination alone. . . . [these stories] promise to make you a great writer." (S. M. Petrov, *I. S. Turgenev,* Moscow, 1957, pp. 21, 22)

Hunter's Sketches not only brought Turgenev into prominence, but they also opened a new page of Russian realism. They were the first successful attempt to show Russian peasants not as mere ignorant, superstitious, impoverished victims of serfdom, but as human beings. For the first time, the peasant entered literature as a full-fledged character, and to the reader, this was a revelation. Belinsky, in his never-ending debate with the aristocratic critics, once wrote concerning the pictorialization of the peasantry in literature:

"Nature is the eternal master copy of art while the greatest and noblest thing in nature is Man. And isn't a muzhik a man? But what, you say, can attract interest in an uncouth, ignorant man? Fancy asking! It's his soul, mind, heart, his feelings, inclinations,—in a word the same things that there are in an educated man." (S. M. Petrov, *I. S. Turgenev,* Moscow, 1961, p. 74)

It had become clear to Turgenev that thorough knowledge of the subject was the cardinal rule of serious writing. Only thus could he hope to be true to life, and only then could he hope to reach the reader. Speculation, invention, idealization simply weren't enough. As soon as Turgenev took something that he knew well (the life of the Orel District peasants) and passed what he knew through his imagination, everything fell into place.

What first impressed readers of *Hunter's Sketches* was their simplicity, placidity and clarity of line. In those respects the author was clearly, consciously following in Pushkin's footsteps. The stories were always compact; the drawing of character was extremely economical, amplified by only the most essential details.

In describing nature Turgenev showed a superb talent. L. Tolstoi later said: "One field where he is such a master that one's hands simply drop in helpless inability to touch the subject after him is nature. One—two strokes, and there is fragrance." No earlier Russian author had been able to achieve either such poignancy or such animation in portraying nature. In Turgenev's work, nature did not serve as a passive background. The stories were not unfolded against it, but amidst it; characters, too, were revealed through it.

This treatment and use of nature focused attention where the author wanted it to be concentrated—on the human being in his vast and complex spiritual and social worlds. The ideal well-being and the fullest possible development of the positive qualities of man comprised the subjective side of *Hunter's Sketches*. It expressed itself in the deftly satirical drawing of the typical carriers of man's negative spiritual elements—the landed nobility and the appointed village elder types ("Burgomaster"), the rich peasant types ("Khor' and Kalinich"), and in such elements as man's cruelty and injustice to man, philistinism, servility, hypocrisy, greed. In concrete terms those were the degrading manifestations of serfdom. In the assertion of man's positive qualities, of his spiritual and intellectual values, the author's subjectivity, on the other hand, found lyric tones of truly spellbinding quality. The possessors of those qualities were mainly the peasants ("The Singers," "The Bezhin Meadow"). The language was simple, light, exact, flowing—a further advance in the linguistic reform begun by Pushkin. At the same time it possessed a style which was entirely new and very attractive.

During the next few years Turgenev continued to add to the *Hunter's Sketches*. In the same year of 1847 *Sovremennik* published "Lgov," "Ermolay and the Miller's

Wife," "The Burgomaster," and "The Office"; in 1848 "Raspberry Water," "Biruk," and others; in 1851, "The Bezhin Meadow," "Kasyan from the Beautiful Mech" and others.

In 1852 *Hunter's Sketches* came out as a book. These stories were a clear indictment of serfdom. The government of Nicholas I recognized this fact by dismissing censor L'vov, who had permitted their publication in book form. Turgenev, too, was heading for trouble. For his obituary on Gogol, Turgenev was arrested for a month in 1852, then exiled to his Spasskoe estate for the entire year of 1853.

What worried the Russian monarchy about Turgenev's writing was not so much the portrayal of the peasants as human beings, but the revelation of their inhuman sufferings at the hands of the nobility, and the thoroughly negative portrayal of that nobility—something that smacked too much of the hated and dangerous Gogol.

No less alarming to the authorities was the author's association with the literary magazine *Sovremennik*. Ever since I. I. Panaev had taken it over, the magazine had been a thorn in their sides. In the 1840's it had been the sounding board for Belinsky's revolutionary aesthetic theories. Now in the 1850's with poet N. A. Nekrasov as its editor, and N. G. Chernishevsky, critic and philosopher, as its guiding spirit, the magazine was fast becoming a literary-political tribune of social and economic democracy. Its prestige was high, and it had a great following among the so-called *raznochintsi,* the new, nongentry intelligentsia that had sprung up during the 1830's and 1840's. The 1850's witnessed a serious challenge to the nobility's intellectual dominance from this new intelligentsia.

Turgenev was united with Chernishevsky and his *raznochintsi* group in his hatred of serfdom. However, he did not oppose monarchy in principle, but wished to get rid of Nicholas I and his "garrison state" rule. On literary matters

Turgenev did not agree with Chernishevsky's emphasis on the Gogol school. He feared that that was a lopsided view, that it unduly cast into the background the Pushkin tradition with its assertion of the positive in life. His aristocratic colleagues in *Sovremennik* wholly misunderstood him, however.

So, in 1855 Turgenev wrote Druzhinin: "It seems to me that on many issues we have divergent viewpoints, and that our personalities are different. . . . Both influences I think are necessary in our literature. The Pushkin influence has for a time receded, but let it assert itself again. The Gogol influence in life and literature is still needed very much. . . ."

And in 1856, to the same Druzhinin: "You remember that I, an admirer and junior follower of Gogol, once talked to you concerning the need for the return of the Pushkin element as a counterbalance to the Gogol one. A striving toward objectivity and total truth is one of the few positive qualities which I thank nature for endowing me with."

Turgenev would have been the last one to sling mud at Gogol. Gogol, to him, was the extension of Pushkin, not Pushkin's negation; what Gogol brought into literature was not vulgarity or baseness (as some critics asserted) but a fresh and necessary stream of clearheaded, uncompromising criticism, aimed at eradicating the negative in life, thus making it possible for life's positive, ideal nature to assert itself fully.

Turgenev advanced this thesis all his life as a critic and correspondent. He was true to it as an author, too. Some of his best novels were products of its application. These were *Rudin* (1855), *The Nest of the Gentry* (1858) and *On the Eve* (1859). Although Gogol had exposed the cruel, parasitic nature of the landed Russian aristocracy, Turgenev, in his three masterpieces, condemned the aristocracy by painting a vivid picture of its moral and spiritual degradation in the 1830's and 1840's, tracing that degradation to the centuries-old, parasitic life based on serfdom.

In 1855, during the Crimean War, Nicholas I died. To Turgenev and many others, Nicholas had been the person- ification of everything evil, and they saw in his passing the beginning of a new era in Russian history.

The new Emperor, Alexander II, soon announced his intention of abolishing serfdom. This intention, to be sure, was dictated by necessity—not by the Czar's goodness of heart. "It's better to abolish serfdom from above," said Alexander II to the Moscow nobility in 1856, "than to wait till it will start abolishing itself from below." The process was to be a gradual one, extended over a period of years, with final freedom set for 1861.

Nekrasov, Chernishevsky and the other *raznochintsi* in the *Sovremennik* sensed foul play. Turgenev, on the other hand, was gratified; he saw a new day dawning in Russia, a flash of light in the darkness. In literary terms this meant that "the ideal" had appeared in life, and that the Gogol approach could be de-emphasized. Nekrasov and Cher- nishevsky could not agree with Turgenev, for they saw nothing positive in the contemplated reforms.

Thus a basic conflict arose between Turgenev and the leaders of the *Sovremennik*. When, in 1861, abolition was announced in the Manifesto of February 19, the *Sovre- mennik*'s worst expectations were confirmed: the serfs were freed, but without land.

That, however, did not shatter Turgenev's faith in the new Emperor. The reform was still better than nothing and, given time, things would improve. The main thing was not to spoil a good beginning, not to hinder the flow of events in the right direction. He was sure that Russia was finally on her progressive way.

This attitude was only a reflection of his socio-political views in a changed historical context. What had united him with Chernishevsky, Nekrasov and the aristocrat-turned-democrat Hertzen in the 1850's, and with Belinsky in the 1840's, had been the common bond of progressivism and humanitarianism, a common desire to see the nation freed of all fetters. Turgenev saw this as a gradual process, involving much hard work on the part of *all* the Russian intelligentsia regardless of their social origin, a process that involved *all* the social groups. Chernishevsky, Nekrasov, Hertzen and Belinsky could not see the nation advancing into the future composed socially as it was then. For one thing they did not see how the nobility could possibly march ahead if for no other reason than that it was dying out. They looked at matters not only from a national point of view, like Turgenev, but from a class point of view as well.

As long as a clash between classes was remote, these differences were secondary, and Turgenev worked well with the *raznochintsi;* but once a clash became imminent as a result of the worsening economic condition of the peasantry and the "phony" liberation, these differences became inescapable. When Chernishevsky began to call on the peasants to rise openly against monarchy and the nobility, Turgenev shied away.

The *Sovremennik* deeply regretted its disagreements with Turgenev. The feeling was mutual. The magazine, considering Turgenev "the pride of our literature," certainly did not want to lose him; Turgenev, who valued the *Sovremennik* as the best literary magazine in the country, would have liked very much to continue, too. Also, he felt closer to Chernishevsky and Nekrasov on more social issues than he did to his liberal aristocratic friends (Botkin or Druzhinin). As a matter of record, following his break with *Sovremennik* in 1862, Turgenev quite consciously never joined the liberal aristocratic camp.

His next novel, *Fathers and Sons,* appeared the same year in a different publication. Written as it was, during the height of the country-wide debate over the forthcoming liberation of the serfs, it reflected the head-on clash between the nobility and the new intelligentsia. The novel did not concern itself with actual problems of those pre-liberation years. The author's point of view as such was absent, too, but subjectively, Turgenev was very much present throughout the work.

If in *Rudin* and *The Nest of the Gentry* the nobility at least still had ideas and a desire to do something, by now it lacked even that. All it could do was sit and watch helplessly as something new, something frightening was moving up to take its place.

This something new and frightening was the *raznochinnaya* intelligentsia which Turgenev represented in the guise of a poor army doctor's son—Bazarov. His understanding of the task at hand was clear, and he had both strength and ability to tackle it. But there was something wrong with him. For one thing, Bazarov offered nothing constructive. He was a nihilist. His philosophy was that of rejection, negation. Bazarov rejected things indiscriminately, whether he knew them to be evil or whether he knew nothing about them because, as he admitted, he "likes to negate," because his "mind is so constructed."

The controversy caused by the novel upon its publication was perhaps the sharpest touched off by any novel in Russian literary history. The *raznochinnaya* intelligentsia, except for a certain segment of it on which the character of Bazarov was actually based (the followers of critic Pisarev), denounced the novel as slander against them. Many of them declared that they would read nothing else written by the author, that he was a traitor to the cause of Russian freedom.

Immediately after *Fathers and Sons,* Turgenev began to go through a long period of moral depression. Having placed such high hopes in the Emancipation Manifesto of February 19, 1861, he had expected gradual changes for the better in the country. But the Emancipation proved to be a very partial success. Worse still was the rapidly increasing opposition of the nobility to its implementation. This, together with the Czarist Government's policy of procrastination, had a most unhealthy effect on the country's economy. In order to forestall any concerted political opposition to its policies, the government moved against the *raznochinnaya* intelligentsia. In 1864, on the Mytnyn Square in St. Petersburg, Chernishevsky was publicly subjected to a so-called civil execution, then condemned to hard labor for several years, and exiled to Siberia for the rest of his days. Pisarev, too, was arrested and thrown into the ill-famed Petropavlovsky Fortress. Both the *Sovremennik* and *The Russian Word* were suppressed.

Although he had nothing to do with it any more, Turgenev found the suppression of the *Sovremennik* painful, and watched with alarm the closing down of public reading rooms, Sunday schools, chess clubs, and the tightening of censorship. It was as though the hated times of Nicholas I were coming back. That was the atmosphere in which Turgenev entered his second period of literary activity.

The author's first post-reform novel was *Smoke* and when it came out in 1867, readers discovered a new Turgenev. The usual manorial setting was absent; the thematic scope had broadened; there was greater lyrical flexibility; and the author's detached attitude was almost gone.

Faced with the greatly increased complexity of individual and social life, with its heightened dramatism and the new, dominant role of politics, the acknowledged "chronicler of the Russian social scene" felt the necessity of finding new forms and new means of expression. Earlier, he had criticized L. Tolstoi for the latter's psychoanalytical method; now he himself began to resort to it. His unsympathetic attitude toward the political satire in Saltikov-Shchedrin's works also changed. He not only approved of it, as the logical outgrowth of Gogol's non-political satire, but added it to his own arsenal.

Smoke was charged with blistering political and social satire. Many characters were built almost exclusively by the use of elements of satire. Here Turgenev's gift for finding common-noun definitions and coining aphorisms revealed itself most brilliantly. In typifying the post-Emancipation aristocracy, the author noted that its attitudes had not changed one iota—that it still considered inalienable the right to abuse human dignity. The nobility allowed only a certain acknowledgment of "form," and felt no need to abandon the teeth-busting ways of Nicholas I. Thus the author created types of the "softly piercing dignitary" and the general whose motto was "politely, but in the teeth."

The post-reform evolution of Russia which had caused Turgenev so much anguish had also strengthened his Western orientation. With the aristocratic reaction sabotaging the reforms, and the *raznochinnaya* democrats aiming at utopian socialist transformations through peasant communes while Russia itself lay prostrate and helpless, Turgenev saw Westernization (in terms of technical, cultural and educational advance) as the only way out.

However, his attitudes toward the two opposing forces were different. The first he bitterly hated, for it stood against everything that was dear to his heart and necessary to westernize Russia. That force had to be shown in all its ugliness—spiritual, political, moral. The *raznochintsi* were something else again. Turgenev shared with them many sentiments and admired their selfless devotion to the people, but doubted their theories and disapproved of their methods. Therefore he had to oppose them too.

Turgenev's last works (prose and poetry) were alternately colored with pessimism, nostalgia for the past, and reassertions of faith in the future. In 1883, after a long illness, he died. Russia mourned him deeply. He left an indelible mark on Russian literature and language. His influence on Russian writers and on his nation has been immense and beneficial, both spiritually and ethically.

—*Neal Burroughs*

Note: The page references on the following pages direct your attention to passages in the text (T for Top of page, M for Middle, and B for Bottom).

PICTORIAL BACKGROUND

The servant, out of a sense of decorum, or perhaps to escape his master's eye, withdrew to the gateway and lit his pipe. Nikolai Petrovich, his head bent, studied the rickety steps of the porch. (p. 3B)

A RUSSIAN INN—1856

Pyotr came back with . . . a thick black cigar which Arkady promptly lit . . . Nikolai Petrovich . . . was obliged to turn his nose away . . . so as not to hurt his son's feelings.

A quarter of an hour later both vehicles drew up before the steps of a new wooden house. . . . This was Maryino . . . or, as the peasants called it, Lone Man's Farm. (p. 13M)

WELL-TO-DO RUSSIAN FARMER'S HOME—1800's

*Pavel Petrovich Kirsanov received his early education at
home, like his younger brother Nikolai. . . . He was extremely
handsome from childhood on . . . was self-confident and had
a droll sarcastic sense of humor. . . . Women lost their heads
over him; men called him a fop and secretly envied him.*
(p. 30T)

A RUSSIAN DANDY OF THE MIDDLE 1800's

Pavel Petrovich suffered torment even while Princess R——
loved him, but when she cooled towards him—and that happened fairly soon—he nearly went mad. He was distraught
with love and jealousy. He gave her no peace and trailed
after her everywhere. She grew tired of his importunities
and went abroad. Despite the pleadings of his friends. . . .
(p. 32M)

ELEGANT SOCIETY OF THE 1800's

Fenichka had put her hair in order, too, and changed her kerchief, but she could have spared herself the trouble. For what in the world can be more fascinating than a pretty young mother with a healthy baby in her arms?

"What a chubby little fellow," Pavel Petrovich said indulgently, and tickled Mitya's twin chins. . . . *(p. 39M)*

RUSSIAN PEASANT MOTHER AND CHILD–1855

And come to grips they did, that very evening at tea. Pavel Petrovich came down to the drawing room ready for battle, irritated and determined. He was only waiting for an excuse to hurl himself at the enemy, but an excuse was long in coming. Bazarov was generally not talkative in the presence of the "old Kirsanov boys" (as he called the brothers). . . . (p. 50B)

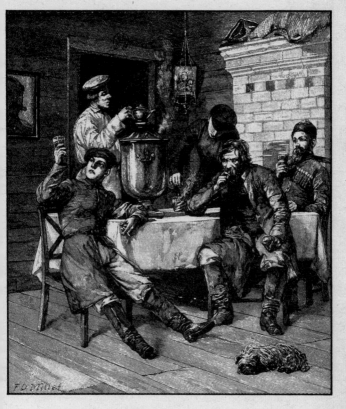

TEA TIME AROUND A RUSSIAN SAMOVAR—1800's

Half an hour later Nikolai Petrovich went into the garden to his favorite arbor. Sad thoughts preyed on him. He now saw clearly, for the first time, that he and his son were drifting apart, and that the rift would grow wider as time went on. It was in vain then that he had sat for days on end in the winter out there in St. Petersburg, poring over new books. . . . (p. 59T)

BUSTLING ST. PETERSBURG IN THE MID 1800's

The Governor received the young men affably, but did not offer them a seat and did not sit down himself. He was always busy and bustling. The first thing in the morning he would get into a tight-fitting uniform and an exceedingly tight cravat; and all day he missed his meals and went without sleep in the eternal bustle and excitement of issuing orders. (p. 65B)

RUSSIAN ARISTOCRAT—1800's

Several days later the ball was held at the Governor's house. Kolyazin was the "hero of the day." The Marshal of the Nobility made known to all and sundry that, strictly speaking, he had come only out of respect, while the Governor contrived (even at the ball, and even when he was sitting still) to "issue orders." Kolyazin's geniality was equalled only by his majestic mien. (p. 76T)

RECEPTION AND BALL AMONG RUSSIAN ELITE—1860's

*Our friends were met in the hallway by two stalwart foot-
men in livery, one of whom immediately ran off in search of
the butler.*

*"Anna Sergeyevna requests you to join her in half an hour,"
announced the butler. "Is there anything you wish in the
meantime?"*

"No, nothing, my dear man," Bazarov answered. . . .
(p. 86M)

GLITTERING INTERIOR OF A WEALTHY RUSSIAN'S HOME—1800's

The twenty-five versts seemed like fifty to Arkady. At last, a village came into view on a sloping hillside. Here lived Bazarov's parents. Nearby, in a young birch wood, stood a little manor house under a thatched roof. Two peasants in caps stood bickering at the first hut. "You're a big swine," one was saying to the other, "and behave worse than a little 'un." (p. 118B)

RUSSIAN VILLAGE—1870's

"When I meet a man who can hold his own against me," he said slowly, "I'll change my opinion about myself. Hate! Why, today, for example, when we were passing the hut of our starosta Philip—it's such a pretty white hut—you said Russia will be a perfect country when the lowliest peasant has a dwelling like that to live in, and that everyone of us should help to bring that about." (p. 138T)

RUSSIAN PEASANT BEFORE HIS HUT—1800's

Father Alexei, a portly handsome man with thick carefully brushed hair and an embroidered girdle over a purple silk cassock, proved to be a very shrewd and quick-witted person. He hastened first to shake hands with Arkady and Bazarov, as though aware beforehand that they had no need of his blessing, and, generally, he bore himself with ease. (p. 142M)

HANDSOME RUSSIAN PRIEST—1870's

Nikolai Petrovich had introduced a fine for damage caused by cattle, but the matter usually ended by the horses being returned to their owners after spending a day or two on the master's fodder. To crown it all, the peasants began to quarrel among themselves. . . . Things would come to a head in a sudden brawl; everybody would come flocking. . . . (p. 149B)

BRAWLING RUSSIAN PEASANTS—1800's

"*Is that supposed to be witty?*" *Pavel Petrovich asked. . . .*

He sometimes asked to be allowed to witness Bazarov's experiments, and once even brought his perfumed face, laved with an excellent lotion, close to the microscope to examine some transparent infusorians in the process of swallowing a green speck and hastily masticating it. . . . (p. 153M)

LABORATORY EQUIPMENT—MIDDLE 1800's

Something whizzed sharply close to Bazarov's ear, followed by an instantaneous report. "I've heard it, so I suppose I'm all right." . . . *He took another step and pulled the trigger.* . . .

Pavel Petrovich gave a slight start and clutched his thigh.

Bazarov threw his pistol down and approached his adversary.

"Are you wounded?" *he asked.* (p. 166M)

AFTERMATH OF A PISTOL DUEL—1870

Sometimes Bazarov would take a walk through the village and, in his usual bantering way, enter into conversation with one of the peasants. "Well," he would say to him, "trot out your views on life, old man; you're said to have in you all the power and future of Russia; you're to start a new era in history; you're going to give us a real language and real laws!" (p. 198B)

A VISITOR CHATTING WITH RUSSIAN PEASANTS—1800's

The change for the better did not last long. The patient suffered a relapse. Vasily Ivanich sat by Bazarov's bedside. Something more than ordinary anguish seemed to be preying on the old man's mind. He tried several times to speak but could not.

Vasily Ivanich . . . dropped on his knees before Bazarov. . . . (p. 207M)

A TIME TO WEEP

A week before in the little parish church a double wedding had taken place . . . that of Arkady and Katya, and of Nikolai Petrovich and Fenichka—and on this day Nikolai Petrovich was giving a farewall dinner in honor of his brother, who was leaving for Moscow on business. Anna Sergeyevna had gone to Moscow, too, immediately after the wedding. (p. 213M)

A RUSSIAN VILLAGE CHURCH—1800's

In this grave lies Yevgeny Bazarov. Here, from the nearby village, often comes a decrepit old couple—husband and wife. Supporting each other, they plod on with weary footsteps. They come to the enclosure, fall down upon their knees and cry long and bitterly, and long do they gaze at the mute tombstone under which their son lies. (p. 217M)

TYPICAL RUSSIAN TOMBSTONES—1800's

VISUAL GLOSSARY

1—mobcap (p. 127T)   3—fez (p. 169M)
2—scratch wig (p. 90B)   4—fuchsia (p. 77M)
5—harpsichord (p. 130T)

6—sulky (p. 100B)   7—troika (p. 151M)
8—lancet (p. 125B)

9–chubouk (p. 120T)   11–cassock (p. 142M)
10–muzhik (p. 35M)   12–siskin (p. 38M)

LITERARY ALLUSIONS AND NOTES

The notes which follow contain brief explanations of some
of the literary allusions in *Fathers and Sons,* as well as historical, mythological, biographical, and other allusions which,
without explanation, might impede understanding. Since,
moreover, the novel in the original Russian contains a
sprinkling of foreign—mostly French—expressions which
have been included in the English translation, an attempt has
been made in these notes to give their meaning in English in
a fairly free rendering.

cum laude **(p. 2B):**
with praise, with honors; used on diplomas at graduation
to indicate the special merit of the work of the recipient.

Ministry of Appanages (p. 3T):
Ministry of Dependent Territories.

patronymic (p. 5B):
the father's first or given name; the middle name of every
Russian man or woman.

Il est libre, en effet **(p. 10T):**
He is, in effect, free.

Catherine the Great (p. 11B):
Catherine (1729–1796) was Empress of Russia (1762–
1796).

Pushkin (p. 12B):
Alexander Sergeyevich Pushkin (1799–1837), Russian
poet, novelist and dramatist, was considered by many to be
Russia's greatest writer. *Eugene Onegin* (1825–1831), a
long narrative poem (on which Tchaikovsky based an
opera), is considered his masterpiece and is characterized
by brilliant descriptions of and comments on the society of
his day.

s'est dégourdi (p. 16T):
    is more at ease.

Galignani's Messenger (p. 17B):
    English magazine published in Paris by Giovanni Antonio
    Galignani (1752–1821) and his two sons, John Anthony
    and William.

nihilist (p. 23M):
    Though Turgenev popularized the label, he did not originate
    it. The Russian author and critic, Avrahm Yarmolinsky
    traces it back to St. Augustine (354–430), who used i
    to denote unbelievers. The translator Bernard Guerney say
    that as political terms "nihilist" and "nihilism" were firs
    used by N. E. Nadezhdin in 1829.

Vous avez changé tout cela (p. 24T):
    You have changed all that.

Hegelists (p. 24T):
    or *Hegelians* were followers of the German philosophe
    Georg Wilhelm Friedrich Hegel (1770–1831). His studie
    of nature, human history, and psychology gave rise to hi
    ideas of government: that the state is superior to all in
    dividuals and that the highest development of the state i
    a monarchy.

Wellington (p. 34B):
    Duke of Wellington (1769–1852), British general; con
    queror of Napoleon at Waterloo (1815) and British Prim
    Minister (1828–1830).

Louis-Philippe's table (p. 34B):
    Louis-Philippe (1773–1850) was King of France (1830–
    1848). Evidently, Pavel Petrovich was distinguished enougl
    to have dined at the table of the King of France.

Mais je puis vous donner de l'argent (p. 36B):
    But I can give you the money.

Royal Streltsi (p. 39T):
    Royal archers.

pastille on a copper disc (p. 39M):
A pastille is a small cone or mass of aromatic material which when lighted fumigates or scents the air of a room.

pater familias **(p. 46M):**
father of a family; head of a family.

Büchner's *Stoff und Kraft* (p. 48B):
Ludwig Büchner (1824–1899) was a German philosopher and physician who developed a highly materialistic philosophy. *Kraft und Stoff* (1855) was translated into English as *Force and Matter* (1864).

Mathieu **(p. 50M):**
French form of Matvei.

of Alexandrian traditions (p. 51B):
of the traditions of Alexander I, Czar of Russia (1801–1825).

materialism (p. 54B):
an attitude which may be formulated in a number of ways, not necessarily related to one another: the philosophy that attempts to explain life and the universe through the ways in which physical laws affect matter; the doctrine that holds material possessions and physical well-being to constitute the greatest good; the regard for the material aspects of life rather than the spiritual ones.

the very emancipation the government
was fussing over (p. 55M):
Alexander II emancipated the serfs on February 19, 1861.

the savage Kalmyk and the Mongol (p. 56M):
members of Buddhist tribes that inhabited the region extending from western China to the Volga River.

Lucifer (p. 56B):
the archangel (often called Satan) who led the revolt of the angels against God and was thrown out of heaven.

Raphael (p. 57T):
Raphael (Raffaello) Sanzio (1483–1520), one of the greatest painters of the Italian Renaissance.

Girl at a Fountain (p. 57T):
a reference to any of the cheap paintings with sentimental or romantic titles which were very popular.

vieilli (p. 58B):
aged ones; old folk; "has-beens."

bon soir (p. 58B):
good evening.

l'énergie est la première qualité d'un homme d'état (p. 63B):
Energy is the most important characteristic (virtue) of a statesman.

Guizot (p. 63B):
François Guizot (1787–1874), French statesman (premier 1847–1848) and historian.

Madame Svechina's St. Petersburg salon (p. 64T):
Sofiya Petrovna Svechina (1782–1859), a Russian writer on mystic and religious themes, was famous also for her literary and intellectual "evenings."

Condillac (p. 64T):
Étienne Bonnot de Condillac (1715–1780) was a French philosopher who tried to achieve a harmony between a scientific concept of psychology and his religious beliefs.

Byronism (p. 65M):
George Gordon, Lord Byron, the English poet (1788–1824), is supposed to have been responsible for a great many fashionable beliefs, moods, attitudes—one of them being a glorification of solitude, loneliness.

il a fait son temps (p. 65M):
He's (Byron's) had his day.

Pan-Slavist (p. 65M) **and Pan-Slavism** (p. 65 footnote):
Pan-Slavism was a movement which sought to unite all Slavic peoples politically and culturally. It was opposed by those who advocated the introduction into Russia and other

Slavic countries of the political and cultural ideas of western Europe.

émancipée (p. 67M):
an emancipated woman.

tax-farming (p. 67B):
a process by which the government, when in need of money, received a fixed amount of money from an individual or a corporation and, in return, gave that individual or corporation the power to collect and keep certain taxes.

Liebig (p. 71T):
Baron Justus von Liebig (1803–1873) was a German chemist who made a number of important contributions to organic and agricultural chemistry.

Moskovskiye Vedomosti (p. 71T):
a Moscow newspaper.

George Sand (p. 71M):
This was the pseudonym of Amandine Aurore Lucie Dupin, Baronne Dudevant (1804–1876), popular French novelist. Her early novels were highly romantic; those she wrote later were full of ideas for social reform.

Emerson (p. 71M):
Ralph Waldo Emerson (1803–1882), the American essayist, philosopher, and poet, was apparently as well known among the intellectuals of far-away Russia as the French George Sand.

Cooper's Pathfinder (p. 71B):
A reference to James Fenimore Cooper's the *Pathfinder* (1840).

mon amie (p. 72B):
my female friend.

Proudhon (p. 73T):
Pierre Joseph Proudhon (1809–1865) was a French writer on social questions who influenced the French and, indeed,

all European radical movements—especially the syndicalists and the anarchists. His belief that individual moral responsibility was superior to socially imposed regulations aroused the opposition of such thinkers as Karl Marx.

Macaulay (p. 73M):
Thomas Babington Macaulay (1800–1859), English politician (Whig), historian, and essayist.

Et toc, et toc, et tin-tin-tin! **(p. 74T):**
words from a drinking song: "Let's touch and clink our glasses together."

Bedlam (p. 74B):
a place of confusion or a lunatic asylum; from the hospital of St. Mary of Bethlehem (Bedlam) in London which was once used as an asylum for the insane.

en vrai chevalier français **(p. 76M):**
as a true French cavalier.

enchanté **(p. 76B):**
delighted to meet you.

"Zut," "Ah fichtre," "pst, pst, mon bibi" **(p. 76B):**
mild French ejaculations.

si j'aurais . . . si j'avais **(p. 76B):**
confused tense forms of the verb meaning *to have*.

absolument **(p. 76B):**
absolutely. Until fairly recently, even dictionaries of English were careful not to confuse *absolute* or *absolutely* with *certain* or *certainly*. In modern editions, however, the distinction seems to have disappeared.

comme des anges **(p. 77T):**
like angels.

quadrille (p. 77M):
a dance for four couples.

Optime **(p. 85T):**
Fine! Excellent!

Saint's Day (p. 85T):
In many countries the day the church celebrates the birthday of a particular saint is celebrated especially by anyone named after that saint.

What *grand genre!* (p. 87T):
What a grand type! What a distinguished lady!

old-fashioned game of *preference* (p. 91B):
a card game resembling whist, sometimes called *five hundred*.

piling up forfeits (p. 93T):
piling up debts.

quitrent (p. 96M):
a small fixed rental paid in a number of European countries by a person to his feudal superior which freed that person from the obligation of performing certain feudal services for the lord.

Toggenburg (p. 98M):
One of the ballads of the German poet and dramatist Friedrich von Schiller (1759–1805) tells the story of Toggenburg, a knight who comes back from a crusade to find his sweetheart a nun, and who spends the rest of his life as a hermit watching for her to appear at a window so that he may get an occasional glimpse of her.

Minnesingers . . . troubadours (p. 98M):
German and French words for those lyric poets and musicians who in the Middle Ages wrote and sang of love and adventure. They are kin to the bards, skalds, minstrels, and jongleurs of all nations and all times.

***notions générales* (p. 107B):**
general ideas.

***Traité élémentaire de physique expérimentale* (p. 108T):**
Elementary Treatise in Experimental Physics.

**You can't really expect the gods
to bake bricks! (p. 115M):**
the equivalent of "Somebody has to do the dirty work."

homme fait **(p. 122T):**
an impressive man.

Croesus **(p. 122B):**
a fabulously wealthy ruler of the ancient world.

Suum cuique **(p. 123T):**
To each his own.

stop playing Lazarus to the rich man (p. 124T):
Lazarus was the beggar (Luke xvi) who desired "to be
fed with the crumbs which fell from the rich man's table."

The Friend of Health **for 1855 (p. 124B):**
a medical periodical. Notice that old Bazarov's "current"
medical literature was four years old.

**Schenlein—Rademacher—Hoffmann—
Brown (p. 125T):**
Johann Lukas Schenlein (1793–1864), Johann Gottfried
Rademacher (1772–1850), Friedrich Hoffmann (1660–
1742), and John Brown (1735–1788) were medical the-
orists who were already old-fashioned when the older
Bazarov was speaking.

voilà tout **(p. 125M):**
That's all.

Prince Wittgenstein (p. 125B):
Ludwig Adolf Peter Wittgenstein (1769–1843), Russian
general who fought against Napoleon and against the Turks.

Zhukovsky (p. 125B):
Vasili Andreevich Zhukovsky (1783–1852), Russian romantic poet, was tutor to the children of the Czar. He is
remembered more for his translations into Russian of the
writings of such foreigners as Byron, Walter Scott, Schiller,
and Goethe than for his own poetry.

Paracelsus (p. 126T):
Philippus Aureolus Paracelsus (1493?–1541), whose real
name was Theophrastus Bombastus von Hohenheim, was
a Swiss alchemist and physician who had a remarkable
influence both in his own day and after his death. Opposing
the ideas of Galen, the Greek physician whose doctrines
were popular for almost fifteen centuries, Paracelsus advocated the use of specific remedies for specific diseases,
introduced opium, mercury, sulphur, iron, and arsenic as
medicines, and wrote about the hereditary characteristics
of syphilis and the relationship between head injuries and
paralysis. One of Robert Browning's most famous poems,
Paracelsus, is a portrait of the scientist.

***In herbis, verbis et lapidibus!* (p. 126T):**
In plants, words, and stones—or minerals [the physician
finds his medicines].

Horace (p. 128T):
Quintus Horatius Flaccus (65–8 B.C.), Roman poet, is
admired by lovers of literature to this very day.

Morpheus (p. 128M):
Greek god of dreams, son of Hypnos, god of sleep.

Maundy Thursday (p. 129T):
The Thursday before Easter, the anniversary of the establishment of the Eucharist, is accompanied by various
ceremonies in different parts of Christendom—blessing of
salt, washing of beggars' feet, distributing of Maundy
money by the king to the poor.

John the Baptist's head (p. 129M):
At the instigation of Salome, daughter of King Herod and
Queen Herodias, John the Baptist was beheaded (Mark vi).
This Biblical narrative was turned into a drama, *Salome,* by
Oscar Wilde and then into an opera by Richard Strauss.

***Alexis, or a Cabin in the Woods* (p. 129M):**
popular French sentimental novel.

Bokhara dressing gown (p. 131T):
Bokhara, in the south central part of Asiatic Russia, has long been famous for its rugs and textiles.

Cincinnatus (p. 131M):
Lucius Quinctius Cincinnatus (5th century B.C.) was a Roman patriot who, on two separate occasions, was called from working on his farm to save his countrymen from their enemies.

Jean Jacques Rousseau (p. 131M):
The French philosopher (1712–1778), born in Switzerland, was a social and educational theorist and novelist. In his social and educational thinking, he stressed the value and dignity of work, especially manual labor.

***homo novus* (p. 131B):**
a new man.

***amice* (p. 134T):**
friend.

icterus—jaundice (p. 134T):
Icterus is the original Greek word for jaundice, a liver disease.

centaury—St. John's wort (p. 134T):
medicinal herbs.

***Robert le Diable* (p. 134M):**
French opera (1831) by the German composer Giacomo Meyerbeer (1791–1864).

Le vin . . . le jeu, les belles, Voilà . . .
***mes seuls amours!* (p. 134M):**
Wine, play (gambling), beautiful women—these are my only loves.

Suvorov (p. 135M):
Alexander Vasilyevich Suvorov (1729–1800), who rose from the ranks to become field marshal, was one of the most highly admired military heroes in the history of Russia.

Castor and Pollux (p. 140B):
Twin brothers, called the Dioscuri, sons of Zeus and Leda, were famed not only as athletes and warriors but also for their devotion to each other. According to Greek mythology, one member of every twin is immortal. When Castor was killed, Pollux asked Zeus to let his twin brother share his immortality with him. One version of the story says that Zeus allowed the brothers to share their immortality, spending half their time in Hades and half in heaven. Another version holds that Zeus rewarded their devotion to each other by placing them in the heavens as the twin stars, the Gemini.

the St. Vladimir (p. 142M):
a military award.

starosta (p. 143T):
village elder.

Du calme, du calme **(p. 150M):**
Take it easy; be calm.

Baltic nobles (p. 153M):
nobles of Latvia, Estonia, Ingermanland, and Courland— all on the eastern shores of the Baltic Sea.

Celadons (p. 159M):
Celadon was a name used frequently by poets to designate a lover, especially a rustic lover. In "The Seasons" by James Thomson, the Scottish poet, Celadon's lady love, Amelia, is struck dead by lightning while she is in his arms.

seminary rat (p. 161T):
term of mild contempt for a theological student.

comme il faut **(p. 162M):**
as it should be done; with propriety.

A bon entendeur, salut **(p. 166T):**
A word to the wise is sufficient; you had better take me seriously.

utile dulci (p. 166T):
work and fun; the useful with the pleasurable.

vastus externus (p. 167T):
name of a muscle in the leg.

vertige (p. 167M):
vertigo (dizziness).

Mrs. Radcliffe (p. 168B):
Ann Radcliffe (1764–1823), British writer of romantic "gothic" novels, who excelled in the description of scenes of mystery and terror.

Sir Robert Peel (p. 169T):
British statesman (1788–1850); Home Secretary (1822–1827); Prime Minister (1834–1835 and 1841–1846); founded London police (called Bobbies after his first name) in 1829.

Couchez-vous (p. 170T):
Go to bed.

C'est la même famille (p. 170M):
She is of the same family; there's a family resemblance.

au dix-neuvième siècle (p. 175B):
in the nineteenth century.

Heine (p. 177B):
Heinrich Heine (1797–1856) was one of the great lyric poets of Germany. His work was often characterized by a kind of bitter humor, a mixture of tears and laughter.

kvass (p. 183T):
a fermented drink made from barley or rye.

**Gogol's letters to the Governor
of Kaluga's lady (p. 184M):**
Nikolai Vasilyevich Gogol (1809–1852), one of the greatest writers in the history of Russian literature, was the author of masterpieces like *The Inspector-General* (1836), a comedy, *The Overcoat* (1842), a highly in-

fluential short story, and *Dead Souls* (1842), a remarkable picaresque novel. In his later years he wrote a series of imaginary letters, *The Correspondence with Friends,* which Mirsky calls "painful, almost humiliating reading, in spite of the occasional flashes of imagination that break through its heavy and poisonous mist." It was this collection of letters that contained a number to the wife of the Governor of Kaluga.

terra firma (p. 186B):
solid ground.

et voilà tout (p. 194B):
and that's all.

borsch (p. 197B):
or *borscht* is a soup made of beets.

**It's the earth, sir, that be standing
on three fishes (p. 199T):**
a reference to an old legend, similar to the Greek legend of the earth resting on the shoulders of Atlas.

Goulard's extract (p. 200M):
an acetate of lead solution used as a lotion for inflammations.

lunar caustic (p. 201T):
silver nitrate, used for cauterizing infections.

Pyaemia (p. 204B):
a form of blood poisoning produced by microorganisms in an open wound.

Elysium (p. 206T):
in Greek and Roman mythology, the place where the good people live after they die.

wertester Herr Kollege (p. 209T):
most worthy colleague.

jam moritur (p. 209M):
He is already dying.

Der Herr scheint des Deutschen
machtig zu sein (p. 209M):
The gentleman seems to be proficient in German.

Aesculapius (p. 209B):
Greek and Roman god of medicine.

très distingué (p. 216T):
very distinguished.

in the temporary opposition (p. 216M):
He doesn't hold office now, so that he's of the party in opposition to those that do.

CRITICAL EXCERPTS

Selected from the hundreds of articles, biographies, and volumes of criticism written about Ivan Turgenev, here are some excerpts that should prove challenging to you. We have included page references to *Fathers and Sons*, indicated in parentheses, so that you can review sample passages to help you decide whether to accept or reject the quoted comments.

1. *A summary of contemporary critics (1862):*

The Sovremennik *found the novel lacking in any merits, including the purely literary ones.* Sovremennik's *critic M. A. Antonovich wrote: "You failed to grasp the problem confronting you. Instead of picturing the relations between the 'fathers' and the 'sons' you wrote a panegyric for the 'fathers' and an indictment of the 'sons.' You also failed to understand the 'sons' . . . the novel is nothing but severe and destructive criticism of the young generation."*

To Antonovich, Bazarov was a "vicious caricature," a "depraved cynic," an "uncouth egotist who loves drinking parties and is addicted to liquor," a "cold individual" incapable of love. "The author," he continued, "was incapable of drawing his hero so that he would remain true to himself. . . . He has filled his mind with thoughts and his heart with feelings that are completely out of accord with his character and his other thoughts and feelings."

A. I. Hertzen, too, criticized the book. He wrote his friend: "You were awfully angry with Bazarov; you caricatured him viciously, and had him utter absurdities. You wished to have him end up being shot and finished him off with typhus. But he nonetheless came out superior to that emptiest of men with a fragrant mustache, and to the nincompoop father, and to the pleasure-loving Arkady. It seems to me that you, like an over-eager duelist, having confronted an insolent, broken, bilious man, and upon hearing a mixture of plebeian and middle-class speech, took it all as a challenge and rushed forward. But where is your substantiation? How came it that his young nature became externally callous, angular, irritable? . . . What was it that prevented everything tender, expansive from coming out? Not Büchner's book to be sure?"

D. I. Pisarev, on the other hand, evaluated Bazarov positively. *"Bazarov typified our young generation,"* he wrote in his magazine The Russian Word. *"In him are combined those qualities which are in small doses spread throughout the mass, and the image of this man shapes up clearly in the reader's mind."*

However, within the democratic camp, Pisarev stood alone in his praise of the novel, and although he gratified the author, he could not relieve the heavy feeling produced by the adverse reaction of his erstwhile admirers and friends. *"I then experienced,"* Turgenev wrote years later, *"diverse, but equally depressing impressions. I saw animosity which at times turned into indignation in many close and likable people; I received congratulations, almost kisses, from people of the opposite camp, from my enemies."*

But if it was true that the Bazarov attitude of indiscriminate negation was typical of only a part of the new intelligentsia, and that it was unfair for Turgenev to attribute it to the Chernishevsky or the Hertzen followers, negation was characteristic of the new raznochinnaya intelligentsia as a whole. It was not a quality peculiar to some "specially constructed minds," but became the general frame of mind of those who could see hardly anything good in a life so permeated with evil. Negation was the mark of the times. Negation had largely created Russian realism; it produced the Gogol school; it was also the quality that gave substance to Turgenev's works. It was also true that the new intelligentsia was, by and large, somewhat coarse and sometimes uncouth, which was understandable considering the social environment they had so recently come from and the life of toil they were leading.

Just the same, Bazarov did not typify the new intelligentsia as a whole. But that was not because the author purposely wanted to draw a caricature, not because he was using his art

to attain some dubious political ends. That would have been
beneath Turgenev, the great realist to whom "total truth" was
sacred. He was not against Bazarov; the novel, especially
the last part, proves that.

"The main figure, Bazarov," wrote Turgenev, "was based
on one young provincial doctor (he died shortly before 1861)
who had made a great impression on me. That magnificent
man was to my mind a personification of that very new, still
fermenting, concept which later became known as nihilism. . . . The impression made on me by this personality was
very strong and at the same time not quite clear. . . . One
fact baffled me: nowhere in our literature did I find even a
hint of what I sensed to be everywhere."

Turgenev was never against anything new, anything beneficial for Russia. He had simply violated the primary rule
of realism, the rule he himself cherished most; i.e., he tried
to picture something that he did not fully understand. The
author himself admitted as much with deep regret. Later,
he could never live down the pain over whatever harm (coining the term "nihilist" for one thing) the cause of Russian
democracy suffered as a result of his partially unsuccessful
typification of Bazarov. Hertzen was certainly right when
he wrote Turgenev that the latter confused "a serious, realistic
and mature ideology" with "some sort of crude, boastful
materialism."

As far as literary merit was concerned, M. A. Antonovich
had found none apparently out of sheer spite, for the novel
was written brilliantly. Turgenev's keen humor, acrid satire,
mastery of conversation and description, were there for all to
see. The one thing that the novel lacked was a plot, but that
didn't so much matter. The composition was masterful. Turgenev always paid scrupulous attention to the composition of
his works, aiming at strict harmony between the parts and
compactness in the whole. That is why this novel, like all his
novels, was short. To achieve compactness the author used
the flashback, one of his favorite techniques. The story unfolded smoothly and swiftly with no psychoanalytical digres-
sions. This was also typical of Turgenev who incidentally

thought that L. Tolstoi would have been a better writer had he spent less time in psychoanalyzing his characters.

> An Introduction to *Fathers and Sons*, Neal Burroughs.

2. *More by Antonovich:*

   Turgenev does not know how to define his problem: instead of depicting the relations between "fathers" and "children," he wrote a panegyric to the "fathers" and an exposé of the "children" and, besides, has actually failed to understand the latter; instead of an exposé, the result in his hands turned out to be a calumny . . . the novel is nothing else but a merciless and . . . destructive criticism of the younger generation.

> "An Asmodeus of Our Time," M. A. Antonovich, a review in *Contemporary*, an organ of the younger radicals (1862).

A panegyric is a eulogy, a shower of praise. What arguments could you adduce from the portraits of Nikolai Petrovich (in Chapters 1–11 and 22–24) and of Bazarov's parents (in Chapters 20–21 and 27–28) that Turgenev has delivered the exact opposite of a panegyric—that instead of praising the "fathers," he has criticized them mercilessly or, at most, made us pity them? Similarly, what rebuttal could you make to the view of Antonovich that the treatment of Arkady—certainly one of the "children"—was a calumny? Or, if you are inclined to share Antonovich's point of view, what other interpretation can be given to these passages?

3. *Justice demands the admission that* Fathers and Children, *the work of the well-known writer Ivan Turgenev, has exerted a salutary influence on minds. Standing at the head of contemporary men of talent and enjoying the sympathy of cultural society, Turgenev, unexpectedly to the younger generation which had recently been applauding him, has by means of this work branded our hobbedehoy revolutionaries with*

the mordant name of nihilists, *and has shaken both the doctrine of materialism and its proponents.*

> Special comment in the Report for 1862 of the nefarious Section III (the unspeakable secret police).

When Bazarov was labeled a *nihilist* (p. 23M) or when he said (p. 53T), "These days negation is more useful than anything else—so we negate," he was—or perhaps he was not —shaking "the doctrine of materialism and its proponents." Considering not only these labels and words, but also all the other words and actions of Bazarov throughout the book, what do you think of the judgment of the secret police?

4. *Examine carefully A. I. Hertzen's criticism of* Fathers and Sons *in his letter to Turgenev cited by Neal Burroughs.*

Do you agree with Hertzen in his estimate of Bazarov's superiority to Pavel Petrovich and Nikolai Petrovich as well as to Arkady? How fair is Hertzen in calling Nikolai Petrovich a nincompoop? Does the picture we get of him at Maryino (pp. 1–62) substantiate this characterization? What label would describe Arkady better than the "pleasure-loving" one used by Hertzen? Why, indeed, is "pleasure-loving" perhaps even unfair? What sort of impression of Arkady does Turgenev want us to go away with as indicated by his description of him on p. 215T?

5. *Examine carefully Pisarev's evaluation of Bazarov cited by Neal Burroughs.*

How can Pisarev say that the Bazarov who speaks so coldbloodedly and scientifically to Pavel Petrovich (pp. 51T–58B) is the same sort of character who impulsively kisses Fenichka (p. 159T) and in a fit of uncontrolled passion declares his love for Odintsova (p. 110M)?

6. *Who has not felt the fascination of Turgenev's women! And yet all of them give themselves to the strong male. With such "superior people," as with beasts, the males fight with*

each other, the woman looks on, and when it is over, she submits herself the slave of the conqueror.

> *All Things Are Possible,* Leo Shestov, translated by S. S. Koteliansky, with a Foreword by D. H. Lawrence, Robert M. McBride, 1920.

7. *[Turgenev's] greatest [story] is* Fathers and Children, *with its masterly sketch of Bazarov, the nihilist . . . who tries in vain to subject all his impulses to scientific law. Unfortunately, the younger generation took offense at the character and severely castigated the author. . . .*

> "Russian Literature," Clarence A. Manning, in *Encyclopedia of Literature,* Joseph T. Shipley, Editor, Philosophical Library, 1946.

8. Fathers and Sons *is Turgenev's only novel where the social problem is distilled without residue into art. . . . Here the delicate and poetic narrative art of Turgenev reaches its perfection, and Bazarov is the only one of Turgenev's men who is worthy to stand by the side of his women. But nowhere does the essential debility and feminineness of his genius come out more clearly than in this, the best of his novels. Bazarov is a strong man, but he is painted with admiration and wonder by one to whom a strong man is something abnormal. Turgenev is incapable of making his hero triumph, and to spare him the inadequate treatment that would have been his lot in the case of success, he lets him die, not from any natural development of the nature of the subject, but by the blind decree of fate. For fate, blind chance, crass cruelty preside over Turgenev's universe. . . . Even the heroic Bazarov dies as resigned as a flower in the field, with silent courage but without protest.*

> *A History of Russian Literature* (revised), D. S. Mirsky, Francis J. Whitfield, Editor, Alfred A. Knopf, 1949.

Mirsky, in his remark that "crass cruelty presides over Turgenev's universe," was probably thinking about the blows inflicted by the Fates on Pavel Petrovich, Nikolai Petrovich, Odintsova, and Bazarov's parents. On the other hand, why would a careful consideration of the careers of such people as Katya, Arkady, and Fenichka give a reader good reason to disagree with Mirsky's remark?

9. *Madame Odintsova's feeling for Bazarov is extremely complex. He attracts her as no man has attracted her before. But the very strength of her sentiment rouses to combat it, that strong self-protective spirit of independence which has up to then been the ruling force in her life. Torn between the two, she knows not whether she loves him or not. Suddenly she gets a message to say that he is dying. She feels impelled to go to him at once; but, as she enters the sickroom and sees his altered deathly countenance, she is conscious only of a chill dismay; and the thought flashes through her, "If I really loved him, I should not have felt like this." One stroke: but no amount of explanation could have so vividly revealed her ultimate coldness; and also that honesty of mind which made her recognize it.*

> *Poets and Story Tellers,* David Cecil, The Macmillan Company, 1949.

10. *Turgenev is in some ways the greatest of the Russian writers. Constance Garnett, who translated all his work, assured me that he used the Russian language with a beauty and a perfection that no other writer has approached. And this unequalled sense of language extended also to form. He was the most perfect artist of them all.*

> Introduction by David Garnett to *Three Famous Plays: A Month in the Country; A Provincial Lady; A Poor Gentleman,* Gerald Duckworth, 1951.

11. *The critics who recognized Bazarov's death as a mere accident and, therefore, as the chief fault of the novel made the fundamental mistake of overlooking its tragic theme; and those who accused Turgenev of libeling the younger generation because Bazarov did not act, overlooked the main reason for his tragedy, namely that Turgenev conceived him as a man born ahead of his time. Indeed, the venom with which the adherents of the progressive movement in Russia attacked Turgenev is largely explained by their subconscious realization of their own helplessness.*

> Turgenev, *A Life*, David Magarshack, Grove Press, 1954.

12. *One of the most moving scenes in* Fathers and Sons *is the last one which describes the visit of his old parents to Bazarov's grave. To Turgenev it was the most convincing proof of true and unselfish love.*

> Turgenev, *A Life*, Magarshack.

We are all affected deeply by such scenes (p. 217) as the one Magarshack refers to. How would you, however, answer the person who insisted that Bazarov's parents expressed their love for him most deeply in Chapters 20 and 21 (pp. 120–146) when he was still very much alive?

13. *From the moment when we first see Bazarov taking his time about offering his bare, red hand to his host, and turning down the collar of his nondescript coat to show his long, thin face, with its sandy side-whiskers and cool green eyes, to the moment, a few months later, when the dying atheist raises one eyelid in horror as the priest administers the last sacrament, we are in the presence of a figure that shows the fullest measure of Turgenev's powers of characterization. He believed that a novelist must be "objective," concerned to represent the world about him rather than his response to it, that his art required an interest in and a cumulative knowledge of other peoples' lives, as well as an understanding of the forces*

that shaped them. Bazarov, the tough-minded, hard-fisted medic, with his brutal honesty, his faith in a crudely empirical science that he uses as a cudgel wherewith to hit out at the genteel culture he abominates, this professed "Nihilist," is an example of what the objective method can achieve. In some respects, he is perhaps fashioned after an image at the back of Turgenev's mind, the image of the man he admired and could not be.

> Turgenev, The Man, His Art and
> His Age, Avrahm Yarmolinsky,
> The Orion Press, 1959.

How would you answer a critic who insisted that Bazarov was not as fully developed a character as Yarmolinsky seems to think? For example, was he fully developed emotionally? What was there in his character that made it impossible for him to have a normal relationship with Odintsova, probably the only woman he ever loved? Does the conversation between the two (pp. 184B–186B) indicate a fully developed emotional relationship? His attitude toward the world about him might provoke even more uncertainties about how fully developed Bazarov was. What really was his view of society? "Yes," says Pavel Petrovich (p. 54M), "you talk to him [the peasant] and despise him at the same time." What you are really asked to consider here is why Turgenev's liberal friends were shocked by *Fathers and Sons* when it first appeared, and why its later readers were able to find virtues in the novel which its earliest readers could not see.

14. *The publication of his strongest novel,* Fathers and Sons, *dominated by its "nihilist" . . . hero, Bazarov, cost him his popularity with the radicals, who accused him of having caricatured them. Deeply offended for Turgenev regarded Bazarov as anything but a caricature; this character was in fact his reply to the familiar criticism that he could create Russian heroines but no Russian hero from this year, 1862 onwards, Turgenev remained abroad, except for brief visits,*

and deliberately alienated himself from Russian life and literature. . . .

> *Literature and Western Man*, J. B.
> Priestley, Harper and Brothers,
> 1960.

How do the actions of Bazarov in his conversations with Pavel Petrovich (Chapters 6, 10, and 24), in his hunting for biological specimens (p. 19M), in his relationships with Odintsova (Chapters 15–19 and Chapter 27) support or refute the charge that Bazarov was a caricature?

On the basis of Turgenev's descriptions of Fenichka (pp. 40T–42, 154M–159), Yevdoxia Kulshina (pp. 69–75), Bazarov's mother (pp. 128B–130), or Odintsova (pp. 77T–119), would you agree with those critics who had insisted, on the basis of his previous stories, that Turgenev was very much better at picturing women than men?

15. *Were the question put: Which work of Turgenev's created the greatest sensation?—it seems inconceivable that any other title could be named in answer save* Fathers and Sons . . . *which not only awakened more interest than any previous or subsequent work of Turgenev's but aroused more controversies than any other Russian novel of the nineteenth century, controversies the heat of which persisted literally for decades and which has not died out in certain quarters to this very day.* Fathers and Sons, *we are assured by a contemporary witness, was read (and even bought) by those who had never opened a book since their school days. . . . What sort of book was it—progressive or retrograde? Whom was the author glorifying, both critics and readers wanted to know, and whom was he denigrating?*

. . . Crabbed Age and Youth cannot live together, and at first glance Fathers and Sons *may have congealed into a classic on that theme.*

Yet the book was very much more than that in its beginnings: the conflict it dealt with was more than merely intratribal, merely regional. All of Russia (literate Russia, that

*is) was split into two camps: Slavophiles and Westernizers.
. . . The Slavophiles were, in short, all those who were perfectly willing to do anything on earth for the dear little muzhik
except get off his back. The Westernizers, on the other hand,
were fighting to spread enlightenment; believing that the
future and progress of Russia lay toward the West, they
wanted to emulate Peter the Great by breaching a few more
windows into Europe and letting the light and fresh air of
civilization into benighted and stifling Russia.*

> (Foreword by Bernard Guilbert
> Guerney), *Fathers and Sons*, Ivan
> S. Turgenev, Bernard Guilbert
> Guerney, Translator, The Modern
> Library, 1961.

If, as Guerney says (and the title of the book seems to
confirm), *Fathers and Sons* harps on the theme that "crabbed
Age and Youth cannot live together," then why do Bazarov
and Arkady, both of the younger generation, eventually
separate (pp. 194T–195M)? Why does Nikolai Petrovich,
a member of the older generation, find happiness not only
with young Fenichka as his wife (pp. 175, 213–214B), but
also with Arkady (pp. 213–214B), who was originally an
ally of Bazarov's? Guerney implies that Bazarov was an
adherent of the Westernizers. What arguments could you
advance to support the assertion that in certain respects
Pavel Petrovich was more "western" in outlook than Bazarov?
Should they not, then, have been intellectual allies rather
than adversaries?

"What sort of book was it," asks Guerney, "progressive or
retrograde? Whom was the author glorifying . . . and whom
was he denigrating?" What answer would you make to a
critic who insisted that because people—as Guerney and
others have pointed out—were confused, Turgenev's book
was really a failure? How can *Fathers and Sons* have any
claim to distinction or even to ordinary effectiveness, if the
very people Turgenev was most anxious to impress found his
novel not only mystifying but positively repelling?

16. *"Within the limits of my power and ability, I strove conscientiously and impartially to represent and incarnate in appropriate types both what Shakespeare called 'the body and pressure of the time' and the rapidly changing countenance of the educated Russians, who have been the predominant object of my observations."* Thus wrote Turgenev toward the end of his life as he looked back at his novels. These form indeed a kind of imaginative social history of Russia during the middle decades of the past century, the age of halfhearted reforms that were changing the old order, threatened by rising political unrest. It is history in terms of the destinies of certain men and women of the privileged classes. The tales display a rare insight into behavior and feeling, the ability to evoke the very essence of a climactic moment or situation. The human dramas are played out against the background of the natural scene, and the vicissitudes of the individuals are set within the larger context of the fate of Russia herself, the huge, mute sphinx. Turgenev believed himself to be an objective, impartial observer of life, but his work reveals a clear-cut point of view: that of a good European, loving freedom *"above all else,"* to use his own phrase, abhorring doctrinaire fanaticism, whether reactionary or radical, a gradualist pinning his faith to enlightenment, civilization, *as the country's sole hope.*

Russians: Then and Now, A Selection of Russian Writing From the Seventeenth Century to Our Own Day, Avrahm Yarmolinsky, Editor, The Macmillan Company, 1961.

If, as Yarmolinsky says, Turgenev believed himself "a good European, loving freedom 'above all else,'" then which of the two chief antagonists in *Fathers and Sons*—Pavel Petrovich or Bazarov—seems to you to have been a more enthusiastic advocate of the doctrine of individual liberty?

18

THE next day when Odintsova came down to breakfast, Bazarov sat bent over his cup for a long time, then suddenly looked up at her. She turned to him as though he had nudged her, and he thought her face looked paler. She presently retired to her room and did not come down again till lunch. It had been raining since morning, and it was impossible to go out for a walk. The whole company gathered in the drawing room. Arkady found a recent issue of a magazine and began reading it aloud. The princess, as usual, first looked surprised, as though he were doing something indecorous, then glared at him, but he paid no attention to her.

"Yevgeny Vasilich," said Anna Sergeyevna, "come up to my room. I wanted to ask you. . . . You spoke yesterday about a manual. . . ."

She got up and made for the door. The princess looked round with an expression that seemed to say: "Just look how amazed I am!" then turned back to stare at Arkady, but he raised his voice and, exchanging glances with Katya who sat next to him, went on reading.

Odintsova walked swiftly to her study. Bazarov followed her with downcast eyes, and only his ear caught the faint swish and rustle of her silk gown gliding in front of him. Odintsova lowered herself into the same armchair that she had occupied the night before, and Bazarov, too, sat down in his former seat.

"What was the name of that book?" she asked after a slight pause.

"Pelouse *et* Frémy, *Notions générales* . . ." replied Bazarov. "I'd also recommend Ganot, *Traité élémentaire de physique expérimentale*. The plates in this work are clearer and as a textbook it is . . ."

Odintsova put out her hand.

"Excuse me, Yevgeny Vasilich, but I didn't call you here to discuss textbooks. I wanted to resume the talk we had yesterday. You went away so suddenly. You won't be bored, will you?"

"I'm at your service, Anna Sergeyevna. But what was it we were talking about yesterday?"

Odintsova threw him a sidelong glance.

"We were talking, I believe, about happiness. I was telling you about myself. Speaking of happiness by the way, why is it that even when we are enjoying, say, some good music, or a lovely evening, or a conversation with people we like—why does it all seem more like a hint of some vast happiness existing elsewhere, rather than real happiness, that is, the kind we ourselves possess? Why is it? Or perhaps you haven't experienced anything of the sort?"

"You know the saying: 'our neighbour's crop seems better than our own,' " retorted Bazarov. "You admitted yourself yesterday that you were dissatisfied. Such thoughts really don't enter my mind."

"Perhaps you think them absurd?"

"No. They simply don't enter my mind."

"Really? Do you know, I'd very much like to know what *you* think about."

"What? I don't follow you."

"Listen, I have long wanted to talk things over with you. You do not have to be told—you know it yourself—that you are not of the common run of men; you are still young—all your life is before you. What do you intend to do? What does the future hold for you? I mean—what goal are you aiming at, where are you going, what is in your mind? In short, who are you, what are you?"

"You astonish me, Anna Sergeyevna. You know that I am studying natural science; as for who I am. . . ."

"Yes, who are you?"

"I've already told you that I'm going to be a country doctor."

Anna Sergeyevna made a gesture of impatience.

"Why do you say that? You don't believe it yourself. That might be all right coming from Arkady, but not from you."

"In what way is Arkady . . . ?"

"Stop it! Can you possibly be content with such a modest career, and haven't you always said that you don't believe in medicine? You, with your ambition—a country doctor! You say that just to put me off, because you don't trust me. Do you know, Yevgeny Vasilich, I might be capable of understanding you. I was once poor and ambitious myself, just as you are; perhaps I have gone through the same trials as you have."

"That's all very well, Anna Sergeyevna, but you must excuse me. . . . I am not used to unburdening my mind, and then, you and I are so far apart."

"Why far apart? You'll be telling me again that I'm an aristocrat? Oh, come, Yevgeny Vasilich, haven't I shown you that . . ."

"And besides," Bazarov interrupted, "what's the use of talking and thinking about the future, which mostly doesn't depend upon us? If an opportunity turns up to do something, all very well and good, if not—then at least you have the satisfaction of knowing that you didn't babble about it beforehand."

"You call a friendly talk babble. . . . Or perhaps you consider me, as a woman, unworthy of your confidences? You despise the lot of us, don't you?"

"You I don't despise, Anna Sergeyevna, and you know it."

"I know nothing . . . but supposing I do understand your reluctance to talk about your future . . . but what is taking place in you now. . . ."

"Taking place!" Bazarov repeated. "As if I were a state or society! In any case, it isn't interesting; besides, a man can't always express what is 'taking place' in him."

"I don't see why one should not be able to speak one's mind."

"Can *you?*" Bazarov asked.

"I can," Anna Sergeyevna answered after a slight hesitation.

Bazarov bowed his head.

"You are happier than I."

Anna Sergeyevna looked at him questioningly.

"Just as you like," she resumed, "but I have a feeling that we shall be good friends. I'm sure that this—how shall I call it—constraint of yours, this reticence, will finally vanish."

"So you have noticed my reticence, and did you say . . . constraint?"

"Yes."

Bazarov got up and went over to the window.

"And would you like to know the reason for this reticence, would you like to know what is taking place within me?"

"Yes," Odintsova repeated, a nameless fear assailing her.

"You won't be angry?"

"No."

"No?" Bazarov stood with his back to her. "Then know that I love you stupidly, madly. . . . Now you've had it your way."

Odintsova put out both her hands before her, and Bazarov pressed his forehead against the windowpane. He breathed with difficulty; he was visibly trembling in every limb. But this was not the tremor of youthful timidity, the sweet dismay of first confession that overcame him: this was passion surging through him in violent, heavy waves, a passion that resembled rage, and perhaps was akin to it. Odintsova was both terrified and sorry for him.

"Yevgeny Vasilich," she murmured, and could not keep a note of tenderness out of her voice.

He spun around, looked at her with eyes filled by his passion, and, seizing both her hands, suddenly drew her into his arms.

She did not immediately free herself from his embrace; a moment later, however, found her standing in a far corner, from which she looked over at Bazarov. He lunged towards her. . . .

"You didn't understand me," she whispered in swift panic.

Another step on his part, it seemed, and she would scream. Bazarov bit his lip and strode out of the room.

Half an hour later the maid brought Anna Sergeyevna a note from Bazarov; it contained one line: "Must I go today, or may I stay till tomorrow?"

"Must you go? I did not understand you. You did not understand me," Odintsova wrote in answer, while she thought: "I did not understand myself."

She did not appear until dinner, and kept pacing up and down her room, her hands behind her back, stopping now and then before the window or the mirror and slowly wiping her neck with a handkerchief as though conscious of a burning stain. She asked herself what had prompted her to incite him to open his heart, and whether she had suspected anything. "It's my fault," she said aloud, "but how was I to foresee it?" She blushed at the memory of Bazarov's almost savage face when he rushed up to her.

"Why not?" she said suddenly, stopping and tossing her curls. She saw herself in the mirror; the defiant poise of her head, the mysterious smile of half-closed eyes and parted lips seemed at that moment to tell her something which made her feel embarrassed. . . .

"No," she decided at length. "God knows where it may have led us. This is no joking matter; tranquillity is the best thing in the world after all."

Her tranquillity had not been disturbed; but she grew sad and even wept a little, without knowing why—but not because she felt insulted. If anything, she felt guilty. Prompted by various vague emotions, a sense of departing life, a craving for novelty, she had let herself go to a certain limit, forced herself to glance at what lay beyond it, and had seen there not even an abyss, but merely emptiness . . . or ugliness.

19

FOR all her self-possession and freedom from prejudice Odintsova nevertheless felt embarrassed when she came into the dining room for dinner. The dinner, however, passed off quite satisfactorily. Porfiry Platonich dropped in and related several anecdotes; he had just returned from town. One item of news that he imparted was that the Governor had ordered his special commissioners to wear spurs, in case he had to send them somewhere urgently on horseback. Arkady talked in an undertone with Katya and paid diplomatic attentions to the princess. Bazarov maintained a sullen dogged silence. Odintsova once or twice looked openly at his grim, angry face with its downcast eyes, every feature of which bore the stamp of disdainful resolution, and thought: "No . . . no . . . no. . . ." After dinner she went out into the garden with the rest of the company, and seeing that Bazarov wanted to speak to her, she stepped aside and stopped. He came up to her, and with his eyes still downcast, said huskily:

"I must apologize to you, Anna Sergeyevna. You must be very angry with me."

"No, I am not angry with you, Yevgeny Vasilich," answered Odintsova, "but I'm distressed."

"All the worse. At any rate I've been punished enough. My position, you will admit, is a ridiculous one. You wrote me: 'Must you go?' I cannot and do not want to stay. I shall be gone tomorrow."

"Yevgeny Vasilich, why. . . ."

"Why am I going?"

"No, I didn't mean that."

"The past cannot be retracted, Anna Sergeyevna . . .

sooner or later it was bound to happen. Consequently, I must be going. I know only one condition under which I could stay, but that can never be. You will pardon my impudence— but you don't love me, do you, and never will?"

Bazarov's eyes gleamed for an instant under his dark brows.

Anna Sergeyevna made no reply. The thought flashed through her mind, "I am afraid of that man."

"Good-bye, madam," Bazarov said, as if reading her mind, and turned towards the house.

Anna Sergeyevna followed slowly in his steps, and having called Katya, took her arm. She kept Katya by her side until evening. She refused to play cards, and most of the time she laughed, which was not at all in keeping with her pale and harassed look. Arkady watched her wonderingly, the way young men do; that is, he kept asking himself; "What does it all mean?" Bazarov shut himself up in his room; he came down to tea, however. Anna Sergeyevna wanted to say something kind to him, but she was at a loss how to break the ice.

An unexpected incident helped her out of her difficulty: the butler announced the arrival of Sitnikov.

The young progressive's precipitate entrance into the room defies description. With his usual impertinence, he had decided to pay a visit in the country on a woman whom he hardly knew and who had never invited him; he had managed to learn that she was entertaining clever acquaintances of his. He was nevertheless extremely nervous, and instead of offering the apologies and greetings that he had prepared beforehand, he mumbled some drivel about Yevdoxia Kukshina having sent him to inquire about Anna Sergeyevna's health and that Arkady Nikolaich had also expressed his highest opinion. . . . At this point he faltered and was thrown into such confusion that he sat down on his own hat. But because nobody threw him out, and Anna Sergeyevna even presented him to her aunt and sister, he quickly regained his composure and was soon chattering away for all he was worth. Vulgarity is often a welcome interlude in life: it slackens strings that are too highly strung and sobers self-confident or presumptuous feelings by a reminder of their kinship with it. With the arrival of Sitnikov, everything became, as it were, duller, and simpler; everybody even ate a heartier supper, and the company retired to bed half an hour before the usual time.

"I will now repeat," said Arkady from his bed to Bazarov, who had also undressed, "what you said to me one day: Why are you so sad? I suppose you've fulfilled some sacred duty?"

Between the young friends there had lately arisen a mock habit of careless badinage, which is always a sign of veiled resentment or unspoken suspicions.

"I'm going down to my father's tomorrow," Bazarov announced.

Arkady propped himself up on his elbow. He was surprised and yet somewhat glad.

"Ah!" he said. "Is that why you're sad?"

Bazarov yawned. "Curiosity killed the cat."

"What about Anna Sergeyevna?" Arkady went on.

"What about her?"

"I mean, is she letting you go?"

"I don't have to ask her permission, do I?"

Arkady became thoughtful. Bazarov went to bed and turned his face to the wall.

Several minutes passed in silence.

"Yevgeny," Arkady suddenly said.

"Well?"

"I'm going tomorrow, too."

Bazarov did not say anything.

"Only I am going home," Arkady went on. "We'll go together as far as the Khokhlov settlement and there you will get Fedot to give you a team. I'd like to meet your folks, but I'm afraid I'd be in their way and yours. You'll come down to our place again, won't you?"

"I've left my things there," Bazarov said by way of reply, without turning his head.

"Why doesn't he ask me why I'm leaving? And as suddenly as he is?" thought Arkady. "Come to think of it, why am I leaving and why is he?" he pursued his thoughts. He could not find a satisfactory answer to his question and his heart filled with bitterness. He realized that it would be hard for him to give up this life to which he had grown so accustomed; but to remain by himself would be rather awkward. Something has happened between them, he told himself. Why should I hang around after he's gone? I'll only get on her nerves, and lose all. He pictured Anna Sergeyevna; then another image gradually began to take shape through the lovely vision of the young widow.

"I'll miss Katya, too," Arkady whispered into his pillow, on which he had already dropped a silent tear. He suddenly tossed back his hair and said aloud: "Why the hell did that ass Sitnikov have to come here?"

Bazarov stirred in his bed, then said:

"My dear chap, you're still an innocent, I see. The Sitnikovs of this world are necessary to us. I need fatheads like him, don't you see? You can't really expect the gods to bake bricks!"

"Humph," thought Arkady to himself, and in a flash all the abysmal depth of Bazarov's conceit was brought home to him. "So you and I are the gods? Or rather, you're the god and I suppose I'm the fathead?"

"Yes," Bazarov repeated gloomily, "you're still an innocent."

Odintsova evinced no great surprise when Arkady told her the next day that he was leaving together with Bazarov; she looked absentminded and tired. Katya looked at him gravely and silently; the princess crossed herself under her shawl in a way that he could not help noticing; as for Sitnikov, he was dumbfounded. He had just come down to lunch in a brand-new suit, this time not of the Pan-Slavist mode; the night before he had left the servant in attendance gasping at the profusion of finery he had brought with him, and now his comrades were deserting him! He minced a little, then began to dart here and there like a hunted hare on the fringe of a forest and suddenly, almost frantically, and almost in a shriek, announced that he was going, too. Odintsova did not detain him.

"I have a very comfortable carriage," the wretched young

man added, addressing Arkady. "I can give you a lift, and Yevgeny Vasilich can take your tarantass; that'll be a good arrangement."

"But it's altogether out of your way, and it's quite a distance to my place."

"That's all right; I have plenty of time. Besides I've got some business to attend to down there."

"Tax farming, I suppose?" Arkady said in a tone too patently contemptuous.

But Sitnikov was too distraught to react with his customary snigger.

"I assure you the carriage is most comfortable," he muttered, "and there'll be room for everybody."

"Don't upset M'sieu' Sitnikov by refusing," said Anna Sergeyevna.

Arkady looked at her and inclined his head significantly.

The guests departed after lunch. Taking leave of Bazarov, Odintsova gave him her hand, saying: "We shall be seeing each other again, won't we?"

"As you please," Bazarov answered.

"In that case, we shall."

Arkady came out on the porch steps first, and got into Sitnokov's carriage. The butler deferentially helped him in. Arkady felt like hitting the butler—and he also felt like crying.

Bazarov got into the tarantass. On reaching the Khokhlov settlement, Arkady waited until Fedot, the innkeeper, had harnessed the horses, and then, going up to the tarantass, said to Bazarov with his old smile, "Take me along with you, Yevgeny. I want to go to your place."

"Get in," Bazarov said through his teeth.

Sitnikov, who had been lounging near his conveyance, whistling gaily to himself, gaped on hearing this bit of news, while Arkady coolly transferred his belongings, took his seat beside Bazarov, and with a polite bow to his late companion, shouted, "Get a move on, coachman!" The tarantass rolled away and was soon lost to view. Sitnikov, completely flabbergasted, stole a look at his coachman, but the latter was trailing the thong of his whip over the outrunner's tail. Whereupon Sitnikov jumped into his carriage, yelled at two passing peasants, "Put your hats on, you chumps!" and dragged himself off to town. He arrived late in the day and, on the morrow, told Kukshina what he thought of "those two damned prigs and boors."

On taking his seat in the tarantass next to Bazarov, Arkady gave his hand a hard squeeze and did not say anything for a long time. Bazarov seemed to have understood and appreciated both the handshake and the silence. He had not slept a wink the previous night, nor had he smoked, and he had eaten practically nothing for several days. His profile looked haggard and gaunt beneath a cap pulled down almost over his eyes.

He broke the silence at last: "Well, my dear chap, let's have a cigar. Is my tongue yellow? Have a look?"

"It is," Arkady said.

"I thought so . . . and this cigar is tasteless, too. The machine's run down."

"You *have* been looking bad these last few days," Arkady said.

"Never mind! We'll pick up. It's a bit tiresome though, my mother's such a tenderhearted soul: unless you grow a big belly and eat ten times a day, she gets terribly upset. Father's not a bad sort, though; he's been places and seen a thing or two. No, no use smoking," he added, throwing the cigar into the dusty road.

"It's twenty-five versts to your estate, isn't it?" Arkady asked.

"Yes. But ask that oracle." He pointed to Fedot's man sitting on the box.

The oracle, however, answered, " 'Oo knows—the versts round here ain't never been measured," and went on swearing softly at the outrunner for kickin' 'er noddle," meaning tossing her head.

"Yes," Bazarov resumed, "that will be a lesson to you, my young friend, an instructive lesson. God, how silly it is! Every man hangs by a thread, a chasm may yawn at his feet any minute, and he goes about looking for all kinds of trouble—spoils his own life."

"What are you hinting at?" Arkady asked.

"I'm not hinting at anything, I'm telling you straight that we've both been acting the fool. What's the use of talking! But I noticed at the clinic that the man who gets angry at his pain is sure to conquer it."

"I don't quite follow you," Arkady said. "You don't seem to have anything to complain about."

"Since you don't quite follow me, let me tell you this: in my opinion it's better to break stones in the road than let a woman get hold even of your little finger. That's all . . ." Bazarov very nearly came out with his pet word "romanticism," but checked himself and said, "nonsense. You won't believe me now, but let me tell you this: you and I have been in feminine society and we've enjoyed it; but giving up that kind of society is like taking a cold shower on a hot day. A man has no time to waste on such trifles; a man must be fierce, says a good old Spanish proverb. Look here," he went on, turning to the muzhik on the box, "you brainy fellow— have you got a wife?"

The peasant turned to our friends a flat face with weak-sighted eyes.

"A wife? Yes. 'Course I has."

"Do you beat her?"

"Beat my wife? All depends. Never beat 'em for nothin'."

"Splendid. Well, and does she beat you?"

The man jerked the reins.

"Fancy saying a thing like that, sir. Must have yer little joke. . . ." He was evidently offended.

"Hear that, Arkady Nikolaich! And you and I have taken a beating . . . that's the advantage of being educated men."

Arkady gave a forced laugh, and Bazarov turned away, and did not open his mouth again for the rest of the journey.

The twenty-five versts seemed like fifty to Arkady. At last, a village came into view on a sloping hillside. Here lived Bazarov's parents. Nearby, in a young birch wood, stood a little manor house under a thatched roof. Two peasants in caps stood bickering at the first hut. "You're a big swine," one was saying to the other, "and behave worse than a little 'un." "And your wife's a witch," the other retorted.

"Judging by their unconstrained behavior," Bazarov pointed out to Arkady, "and the playful turns of speech, you can tell that my father's peasants are none too downtrodden. Here he is himself, coming out on to the steps of his house. Must have heard the bell tinkling. It's him. I recognize his figure. Tut-tut! but hasn't he gone grey, poor fellow!"

20

BAZAROV leaned out of the tarantass, while Arkady craned his neck from behind his friend's back and saw a tall, spare man with disheveled hair and a fine aquiline nose, wearing an old unbuttoned military coat; he was standing on the porch steps with his legs wide apart, smoking a long pipe and screwing his eyes up against the sun.

The horses stopped.

"You've come at last," said Bazarov's father, continuing to smoke, though the *chubouk* fairly danced between his fingers. "Well, get out, get out, let's kiss."

He embraced his son.

"Yevgeny darling, Yevgeny," came a quavering woman's voice. The door flew open, and on the threshold there appeared a round little old lady wearing a white cap and a short, brightly colored jacket. She cried out, swayed, and would probably have fallen had not Bazarov supported her. Her plump little arms instantly went round his neck, her head was pressed to his breast and everything around was hushed. All that could be heard were her broken sobs.

Old Bazarov breathed hard and screwed his eyes up more than ever.

"That'll do, Arisha, that'll do," he said, exchanging a look with Arkady, who was standing motionless by the carriage, while the man on the box even turned his head away. "Come, come. Please stop it."

"Ah, Vasily Ivanich," the old lady stammered, "it's such a long time since I've seen my darling, my dearest boy . . ." and without unclasping her arms she drew back her tear-stained, puckered, radiant face, surveyed him with a blissful, droll kind of look and fell on his neck again.

"Well, yes of course, it's all in the nature of things," said Vasily Ivanich, "but let us better go in. Yevgeny has brought a visitor with him, I see. Excuse me," he added, turning to Arkady with a little scrape of his foot; "feminine weakness, you know; a mother's heart after all . . ."

Yet his own lips and brows twitched and his chin quivered. He was visibly striving to master his feelings and feign indifference. Arkady bowed.

"Come along, Mother, really," Bazarov said and conducted the old lady, overcome with emotion, into the house. Placing her in a comfortable armchair, he hurriedly embraced his father once more and presented Arkady.

"Heartily glad to make your acquaintance," Vasily Ivanich said. "You're welcome to whatever we have: it's a simple life we lead, on a military footing. Arina Vlasyevna, calm yourself. You mustn't be so soft! What will the gentleman think of you?"

"My dear sir," the old lady stammered through her tears, "I haven't the pleasure of knowing your name. . . ."

"Arkady Nikolaich," Vasily Ivanich prompted gravely in an undertone.

"I beg your pardon, it's so silly of me." The old lady blew her nose, then bending her head to right and left she carefully wiped one eye after the other. "Please excuse me. Really, I thought I'd die without seeing my darling b . . . b . . . boy."

"Well, you have him now, madam," Vasily Ivanich threw in. "Tanya," he said to a barefooted girl of thirteen in a bright red cotton frock who was peeping timorously from behind the door, "bring the mistress a glass of water—on a tray, understand? And you gentlemen," he added with old-fashioned facetiousness, "pray come into a retired veteran's study."

"Let me give you just one more hug, Yevgeny dear," murmured Arina Vlasyevna. Bazarov bent over her. "My, what a handsome fellow you've grown to be!"

"I don't know about handsome," Vasily Ivanich remarked, "but he's a man *homme fait,* as the saying goes. And now, Arina Vlasyevna, I hope that your maternal heart has had its fill, and you will see about filling our dear guests, for, you know, fair words butter no parsnips."

The old lady got up from her armchair. "This very minute, Vasily Ivanich—the table will be laid; I shall run into the kitchen myself, and get the samovar ready; I'll see to everything. It's three years since I've set eyes on him or taken care of him. Can you imagine?"

"There, there, see to it, my little hostess, but mind you don't put us to shame; and you gentlemen, will you please follow me. Ah, here's Timofeich come to pay you his compliments, Yevgeny. I suppose he's overjoyed too, the old dog. Eh? Aren't you glad, you old dog? Please come this way."

And Vasily Ivanich bustled along with a shuffle and scrape of his worn-down slippers.

The entire house consisted of six tiny rooms. The one to which he brought his guests was called the study.

A heavy-legged table, littered with papers that were dark and almost sooty with ancient dust, occupied the whole length of the wall between the two windows. The walls were hung with Turkish weapons, riding crops, a sword, two maps, some anatomical charts, a portrait of Hufeland,[*] a hair-woven monogram in a black frame, and a framed diploma; a leather sofa with depressions and rents in it here and there stood between two huge bookcases of silver birch; the shelves were littered with books, small boxes, stuffed birds, jars and vials. In one corner stood a broken electrical machine.

"I warned you, my dear guest," began Vasily Ivanich, "that we live here, so to speak, as at a bivouac. . . ."

"Do stop it. What are you apologizing for?" Bazarov broke in. "Kirsanov knows very well we're no Croesuses and that your home is not a palace. Where are we going to put him, that's the question?"

---

[*] C. W. Hufeland (1762-1836), a German doctor concerned with longevity.

"Why, Yevgeny, to be sure—I have a splendid little room in the wing: your friend will be comfortable there."

"So you've got a new wing, have you?"

"To be sure, sir; where the bathhouse is, sir," Timofeich put in.

"That is, next to the bathhouse," Vasily Ivanich added hastily. "It's summertime now. I'll just run down there and have the place fixed up; and you, Timofeich, bring the gentlemen's things in meanwhile. You'll use my study, of course, Yevgeny. *Suum cuique.*"

"There you are! A funny old boy, and as kind as they make them," Bazarov said, as soon as Vasily Ivanich had left the room. "He is as eccentric as your father, but in a different way. He's much too chatty though."

"And I think your mother is a wonderful woman," Arkady remarked.

"Yes, she's an artless soul. You'll see what a dinner she'll give us."

"We weren't expecting you today, sir, and didn't order any beef," said Timofeich, who had just brought in Bazarov's suitcase.

"We'll manage without the beef; if you haven't got it, you haven't. Poverty is no crime, they say."

"How many serfs does your father own?" Arkady asked suddenly.

"The estate is not his, it's Mother's; as far as I remember, fifteen."

"Oh, no, there's twenty-two all told," Timofeich said, displeased.

There was a sound of shuffling slippers, and Vasily Ivanich reappeared.

"Your room will be ready for you in a few minutes," he announced solemnly, "Arkady . . . Nikolaich?—did I get it right? And here's your servant," he added, pointing to a lad with a close-cropped head wearing a blue kaftan torn at the elbows and somebody else's boots, who had come in with him. "His name's Fedya. Permit me to repeat, though my son won't allow it: it's the best we can offer you. He can fill a pipe though. You smoke, don't you?"

"I mostly smoke cigars," Arkady answered.

"And very wisely, too. I prefer cigars myself, but in these secluded parts they're very difficult to get."

"Oh, stop playing Lazarus to the rich man," Bazarov broke in once more. "Better sit down here on the sofa and let's have a look at you again."

Vasily Ivanich chuckled and sat down. He greatly resembled his son, except that his forehead was not so high and broad, and his mouth was more generous, and he incessantly fidgeted and shrugged as though his clothes were too tight for him under the arm-pits, and blinked his eyes, cleared his throat and fiddled with his fingers, whereas his son maintained a careless kind of immobility.

"Playing Lazarus," Vasily Ivanich repeated. "Don't imagine, Yevgeny, that I want to move our guest, so to speak, to pity with a sort of—there, what a godforsaken spot we live in. On the contrary, I'm of the opinion that for an active-minded person there is no such thing as a godforsaken spot. At any rate I try my hardest not to become moss-grown, as they say. I keep abreast of the times."

Vasily Ivanich pulled out of his pocket a new lemon-colored *foulard* that he had picked up on his way to Arkady's room, and went on, flourishing the handkerchief: "I say nothing of the fact that I have, for instance, with no inconsiderable loss to myself, made my peasants tenant farmers and gone halves with them in my land. I deemed this to be my duty, and the most judicious thing to do, though other landlords don't dream of it; I allude to the interests of science and education."

"Yes; I see you have there *The Friend of Health* for 1855," observed Bazarov.

"A friend of mine sends it to me for old times' sake," Vasily Ivanich said hastily. "But we also have some idea, for instance, about phrenology," he added, speaking more for Arkady's benefit, and pointing to a small cast of a head, charted with numbered squares, which stood on a shelf. "We're not entirely unacquainted with Schenlein, for example, or Rademacher."

"Do they still swear by Rademacher in this gubernia?" Bazarov asked.

Vasily Ivanich coughed.

"Er—this gubernia. . . . Of course, you gentlemen know better, you are way ahead of us. You are our successors, after all. In my time, a humoralist* like Hoffmann, or a man like Brown with his vitalism seemed very funny to us, yet they had once created a stir. With you some new man has taken the place of Rademacher, and you pay him homage; but in twenty years, perhaps he, too, will look ridiculous."

"Let me tell you in consolation," said Bazarov, "that we now consider medicine ridiculous altogether and pay homage to nothing."

"What do you mean? But you're going to be a doctor, aren't you?"

"I am, but that has nothing to do with it."

Vasily Ivanich tamped down the hot ashes in the bowl of his pipe with his middle finger.

"Well, maybe, maybe—I won't argue. What am I, after all? A retired army surgeon, *voilà tout*, and now I've become a farmer. I served in your grandfather's brigade," he said addressing Arkady once more. "Yes, sir, I've seen a thing or two in my time. Been in all kinds of society and known all kinds of people! The man you see before you—yes, I held the pulse of such men as Prince Wittgenstein and the poet Zhukovsky! As for those in the southern army, those mixed up in the events of December the 14th,** you know" (At this point Vasily Ivanich pursed his lips significantly) "I knew every one of them. Of course, I had nothing to do with it. My business was to wield the lancet and nothing more! But your grandfather was a highly respected man, a real soldier."

"Come, admit that he was just a blockhead," Bazarov put in indolently.

* A specialist in diseases of body liquids (blood, lymph).
** An allusion to the abortive Decembrist uprising of December 14 (old style), 1825.—*Tr.*

"Goodness, Yevgeny, the expressions you use! Of course, General Kirsanov did not belong to . . ."

"Let's drop him," flung in Bazarov. "Coming up here I was pleased to see how well your birch wood has done."

Vasily Ivanich brightened.

"And you'll see what a fine garden I have now! Planted every tree with my own hands. And there's fruit, and berries and all kinds of medicinal herbs. You young people may be smart, but old Paracelsus spoke the holy truth when he said: *In herbis, verbis et lapidibus!* I've given up my practice, as you know, but once or twice a week I have to dig out the old stuff. People come asking for advice, and you can't very well kick them out. Some poor beggar drops in occasionally and wants to be treated. And there are no doctors around here at all. Would you believe it, one of the neighbors, a retired major, goes in for doctoring too. I once asked somebody whether he had ever studied medicine. No, they said, he hasn't, he does it mostly out of charity. . . . Ha! ha! out of charity! Eh! Isn't that great? Ha-ha! Ha-ha!"

"Fedya, fill me a pipe," Bazarov said sternly.

"There's another doctor here who comes to visit a patient," Vasily Ivanich plunged on in a sort of desperation, "and learns that the patient has already been gathered to his fathers: the servant doesn't even let him in, saying there isn't any need now. The doctor was rather taken aback, not having expected it, and asks, 'Tell me, did your master have the hiccups before he died?' 'Yes, sir, he did.' 'And did he hiccup much?' 'Oh, yes.' 'Ah, well, that's good,' and took himself off. Ha-ha-ha!"

The old man laughed alone; Arkady arranged his face into a smile. Bazarov merely puffed at his pipe. The talk went on thus for nearly an hour; Arkady, meanwhile, had looked at his room, which proved to be the bathhouse anteroom, but was cosy and clean. At length Tanya came in and announced that dinner was ready.

Vasily Ivanich got up first.

"Come on, gentlemen! I hope I haven't bored you. Perhaps the hostess will do better."

The dinner, though hastily prepared, proved to be an excellent one, even a lavish one, except for the wine, which was not up to much, as they say: the almost black sherry, which Timofeich had purchased in town from a dealer of his acquaintance, had a copperish—or was it resinous—taste to it; and the flies were a nuisance too. Usually a serf boy kept them off with a large green branch; but today Vasily Ivanich had dismissed him, for fear of criticism on the part of the younger generation. Arina Vlasyevna had smartened herself up; she put on a high mobcap with silk strings, and a sky-blue patterned shawl. She cried a little again on seeing her darling Yevgeny, but before her husband could admonish her, she hastily wiped away the tears so as not to wet her shawl. The young men ate alone, as their hosts had long since dined. They were waited on by Fedya, who obviously felt encumbered by his out-size boots, assisted by a woman with masculine features and blind in one eye, named Anfisushka, who combined the duties of housekeeper, poultry-maid and laundress.

Throughout the meal Vasily Ivanich paced up and down the room, talking with an almost blissful air about the grave concern which Napoleon's policy and the Italian imbroglio inspired in him. Arkady might not have existed for all the attention which Arina Vlasyevna paid him. With her little fist propping up her round face, to which a pair of puffy, cherry-colored lips imparted a very benign expression, she did not take her eyes away from her son and sighed all the time. She was dying to know how long he was going to stay, but was afraid to ask him. "What if he says two days," she thought with a sinking heart. After the roast Vasily Ivanich disappeared for a moment and returned with an uncorked half-bottle of champagne. "Here," he exclaimed, "though we do live in the backwoods, we have something to cheer the heart on a festive occasion." He poured out three goblets and a wineglass, toasted the health "of our inestimable guests," drained his glass at a gulp militarywise, and made Arina Vlasyevna drink her wineglass to the last drop. When it was time for the preserved fruit, Arkady, who had an aversion to sweet things, felt it incumbent on him to try four freshly cooked varieties, especially since Bazarov had flatly declined them and lighted a cigar. Then tea appeared upon the scene with cream and butter and cakes; after which Vasily Ivanich invited everybody into the garden to admire the beauty of the evening. As they passed a bench, he whispered to Arkady, "On this spot I do a little philosophizing as I watch the sunset: a fitting occupation for an anchorite. And there, further on, I have planted a few trees beloved of Horace."

"What trees are they?" asked Bazarov, who had been listening.

"Why, acacias, of course."

Bazarov began to yawn.

"I believe it's time our travellers sought the arms of Morpheus," Vasily Ivanich said.

"In other words, time to turn in!" Bazarov said. "That's a good idea. It really is time."

He kissed his mother on the forehead by way of good night, while she embraced him and blessed him with a furtive triple sign of the cross. Vasily Ivanich saw Arkady to his room and wished him "the blessed slumber I enjoyed myself when I was your happy age." Indeed, Arkady slept like a top in his bathhouse anteroom: the place smelled of mint, and two crickets chirped drowsily behind the stove. Vasily Ivanich went to his study where he settled himself on the sofa at his son's feet with the intention of having a chat; but Bazarov instantly dismissed him, saying he wanted to go to sleep, although he actually remained awake till daybreak. He stared wrathfully into the darkness with wide-open eyes: childhood's memories had no fascination for him, and besides, he had not yet shaken off his recent painful impressions. Arina Vlasyevna, after praying to her heart's content, had a good long talk with Anfisushka, who stood before her mistress as if rooted to the spot. She stared at Arina Vlasyevna with her single eye and conveyed to her in mysterious whispers all her views and fancies concerning Yevgeny

Vasilich. What with joy, the wine and the cigar smoke, the old lady's head was reeling; her husband tried to speak to her, but gave it up as hopeless.

Arina Vlasyevna was a true Russian gentlewoman of the old days; she should have lived some two hundred years before, in the days of old Muscovy. She was very pious and impressionable, and believed in all kinds of omens, fortunetelling, charms, and dreams: she believed in imbecilic zealots, household sprites, spooks, ill-omened encounters, evil spells, folk medicine, charmed salt for Maundy Thursday, and the imminent end of the world; she believed that if the candles did not blow out at vespers on Easter Sunday buckwheat would yield a good harvest, and that mushrooms could stop growing if seen by the human eye; she believed that the devil haunted watery places and that every Jew had a bloodstain on his chest. She was afraid of mice, grass snakes, frogs, sparrows, leeches, thunder, cold water, draughts, horses, goats, red-headed people and black cats, and considered crickets and dogs unclean animals; she ate neither veal, nor pigeon, nor crab, nor cheese, nor asparagus, nor artichokes, nor hares, nor watermelons, because a cut watermelon reminded her of John the Baptist's head; of oysters she could not speak without a shudder; she was fond of a good meal— and kept Lent rigorously. She slept ten hours a day and did not go to bed at all if Vasily Ivanich had a headache. She had never read anything besides *Alexis, or a Cabin in the Woods,* wrote one, or at most two, letters a year, and knew what was what in housekeeping, curing, pickling and preserving, though she never did a thing with her own hands and was generally indisposed to bestir herself. Arina Vlasyevna was very kindhearted and not at all foolish—in her own way. She knew that the world consisted of masters whose business it was to give orders and of common people who had to take them, and so she accepted all demonstrations of servility without a qualm; she was kind and gentle, however, to those under her, never turned a beggar away without giving him something, and never censured people, though she liked to gossip at times.

She had been very attractive in her youth, had played the harpsichord and spoken a little French; but after years of wandering with her husband, whom she had married against her will, she had grown fat and forgotten both music and French. She loved her son and feared him beyond words; the management of the estate she left to Vasily Ivanich, and did not trouble her head any more about it: she would merely moan in distress, and wave him off with her handkerchief while her brows would go up in alarm whenever her husband began talking about his plans and the changes he intended to make. She was obsessed by imaginary fears, was constantly expecting some great calamity, and would start crying as soon as she thought of anything sad. . . . Such women are rare nowadays. God knows whether we should be glad of it or not!

21

ON getting out of bed Arkady opened the window —and the first thing that met his eyes was Vasily Ivanich. Clad in a Bokhara dressing gown girdled with a large handkerchief, the old man was pottering about in the garden. Seeing his young guest he cried out, leaning on his spade:

"Good morning to you, sir! Did you sleep well?"

"Fine," Arkady said.

"Well, and here am I, as you see, working like a Cincinnatus, to clear a patch for my late turnips. Things have now come to such a pass—and thank God for it I say!—when every man must make his living by his own hands; no use relying on others; a man must work himself. And so, Jean Jacques Rousseau was right, it seems. Half an hour ago, my dear sir, you would have found me in quite a different capacity. A peasant woman came, complaining of the collywobbles, as she calls it. We call it dysentery. I gave her—how had I better express it—an opium infusion, and I pulled another woman's tooth out. I offered to etherize her, but she wouldn't have it. I do it all gratis—*en amateur*. It's nothing new to me, though; I'm a plebeian, you know, *homo novus*. I'm not of the blue blood, like my better half. Wouldn't you like to come out here in the shade and take a breath of fresh air before breakfast?"

Arkady joined him outside.

"Welcome, once more," Vasily Ivanich said, touching his greasy skullcap in military salutation. "You're used to luxury and pleasure, I know, but even the great of this world are nothing loath to beguile the time under a cottage roof."

"Good Lord," Arkady protested, "since when do I belong

to the great ones of this world? And I'm not used to luxury either."

"Come, come, sir," parried Vasily Ivanich with a polite grimace. "I may be out of the running now, but I have knocked around the world a bit, and I can tell a bird by its song. I'm something of a psychologist, too, in a way, and a physiognomist. If it weren't for this gift, as I dare call it, I'd have gone to the dogs long ago; it doesn't take much to push a little fellow like me to the wall. Let me tell you frankly: the friendship I notice between you and my son gives me sincere pleasure. I have just seen him: he got up very early as usual—you are probably aware of that custom of his—and went off to explore the countryside. Excuse my curiosity, but have you known Yevgeny long?"

"Since last winter."

"I see. May I also inquire—but why not take a seat? May I inquire as a father, with all frankness, what is your opinion of my Yevgeny?"

"Your son is one of the most remarkable men I have ever met," Arkady said earnestly.

Vasily Ivanich's eyes suddenly dilated and a faint flush mantled his cheeks. The spade dropped out of his hand.

"And so, you believe . . ." he started to say.

"I am sure," Arkady went on quickly, "that your son has a great future before him, that he will make your name famous. I was convinced of it the moment we first met."

"How . . . how did that come about?" Vasily Ivanich said breathlessly. His wide mouth spread in a rapturous smile, which stayed there.

"So you want to know how we met?"

"Yes . . . and generally . . ."

Arkady began talking about Bazarov with still greater warmth and enthusiasm than he had displayed on that memorable evening when he had danced with Odintsova.

Vasily Ivanich sat listening while he blew his nose, rolled his handkerchief between both hands, coughed, and rumpled his hair. Then, unable to contain himself any longer, he leaned over to Arkady and kissed him on the shoulder.

"I can't tell you how happy you've made me," he said smiling all the time. "I want you to know that I . . . adore my son; I say nothing about my old woman, of course: she's a mother—and there everything is said! But I dare not show my feelings in front of him; he doesn't like it. He has an aversion to every display of affection; many people disapprove of this hardness of his, which they regard as a sign of pride or insensibility; but men like him should not be measured by the ordinary rule, don't you think so? Well, for example: another man in his place would keep squeezing money out of his parents, but believe it or not, he never took a kopek more than he needed as long as he lived, I swear!"

"He's an honest, unselfish man," Arkady said.

"Unselfish is the word. As for me, Arkady Nikolaich, I not only adore him, I'm proud of him, and my only ambition is to see the following words written in his biography one day: 'The son of a common army surgeon, who, however, early discovered in him great promise and stinted nothing for his education. . . .'"

The old man's voice broke.

Arkady squeezed his hand.

"What do you think?" Vasily Ivanich asked after a brief silence. "It's not in the field of medicine that he will win the fame you prophesy for him, is it?"

"Certainly not medicine, though here too he will rank with the foremost scientists."

"What field do you think, Arkady Nikolaich?"

"It's difficult to say now, but he will be famous."

"He will be famous!" echoed the old man and became lost in thought.

"Arina Vlasyevna asks you to come and have breakfast," Anfisushka said as she passed by carrying a huge dish of ripe raspberries.

Vasily Ivanich started.

"Will there be cooled cream with the raspberries?"

"Yes, sir."

"See that it's cool though! Don't stand on ceremony, Arkady Nikolaich, help yourself. Where is Yevgeny so long?"

"Here I am," Bazarov spoke up from Arkady's room.

Vasily Ivanich turned round quickly.

"Aha! Thought you'd pay your friend a visit, but you're too late, *amice*—we've already had a long chat together. Now we must go and have breakfast—Mother's calling us. By the way, I want to talk to you."

"What about?"

"There's a muzhik here who is suffering from icterus. . . ."

"That is, jaundice?"

"Yes, a chronic and very refractory case of icterus. I've prescribed centaury and St. John's wort; made him eat carrot, and gave him soda; but these are all palliatives. Something more drastic is needed. Although you make fun of medicine, I'm sure you could give me some good advice. But we'll talk of that later. Let's go and have breakfast now."

Vasily Ivanich jumped to his feet, burst into a gay bit of song from *Robert le Diable*:

> *Le vin, le vin, le vin, le jeu, les belles,*
> *Voilà, voilà, voilà, mes seuls amours!*

"Wonderful, how full of vim he is!" Bazarov said, moving away from the window.

It was noon. The sun beat down hotly through a thin veil of unbroken whitish clouds. A stillness hung over everything; only the cocks in the village crowed away in high feather, evoking in everyone who heard them an odd sensation of drowsiness and ennui; and somewhere high up in the treetops the incessant cheep of a baby hawk sounded like a plaint. Arkady and Bazarov were lying in the shadow of a small haystack, having strewn the ground under them with an armful or two of crisp but still green and fragrant hay.

"That aspen," Bazarov began, "reminds me of my childhood; it stands on the edge of a pit where there used to be a brick barn, and I was convinced at the time that the pit and the tree possessed a peculiar spell; I never felt bored near them. I didn't understand then that I wasn't bored

simply because I was a child. And now that I've grown up,
the spell doesn't work."

"How long did you live here altogether?" Arkady asked.

"For two years running; then we used to come back from
time to time. Ours was a rambling sort of life, mostly knocking
around from town to town."

"And has the house been up long?"

"Yes, a long time. It was built in Grandfather's time—my
mother's father."

"Who was your grandfather?"

"The devil knows. A second major or something. Served
under Suvorov and was full of tales about the march across
the Alps.* Lies, no doubt."

"That accounts for the portrait of Suvorov hanging in the
parlor. But I like little houses like yours, old and snug, with
a peculiar smell all their own."

"Smells of lamp oil and melilot," Bazarov said with a yawn.
"And as for the flies in these dear little houses. . . . Ugh!"

"I say," Arkady went on after a little pause, "were you
disciplined much in your childhood?"

"You see the kind of parents I have. Can't call them strict,
can you?"

"Do you love them, Yevgeny?"

"I do, Arkady!"

"They love you so much!"

Bazarov was silent.

"Do you know what I'm thinking?" he said presently,
clasping his hands behind his head.

"No, what is it?"

"I was thinking that my folks are having a good time in
this world! My father at sixty potters around, talks of 'pal-
liative' remedies, treats sick people, is generous to the
peasants, and generally has the time of his life. Mother, too,
is happy: her day is crammed with so many occupations, and
so many oh's and ah's that she hasn't time to stop and think;
while I . . ."

---

* Reference to the successful 1799 Russian campaign against the French in
Northern Italy.

"What about you?"

"I'm thinking: here am I lying under a haystack. The narrow place I occupy is so small compared to the rest of space where I am not and where nobody cares a rap about me; and the little span of my life is such a speck in eternity, where I haven't been and never will be. . . . Yet in that atom, in that mathematical point, the blood circulates, the brain works, desires are kindled. How monstrous! How preposterous!"

"Let me tell you that what you say applies in equal measure to all people."

"You're right," Bazarov said. "What I meant is that they— my parents, that is— are occupied and don't worry about their own insignificance—it doesn't rankle them . . . whereas I . . . I am disgusted and furious."

"Furious? But why furious?"

"Why? You ask why? Have you forgotten?"

"I haven't forgotten anything, but still I don't think you have any right to be angry. You're unhappy, I agree, but . . ."

"Oh, I see, Arkady Nikolaich, your idea of love is like that of all modern young men: chuck-chuck-chuck little hen, and the moment she comes near, you take to your heels. I'm not that kind. But enough of that. What can't be helped can't be mended by talk." He turned over on his side. "Aha! Here's a sturdy little ant hauling a half-dead fly. Haul away, little one, haul away! Never mind her kicking—make the best of your right as an animal to disregard any feelings of compassion, not like us self-broken humans!"

"You should be the last to talk about that, Yevgeny! Since when have you been broken?"

Bazarov raised his head.

"That's the only thing I'm proud of. I've not broken myself, and nothing in petticoats will ever break me. Amen! That's over and done with! You won't hear another word from me about it."

The two lay for some time in silence.

"Yes," Bazarov began, "man is a queer animal. When you look, from the outside, at the secluded lives our 'fathers' lead here, you wonder—what could be better? Eat, drink and know that everything you do is right and sensible. But no, you get bored to death. You want to grapple with people, if only to scold them."

"Life ought to be arranged in such a way that every moment of it is significant," Arkady remarked thoughtfully.

"That's just it! The significant, though it may sometimes be false, is sweet, and one could even put up with the insignificant . . . but it's the petty strife that gets you down, the petty strife."

"Petty strife needn't exist for a man if he doesn't want to recognize it."

"Hm . . . what you've said is a *platitude reversed.*"

"Eh? What do you mean by that term?"

"Just this: to say, for example, that education is useful, is a platitude; but to say that education is harmful, is a platitude reversed. It looks smarter, but it really amounts to the same thing."

"But where is the truth?"

"Where? I'll answer you like an echo: Where?"

"You're in a melancholy mood today, Yevgeny."

"Am I? Probably it's the sun, and then it's bad to eat too many raspberries."

"In that case what about taking a nap?" Arkady said.

"All right; but don't look at me. A man usually looks foolish when he's asleep."

"Do you care what people think of you?"

"I don't know what to say. A real man shouldn't care; a real man is one you don't think about. You must either obey him or hate him."

"Strange! I don't hate anyone," Arkady said after a moment's reflection.

"And I do, a lot. You're a softhearted, sloppy fellow. You couldn't hate anybody! You're too timid; you haven't enough self-confidence."

"And you are self-confident, I suppose?" Arkady interrupted him. "You have a high opinion of yourself, haven't you?"

Bazarov did not answer at once.

"When I meet a man who can hold his own against me,"
he said slowly, "I'll change my opinion about myself. Hate!
Why, today, for example, when we were passing the hut of
our starosta* Philip—it's such a pretty white hut—you said
Russia will be a perfect country when the lowliest peasant
has a dwelling like that to live in, and that everyone of us
should help to bring that about. But I have come to hate
the lowliest peasant, Philip and Sidor and the rest of them,
for whom I am expected to extend myself, and who won't
even say thank you—not that I need his thanks. All right,
what if he does live in a white hut . . . when I am feeding the
worms—what then?"

"Oh come, Yevgeny. Listening to you today one is inclined
to agree with the people who accuse us of lack of principles."

"You sound like your uncle. Generally there aren't any
principles—you don't seem to have grasped that yet! There
are only sensations. Everything depends on them."

"How do you figure that out?"

"Quite simple. Take me, for example: my attitude is one
of negation—as a matter of sensation! I like negation; my
brain is built that way—that's all! Why do I like chemistry?
Why do you like apples? It's all a matter of sensation. It's
all the same thing. Deeper than that people will never go.
Not everybody will tell you that, and I won't be caught
telling it to you again."

"Well, and is honesty a sensation too?"

"Of course!"

"Yevgeny!" Arkady began in a sad voice.

"Eh? What? Don't like it?" Bazarov interrupted him. "No,
sir! If you're going to mow everything down then go the
whole hog. But no more philosophizing. 'Nature evokes the
silence of sleep,' said Pushkin."

"He never said anything of the kind," Arkady protested.

"Well, if he didn't he might have and should have said it,
being a poet. By the way, he must have served in the army."

"Pushkin was never a military man."

---

* Village elder.

"But, my dear fellow, on almost every page he has 'To battle, to battle! For Russia's honor!' "

"You're just talking nonsense! It's nothing short of slander, really."

"Slander? Pooh! You don't frighten me with words like that! No matter how much you slander a person, he really deserves twenty times more."

"Let's go to sleep!" Arkady said, annoyed.

"With the greatest pleasure," Bazarov retorted.

But neither of them could sleep. A feeling almost akin to animosity stole into the hearts of the two young men. Five minutes later they opened their eyes and looked at each other in silence.

"Look," Arkady said suddenly, "a dry maple leaf has broken off and fallen to the ground; its movements are exactly like the flight of a butterfly. Isn't it curious? A thing so utterly sad and dead resembles a thing so utterly alive and joyous."

"O, my friend, Arkady Nikolaich!" Bazarov exclaimed, "one thing I ask of you. Don't speak so sweetly."

"I speak as best I can. This is downright despotism, if you ask me. If an idea occurs to me, why shouldn't I express it?"

"Very well; but why shouldn't I express mine? I believe that to speak sweetly is indecent."

"What *is* decent then? To swear?"

"Ah! I see you've definitely made up your mind to follow in your uncle's footsteps. How delighted that idiot would be to hear you!"

"What did you call Pavel Petrovich?"

"I called him the right thing—an idiot."

"But that's intolerable!" Arkady exclaimed.

"Aha! The call of the blood," Bazarov said coolly. "I've noticed that it's very strong in people. A man is prepared to renounce everything, and give up all prejudices, but to admit, for example, that his brother is beyond him. Indeed: *my* brother, *mine*—and not a genius? How can that be?"

"It was a simple sense of justice, that made me speak up, not family feeling at all," Arkady retorted testily. "But because you don't understand it, because you haven't got the *sensation*—you can't judge it."

"In other words: Arkady Kirsanov is too exalted of mind for me to understand. I bend my knee and say no more."

"Leave off, Yevgeny; we'll end up by quarrelling."

"I say, Arkady, let's have a good quarrel for once—let's go at it tooth and nail, to utter annihilation."

"We might end up by . . ."

"By coming to blows?" Bazarov said eagerly. "What of it? Here, in the hay, in these idyllic surroundings, far from the world and the eyes of men—not a bad idea. But you'd be no match for me. I'd grab you by the throat . . ."

Bazarov spread his long wiry fingers. Arkady turned around and assumed an attitude of defense, jokingly, as it were. But his friend's face looked so sinister, his sneering lips and gleaming eyes held such an ugly threat in them that Arkady quailed.

"Ah! So that's where you've hidden!" came the voice of Vasily Ivanich, and the old army surgeon appeared before the young men dressed in a homespun linen jacket and a straw hat, also homemade. "I've been looking for you all over. You've chosen a splendid place, however, and an excellent occupation. To lie on the 'earth' and gaze at the 'sky'. . . . Do you know, there's something significant in that!"

"I only gaze at the sky when I'm about to sneeze," Bazarov growled and, turning to Arkady, added in an undertone, "What a pity he interrupted us."

"What nonsense," Arkady whispered and surreptitiously squeezed his friend's hand. "But no friendship will long withstand such clashes."

"When I look at you two young friends," Vasily Ivanich went on, shaking his head and resting his crossed hands on an intricately twisted stick of his own handiwork with a knob in the shape of a Turk's head, "it does my heart good. What fine brawn, what abilities, talents!—brimming youth! Simply . . . Castor and Pollux!"

"Just listen to him—spouting mythology!" Bazarov said. "One can easily tell you were a strong Latinist in your time!

I believe you were awarded a silver medal for composition, weren't you?"

"Dioscuri, Dioscuri!" Vasily Ivanich repeated.

"Come on, Father, enough of this cooing."

"Once in a blue moon doesn't matter," mumbled the old man. "But I've been looking for you, gentlemen, not to pay you compliments, but to inform you, in the first place, that we shall soon be having dinner; and, secondly, I wanted to warn you, Yevgeny. . . . You're a clever man, you understand people, and women too, and mother wanted to have a service read on the occasion of your homecoming. Don't imagine that I'm asking you to attend the service—it's all over now, but Father Alexei . . ."

"The priest?"

"Er, yes, the clergyman; he's . . . going to have dinner with us. I didn't know it, as a matter of fact I was even against it . . . but, somehow, it happened that way . . . he didn't understand me. . . . Well, and Arina Vlasyevna, too . . . He's a very good and sensible man, though."

"He won't eat my portion at dinner, will he?" Bazarov asked.

"Good heavens, no!" Vasily Ivanich laughed.

"Then that's good enough for me. I'll sit down to table with any man."

Vasily Ivanich adjusted his hat.

"I knew beforehand that you were all above prejudice. Look at me, I'm an old man, getting on to sixty-two now, and I haven't any prejudices either." (Vasily Ivanich did not have the courage to admit that he had wanted the service read himself. He was no less pious than his wife.) "And Father Alexei is very eager to make your acquaintance. You'll like him—you'll see. He's not averse to a game of cards and . . . between you and me . . . he even smokes a pipe."

"All right. We'll sit down to a game of *yeralash** after dinner, and I'll beat him."

"He-he-he, we'll see about that! Don't be so sure of yourself."

---
* A card game.

"Why? Going to recall the old days?" Bazarov said with peculiar emphasis.

Vasily Ivanich's bronzed cheeks flushed faintly.

"For shame, Yevgeny. Don't rake up the past. But I don't mind confessing to this gentleman that I did have that passion in my youth—and paid for it too! But isn't it hot? Let me sit down next to you. I'm not in your way, am I?"

"Not at all," Arkady said.

Vasily Ivanich lowered himself with a grunt on to the hay.

"This couch of yours, gentlemen," he began, "reminds me of my army, bivouac days, with the dressing stations rigged up near a haystack like this, that is, if we were lucky enough." He sighed. "Yes, I've been through a lot in my time. There is that curious episode during the plague epidemic in Bessarabia, for example, if you would like to hear it."

"The one you got the St. Vladimir for?" Bazarov said. "We've heard it. By the way, why don't you wear it?"

"I've told you I have no prejudices," Vasily Ivanich muttered—only the day before he had ordered the red ribbon to be ripped off his coat—and proceeded to narrate the plague episode. "He's fallen asleep," he suddenly said to Arkady in a whisper, pointing at Bazarov with a humorous wink. "Yevgeny! Get up!" he added, aloud. "Let's go in to dinner."

Father Alexei, a portly handsome man with thick carefully brushed hair and an embroidered girdle over a purple silk cassock, proved to be a very shrewd and quick-witted person. He hastened first to shake hands with Arkady and Bazarov, as though aware beforehand that they had no need of his blessing, and, generally, he bore himself with ease. He made himself companionable without being offensive; he laughed at seminary Latin and defended his bishop. He drank two glasses of wine, but declined a third; and accepted a cigar from Arkady, but did not smoke it, saying he would take it home. The only disagreeable thing about him was a habit he had of slowly and warily raising his hand to catch flies that settled on his face, and sometimes he squashed them.

He sat down at the card table with pleasure and ended by

winning two rubles fifty kopeks from Bazarov in paper money. (No one in Arina Vlasyevna's house had any notion of using silver money.) The lady sat, as usual, next to her son (she did not play cards), her face propped up by her fist, and got up only to order some new dish to be served. She was afraid to caress Bazarov and he did not encourage her; besides, Vasily Ivanich had admonished her against "bothering" him too much. "Young men don't like it," he had urged. (The dinner given that day need hardly be described; Timofeich, in person, had galloped off at daybreak for a particular brand of Circassian beef; the *starosta* had gone in the opposite direction for burbots, perch and crawfish; for mushrooms alone the peasant women had received forty-two kopeks in copper coins.) Arina Vlasyevna's gaze, bent steadfastly on Bazarov, expressed not only devotion and tenderness—there was a tinge of sadness in it, mingled with curiosity and fear, a sort of meek reproach.

Bazarov had other things to think of besides bothering his head about the expression of his mother's eyes. He rarely addressed her, and when he did, it was with a curt question. Once he asked her to give him her hand "for luck." She slipped her soft little hand into his hard, broad palm.

"Well," she asked after a while, "did it help?"

"Worse than ever," he said with a careless smile.

"He plays a risky game," Father Alexei said rather ruefully, stroking his handsome beard.

"Napoleon's rule, Father, Napoleon's rule," put in Vasily Ivanich, leading with an ace.

"Which brought him to St. Helena," murmured Father Alexei, trumping the ace.

"Would you like some currant juice, darling?" asked Arina Vlasyevna.

Bazarov merely shrugged.

"No!" he said to Arkady the next day, "I'll clear out tomorrow. It's tedious. I want to work, and I can't do it here. I'll go to your place again—I've left all my preparations there. At your place I can at least shut myself up. Here Father keeps on telling me, 'My study's at your disposal—nobody

will be in your way,' but he doesn't leave my side for a
minute. I can't very well shut him out. And Mother, too. I
hear her sighing behind the wall, but if I go out to her I can't
find anything to say to her."

"She'll be very upset," Arkady said, "and so will he."

"I'll be coming back to them."

"When?"

"Before going to St. Petersburg."

"I feel especially sorry for your mother."

"How's that? Has she won you over with her berries?"

Arkady lowered his eyes.

"You don't know your mother, Yevgeny. She's not only a
fine woman; she's very clever, really. This morning she talked
to me for half an hour, and she was so sensible and interesting."

"Enlarging about me most of the time, I suppose?"

"We talked of other things, too."

"Perhaps—these things are clearer to an outsider. If a woman
can sustain a conversation for half an hour it's a good sign.
But I'm going all the same."

"You won't find it easy to break the news to them. They're
talking all the time about what we'll be doing two weeks
from now."

"No, it won't be easy. What the devil made me tease my
father today! He ordered one of his tenant serfs to be flogged
the other day—and quite right, too. Yes, quite right—don't
look at me in such horror—because the man's an unspeakable
thief and drunkard. Father never expected the thing would
reach my ears. He was greatly upset, and now I'll have to
upset him even more. Never mind! He'll get over it!"

Bazarov had said, "Never mind!" but it took him the whole
day to pluck up the courage to tell Vasily Ivanich of his
intentions. At last, when bidding him good night in his
study, he said with a simulated yawn:

"Yes . . . nearly forgot to tell you. . . . Will you please send
a relay of horses down to Fedot's tomorrow?"

Vasily Ivanich was astonished.

"Is Mr. Kirsanov leaving us?"

"Yes; and I'm going with him."

Vasily Ivanich spun around.

"You are going away?"

"Yes. . . . I have to. See about the horses, please."

"Very well . . ." the old man faltered, "a relay . . . very well . . . but . . . but. . . . What's the matter?"

"I must go down to his place for a short time. I'll be back again."

"Yes! For a short time. . . . All right." Vasily Ivanich took out his handkerchief and bending over almost to the ground blew his nose. "Ah, well! I thought you'd stay . . . a little longer. Three days. . . . That's . . . after three years . . . not much, not much, Yevgeny!"

"But I'm telling you I'll be back soon. I have to go."

"You have to. . . . Ah, well! Duty first, of course. . . . So you want the horses sent out? All right. We hadn't expected this, of course. Arina has asked the neighbor for flowers— wanted to decorate your room." (Vasily Ivanich said nothing about how, every day at peep of dawn, standing with slippers on his bare feet, he conferred with Timofeich, and, drawing out one tattered banknote after another with trembling fingers, he gave him orders for the day's shopping, laying particular stress on eatables and red wine, which the young men appeared to be fond of.) "Freedom above all—that's my rule. . . . Mustn't stand in the way . . . mustn't . . ."

He suddenly fell silent and made for the door.

"We'll be seeing each other again soon, Father, really."

But Vasily Ivanich, without turning his head, waved his hand wearily and left the room. Coming into his bedroom he found his wife in bed, and began to say his prayers in a whisper, so as not to waken her. She awoke, however.

"Is that you, Vasily Ivanich?" she asked.

"Yes, Mother!"

"You've come from Yevgeny? Do you know, I'm afraid he's not comfortable on the sofa. I told Anfisushka to give him your camp mattress and some new pillows. I'd give him our feather bed, but he doesn't like a soft bed, if I remember."

"Never mind, Mother, don't worry. He's comfortable. Lord have mercy on us poor sinners," he went on in an undertone, finishing his prayer. Vasily Ivanich pitied his old wife and decided not to tell her before morning what sorrow awaited her.

Bazarov and Arkady left the next day. A gloom was cast upon the whole household from early in the morning. The dishes kept slipping out of Anfisushka's hands; even Fedya was baffled and ended by taking off his boots. Vasily Ivanich was fussier than ever: he was obviously putting on a bold front; he talked loudly and stamped about, but his face had grown haggard and his eyes avoided his son's face. Arina Vlasyevna cried softly; she would have broken down completely had her husband not spent more than two persuasive hours with her in the morning. When Bazarov, after repeated promises to return in not more than a month, had finally torn himself from the clinging embraces and taken his seat in the tarantass, when the horses had started and the bell had begun to jingle and the wheels to turn, when there was nothing more down the road for straining eyes to see and the dust had settled, and Timofeich, bent almost double, had staggered back to his tiny room; when the old couple were left alone in a house which, like them, seemed to have suddenly shrunk and aged—Vasily Ivanich, who a minute before had been bravely waving his handkerchief on the porch steps, sank into a chair and dropped his head on his chest. "He has left us, left us!" he murmured. "Found it too dull here. All alone now, all alone!" he repeated several times, gazing dully before him and stretching his hand out appealingly.

Then Arina Vlasyevna went up to him, and, laying her grey head to his, said, "It can't be helped, Vasya! A son is like a severed branch. He's like the eagle that comes when it wants and goes when it wants; and you and I are like mushrooms on a tree stump—we sit side by side without budging. Only I will remain the same to you always, and you to me."

Vasily Ivanich drew his hands away from his face and embraced his wife, his friend, as he had never embraced her in his youth; she had comforted him in his grief

22

ALL the way to Fedot's our friends rode in silence, merely exchanging a word now and then. Bazarov was none too pleased with himself. Arkady was not pleased with him either. Moreover, his heart was weighed down with that unaccountable feeling of sadness which is familiar only to very young men. The coachman rehitched the horses and, climbing to his seat, asked, "Left or right, sir?"

Arkady started. The road to the right led to town, and thence home; the road to the left led to Odintsova's.

He glanced at Bazarov.

"Shall we go to the left, Yevgeny?" he asked.

Bazarov turned his head away.

"Don't be silly!" he muttered.

"I know it's silly," Arkady said. "But what's the harm? It isn't the first time."

Bazarov pulled his cap down.

"As you like," he said at length.

"To the left, coachman!" Arkady cried.

The tarantass clattered off in the direction of Nikolskoye. Having decided on this foolishness, the friends were more silent than ever, and even seemed to be angry.

By the way the butler received them on the porch steps of Odintsova's house, our friends might have guessed how injudiciously they had acted in giving way to their sudden fancy. Obviously they were not expected. They sheepishly cooled their heels for a rather long time in the drawing room. At last Odintsova came in. She greeted them with her usual affability, but was surprised they had come back so soon. Judging by her speech and movements, she was not exactly delighted. They hastened to announce that they had dropped in on their way to town and would be moving on in about four hours. She merely uttered a deprecatory little sound, asked Arkady to convey her regards to his father, and sent for her aunt. The princess came in looking sleepy, which made her shrivelled old face look fiercer than ever. Katya was feeling indisposed and did not leave her room. It suddenly dawned on Arkady that he had been wanting to see Katya almost as badly as Anna Sergeyevna. The four hours passed in desultory talk on this, that and the other; Anna Sergeyevna listened and spoke with an unsmiling face. Only at leave-taking did something of her former friendliness appear.

"I'm in the doldrums just now," she declared, "but you mustn't take any notice and—I say this to both of you—call again in a little while."

Both Bazarov and Arkady responded with a silent bow, got into their carriage and drove straight home to Maryino, where they arrived safe and sound the next evening. Throughout the journey neither had so much as mentioned Odintsova's name; Bazarov in particular had hardly opened his mouth and kept staring away from the road with a kind of fierce tensity.

At Maryino everybody was delighted to see them. Nikolai Petrovich had been getting worried about his son's long absence. He uttered a cry of joy, kicked his feet and jumped up and down on the sofa when Fenichka came running in, with shining eyes, to announce the arrival of the "young masters." Even Pavel Petrovich experienced a mild thrill and smiled indulgently as he shook hands with the returned wanderers. There followed accounts and questions; Arkady did most of the talking, especially at supper, which lasted until long after midnight. Nikolai Petrovich ordered several bottles of port, recently delivered from Moscow, to be brought up, and applied himself to it so assiduously that his cheeks became crimson, and he laughed all the time with a kind of childish, nervous laugh. The general excitement spread to the servants' hall. Dunyasha dashed in and out like one possessed, slamming doors, while Pyotr, at three in the morning, was still attempting a *Valse-Cossack* on the guitar. The strings made a pleasant plaintive sound in the still air, but the educated valet got no further than an opening ornamental passage—nature had denied him musical gifts, as she had denied him all others.

Things had been going none too smoothly at Maryino and poor Nikolai Petrovich was having a hard time. The farm was giving increasing trouble—and cheerless, futile cares they were. The hired laborers were becoming insufferable. Some demanded to be paid off or given a raise, others quit, taking the advance with them; the horses sickened; the wear and tear on the harness was dreadful; work was done in a slapdash manner; the threshing machine that had been delivered from Moscow proved too cumbersome for practical purposes; a winnowing machine was damaged beyond repair at the first trial; half the cattle sheds were destroyed by fire because a blind old menial had gone to fumigate her cow with a torch on a windy night—the culprit had laid all the blame on her master's mania for newfangled kinds of cheeses and dairy farming. The manager suddenly became lazy and even began to grow fat, like every Russian who eats "free bread." On catching sight of Nikolai Petrovich from a distance, he would make a show of zeal by throwing a bit of wood at a passing pig or shaking his fist at a half-naked urchin, but most of the time he slept. The peasants were in arrears with their rent and stole the master's timber; and barely a night passed without the herdsmen impounding stray peasant horses found grazing on the farm meadows. Nikolai Petrovich had introduced a fine for damage caused by cattle, but the matter usually ended by the horses being returned to their owners after spending a day or two on the master's fodder. To crown it all, the peasants began to quarrel among themselves: brothers demanded a division of property; their wives began to argue with one another. Things would come to a head in a sudden brawl; everybody would come flocking to the office, burst in on the master, often with battered visages and in a drunken state, demanding justice and retribution. A hubbub and a clamor would arise, the wails and whimpering squeals of the women mingling with the curses of the men. One had to arbitrate between the warring parties and shout oneself hoarse, knowing only too well that no proper decision could be reached. There was a shortage of hands for harvesting: a neighbouring farmer of most seemly aspect had contracted to supply reapers at the rate of two rubles per dessyatin, but had cheated Nikolai Petrovich shamelessly. The local peasant women demanded an exorbitant price, and meanwhile the grain was spilling, the mowing still had to be done, and the Guardian Council was threatening and demanding prompt and full payment of interest on the mortgage.

"I'm at the end of my tether!" Nikolai Petrovich often cried in despair. "I can't very well fight them, and my principles don't allow me to call in the police officer. Yet you can't do anything without the fear of punishment!"

"Du calme, du calme," Pavel Petrovich would soothe him, while he wrinkled his forehead, pulled at his mustache and mused.

Bazarov kept aloof from these squabbles. Besides, as a guest, all this was none of his business. The day after he arrived at Maryino he set to work on his frogs, infusorians and chemicals, and was busy with them all the time. Arkady, on the other hand, thought it his duty, if not to help his father, at least to show that he was ready to help. He heard his father out patiently, and once offered some advice, not in the hope that it would be taken, but to show his sympathy. The idea of running a farm was not repugnant to him—if anything, he looked forward to taking up agricultural pursuits. But at the moment his head was filled with other things.

Arkady was amazed to find himself constantly thinking about Nikolskoye. Formerly he would have merely shrugged his shoulders had anybody suggested the possibility of his being bored in Bazarov's company, or under his parental roof; but he really was bored and ached to get away. He took to long fatiguing hikes, but that was no help. Once, during a conversation with his father, Arkady learned that Nikolai Petro-

vich had some letters, and rather interesting ones, from Odintsova's mother to his late wife, and Arkady worried his father
until he had got those letters from him. Nikolai Petrovich had
to ransack a score of drawers and trunks to find them. On
acquiring these musty papers, Arkady seemed to calm down,
as though he had set himself a goal and then achieved it.

"I say this to both of you," he whispered to himself over
and over again. "She said that herself. Damn it all, I'll go . . .
yes, I will!" Then he recollected the last visit, the cool reception, and his old sense of embarrassment and timidity returned. The adventurous spirit of youth, however, a secret
desire to try his luck, to test his strength under his own
auspices, finally overcame his scruples.

Ten days after his return to Maryino, he was once more
on his way to town on the pretext of studying the organization
of Sunday schools—and from there to Nikolskoye. Eagerly
urging on the coachman, he rushed toward his destination like
a young officer into battle. He was gripped by fear and joy,
and bursting with impatience. "The main thing is not to think
about it," he kept saying to himself. The coachman, as luck
would have it, was a jolly man; he stopped at every public
house on the road, saying, "Wet the whistle—or not?" and
having wet the whistle he did not spare the horses. The tall
roof of the familiar house came in sight at last. "What am I
doing?" it suddenly flashed through Arkady's mind. "Too
late to turn back now!" The troika raced down the road, with
the coachman whooping and whistling. With a clatter of hoofs
and a rumble of wheels, they rushed over the little wooden
bridge, and now the drive lined by trimmed fir trees swept towards them. There was the flutter of a pink dress amid the
dark greenery, and a young face looked out from under the
light fringe of a parasol. He recognized Katya, and she recognized him. Arkady told the coachman to stop the gallop-
ing horses, jumped out of the carriage, and went up to her.
"It's you!" she murmured, a slow flush mounting to her cheeks.
"Let's join my sister; she's here in the garden. She will be
glad to see you."

Katya led Arkady into the garden. His meeting her struck

him as a peculiarly happy omen; his joy at seeing her was
as great as if she were someone near and dear to him. Things
could not have turned out better—no butler, no announce-
ment. At a bend in the path he saw Anna Sergeyevna. She
was standing with her back to him. Hearing footsteps, she
turned round slowly.

Arkady felt embarrassed again, but her very first words
immediately set him at his ease. "Hullo, you runaway!" she
said in her kind, steady way, and went forward to meet him,
smiling and screwing up her eyes against the sun and wind.
"Where did you find him, Katya?"

"I have brought you something, Anna Sergeyevna," he
began, "something you least of all expect. . . ."

"You have brought yourself. That's best of all."

23

HAVING seen Arkady off with mock regret and given him to understand that he was under no delusion as to the true object of his journey, Bazarov withdrew into complete seclusion. He was seized by a fever of activity. He no longer argued with Pavel Petrovich, particularly since the latter had assumed a more aristocratic air than ever in his presence, and expressed his opinions by sounds rather than words. Only once did Pavel Petrovich venture a bout with the *nihilist* on the then fashionable topic of the rights of the Baltic nobles, but abruptly checked himself, saying with frigid suavity, "But we cannot understand one another. At least, I'm sorry to say, I do not understand you."

"To be sure!" Bazarov exclaimed. "A man is capable of understanding everything—how the air flows and what takes place on the sun; but how another man can blow his nose differently than he does—that he cannot understand."

"Is that supposed to be witty?" Pavel Petrovich asked and walked away.

He sometimes asked to be allowed to witness Bazarov's experiments, and once even brought his perfumed face, laved with an excellent lotion, close to the microscope to examine some transparent infusorians in the process of swallowing a green speck and hastily masticating it with the aid of the flexible cilia situated in the gullet. Nikolai Petrovich visited Bazarov much more often than his brother; he would have come every day "to learn" as he put it, had he not been so busy with the farm. He stayed out of the way of the young naturalist: he would usually sit in a corner, watching attentively, only occasionally permitting himself a discreet question. During meals he tried to turn the conversation to physics, geology or chemistry, since all other topics, including farming, not to mention politics, were fraught with the risk of mutual annoyance, or clashes. Nikolai Petrovich sensed that his brother's hatred of Bazarov had not abated in the least. A trivial incident, among many others, confirmed his suspicions. Cases of cholera had appeared in the neighborhood and even claimed two victims at Maryino. One night Pavel Petrovich was seized by a rather severe attack. He suffered till morning, but did not resort to Bazarov's skill. When the latter met him the next morning and asked why he had not sent for him, Pavel Petrovich, still pale but carefully groomed and shaved, replied, "If I remember rightly, you yourself said that you do not believe in medicine." And so the days passed. Bazarov worked doggedly and gloomily—but there was one person in Nikolai Petrovich's house he talked to cheerfully. That person was Fenichka.

He usually met her early in the morning in the garden or in the yard. He never went to her room, and she had gone up to his door only on one occasion to ask whether or not she could bathe Mitya. She not only trusted him, but she was not afraid of him; indeed, she felt more at her ease with him than with Nikolai Petrovich. Why that was so it was difficult to say; perhaps it was because she was intuitively aware that Bazarov lacked those attributes of the grand gentleman, that higher something which at once fascinated and awed her. To her he was just an excellent doctor and a simple man. She tended her child in his presence without constraint, and once, when she suddenly felt dizzy and her head began to ache, she took a spoonful of medicine from his hands. In Nikolai Petrovich's presence she seemed to shun Bazarov: she did so not out of guile, but through a sense of propriety. Pavel Petrovich she feared more than ever. He had begun to watch her lately, and would crop up suddenly behind her back, with a set wary look and his hands in the pockets of his immaculate suit. "He just freezes you up," Fenichka complained to Dunyasha, who would sigh by way of reply, thinking of another "unfeeling" man. Bazarov had unsuspectingly become the *cruel tyrant* of her heart.

Fenichka liked Bazarov; and he liked her, too. Even his face would change when he talked to her: it assumed a serene, almost gentle expression, and his customary nonchalance was tinged with playfulness. Fenichka grew prettier every day. There is a time in a young woman's life when she suddenly begins to bloom and blossom forth like a summer rose; this time had come for Fenichka. Everything favored it—even the sultry July heat. Clad in a light white dress, she looked whiter and lighter herself: she did not tan in the sun, and the heat, which she tried in vain to avoid, imparted a tender bloom to her cheeks and ears and diffused a soft lassitude through all her body, which was reflected by a dreamy languor in her pretty eyes. She could hardly do anything; her hands were forever slipping listlessly to her lap. She could barely walk about, and uttered amusing little exclamations of helplessness.

"You should bathe more often," Nikolai Petrovich used to tell her.

He had fixed up a bathing tent at one of the ponds that had not yet dried up.

"Oh, Nikolai Petrovich! By the time you get to the pond you're almost dead, and by the time you get back it kills you. There isn't a bit of shade in the garden."

"That's true, there isn't any shade," Nikolai Petrovich would say, stroking his eyebrows.

One morning at a little past six, Bazarov, returning from his walk, came across Fenichka in the lilac arbor, which was long past bloom but was still thick and green. She was sitting on a bench with a white kerchief thrown over her head as usual; next to her lay a pile of red and white roses still wet with dew. He wished her good morning.

"Ah! Yevgeny Vasilich!" she said, raising a corner of the kerchief to take a look at him, her arms baring to the elbow as she did so.

"What are you doing here?" Bazarov said, sitting down beside her. "Making a bouquet?"

"Yes, for the breakfast table. Nikolai Petrovich likes it."

"But breakfast's a long way off yet. My, what a lot of flowers!"

"I've picked them now because it will be hot later on and I daren't go out of doors. This is the only time I can breathe freely. This heat makes me awfully weak. I wonder if I'm well?"

"What an idea! Let's feel your pulse." Bazarov took her hand, found the steadily throbbing vein and did not even bother to count the beats. "You'll live to be a hundred," he said, releasing her hand.

"Oh, God forbid!" she exclaimed.

"Why? Wouldn't you like to live long?"

"But a hundred years! Grandma lived to eighty-five—but what a martyr she was! Black and deaf and bent and coughing all the time; simply a burden to herself. What's the use of such a life!"

"Better to be young then?"

"Why, of course!"

"In what way is it better? Tell me!"

"What a question! Well, I'm young now . . . I can do anything. I can come and go and carry things and I don't have to ask anyone to do them for me. What could be better?"

"To me it's all the same whether I'm young or old."

"How can you say that? What a thing to say!"

"But judge for yourself, Fedosya Nikolayevna. What need have I for my youth? I live all alone, a poor lonely man. . . ."

"That only depends on you."

"That's just the trouble—it doesn't! If only somebody would take pity on me."

Fenichka gave him a sidelong glance, but said nothing. "What's that book you have?" she asked presently.

"This one? It's a learned book, difficult stuff."

"And you are learning all the time! Don't you find it dull? You must know everything there is to know, I should imagine."

"Evidently not. Try and read some of it."

"But I won't understand a thing. Is it in Russian?" Fenichka said, taking the heavily bound volume in both hands. "What a thick book!"

"Yes, it's in Russian."

"All the same, I won't understand it."

"I didn't mean you to understand it. I want to look at you while you are reading. The tip of your nose wriggles very prettily when you read."

Fenichka, who had begun to spell out an article, "On Creosote," burst out laughing and dropped the book. It slipped down from the bench to the ground.

"I like to see you laugh, too," Bazarov said.

"Oh, stop it!"

"I like to hear you speak. It's like the babbling of a brook."

Fenichka turned her head away. "Oh, how can you!" she murmured, toying with the flowers. "What do you find in my talk? You have spoken to such clever ladies."

"Ah, Fedosya Nikolayevna! Believe me, all the clever ladies in the world are not worth your little finger."

"Oh, what a thing to say!" Fenichka whispered.

Bazarov picked the book up from the ground. "This is a doctor's book. You shouldn't throw it around!"

"A doctor's book?" Fenichka echoed and turned round to him. "Do you know what? Since you gave me those drops— do you remember?—Mitya's been sleeping wonderfully! I don't know how to thank you; you're so kind, really."

"Doctors should really be paid," Bazarov said with a smile. "Doctors, you know, are a selfish lot."

Fenichka looked up at Bazarov with eyes that seemed darker, a pale gleam that set off the upper part of her face. She did not know whether he was joking or in earnest.

"If you wish, we shall be only too pleased. . . . I'll talk it over with Nikolai Petrovich."

"You think it's money I want?" Bazarov broke in. "No, I don't want any money from you."

"What then?" Fenichka said.

"What?" repeated Bazarov. "Guess."

"I'm no good at guessing!"

"Then I'll tell you; I want . . . one of those roses."

Fenichka laughed again and even flung up her hands, so amusing did Bazarov's request seem to her. Although she laughed, she felt flattered. Bazarov looked at her intently.

"Why, certainly," she said at length, and bending over the bench she began to turn the flowers over. "Which would you like, a red one or a white one?"

"A red one, and not too big."

She straightened up.

"Here you are," she said, but instantly snatched her hand back and, biting her lip, glanced at the entrance to the arbor, then listened.

"What is it?" Bazarov said. "Nikolai Petrovich?"

"No. He's gone out to the fields. . . . I'm not afraid of him. But Pavel Petrovich . . . I thought for a moment . . ."

"What?"

"I thought he was walking around. No . . . it's nobody. Here, take it." Fenichka gave Bazarov the rose.

"What makes you afraid of Pavel Petrovich?"

"He scares me all the time. He doesn't say a word, just looks at me in a queer sort of way. But you don't like him either. Do you remember how you used to argue with him all the time? I don't know what it's all about, but I can see how you turn him this way and that. . . ."

Fenichka showed with her hands how, in her opinion, Bazarov turned Pavel Petrovich this way and that.

Bazarov smiled.

"What if he got the better of me?" he said. "Would you take my part?"

"How could I take your part? And besides, nobody will ever get the better of you."

"You think so? But I know a hand that could knock me over with one finger if it wanted to."

"What hand is that?"

"Don't pretend you don't know. How nice the rose you gave me smells. Just smell it."

Fenichka craned her slim neck and put her face to the flower.

The kerchief slipped down to her shoulders, uncovering a soft mass of black, lustrous hair, slightly ruffled.

"Wait, I want to smell it with you," Bazarov murmured, and bending down he kissed her on her parted lips.

She started and pressed both hands against his chest, but pressed feebly, and he was able to renew and prolong the kiss.

A dry cough sounded behind the lilac bushes. Fenichka instantly moved to the far end of the bench. Pavel Petrovich passed the entrance, made a slight bow, and said with a kind of savage gloom, "You're here!" as he walked away. Fenichka hastily picked up her roses and left the arbor. "For shame, Yevgeny Vasilich," she whispered as she went out. There was genuine reproach in her voice.

Bazarov recalled another recent scene and was struck with a sense of guilt and contemptuous irritation. But he shook his head, ironically congratulated himself on his initiation into the ranks of chartered Celadons and went to his room.

And Pavel Petrovich left the garden and walked slowly to the woods. He remained there a fairly long time, and when he came in to breakfast Nikolai Petrovich solicitously inquired whether he was well—so dark had his countenance grown.

"You know I sometimes suffer from bilious attacks," Pavel Petrovich calmly replied.

24

SOME two hours later he knocked at Bazarov's door.

"I must apologize for interrupting your scientific studies," he began, settling himself in a chair by the window with both hands resting on a handsome ivory-handled cane (he usually went about without a cane), "but I must ask you to spare me five minutes of your time—no more."

"All my time is at your disposal," replied Bazarov, over whose face a shadow had flitted as soon as Pavel Petrovich crossed the threshold.

"Five minutes will be enough for me. I have come to put just one question to you."

"A question? What is it?"

"Well, then, please listen. At the beginning of your sojourn in my brother's house, when I had not yet denied myself the pleasure of conversation with you, I had occasion to hear your views on many subjects; but, as far as I remember, neither between us nor in my presence was there any talk of duels. May I inquire what your views are on this score?"

Bazarov, who had risen on Pavel Petrovich's entrance, sat down on the edge of the table and crossed his arms.

"My view is this," he said. "From the theoretical standpoint a duel is absurd, but from the practical—that's another matter."

"That is to say, if I understand you rightly, whatever your theoretical opinion of a duel may be, you would not in practice let yourself be insulted without demanding satisfaction?"

"You have understood exactly."

"Very good, sir. I am very pleased to hear you say so. Your statement relieves me of my uncertainty. . . ."

"Indecision, you wanted to say."

"It's all the same; I express myself so as to be understood: I am not a seminary rat. Your statement relieves me of a regrettable necessity. I have decided to fight a duel with you."

Bazarov stared.

"With me?"

"Yes, sir, with you."

"Good heavens, what for?"

"I could explain the reason to you," Pavel Petrovich began, "but I prefer not to. You are simply one too many here in my opinion. I detest you, loathe you, and if that is not enough. . . ."

Pavel Petrovich's eyes flashed. There was a gleam in Bazarov's too.

"Very well, sir," he said. "Further explanations are unnecessary. You have taken it into your head to try out your chivalry on me. I could deny you that pleasure, but never mind."

"I am greatly obliged to you," Pavel Petrovich answered. "I can now hope that you will accept my challenge without compelling me to resort to violence."

"In other words, speaking without allegory—to that cane?" Bazarov said coolly. "Quite right. You don't have to insult me. It would not be wholly safe either. You can remain a gentleman. I accept your challenge as a gentleman too."

"Splendid," Pavel Petrovich said, and put his cane in a corner. "A few words now as to the conditions of our duel—but first I would like to know whether you consider it necessary to resort to the formality of a trivial quarrel, as a pretext for my challenge?"

"No, let us do without formalities."

"I think so too. I do not think it worth while to go into the real reasons for our difference either. We cannot stand each other. What more need be said?"

"What more, indeed?" Bazarov repeated ironically.

"As regards the conditions of the duel—we shall not have any seconds. Where should we find them?"

"Precisely, where should we find them?"

"So I have the honor to propose the following: the duel is to take place tomorrow morning, say at six o'clock by the copse, with pistols; the barrier at ten paces. . . ."

"Ten paces? Very well; we hate each other at that distance."

"We can make it eight," observed Pavel Petrovich.

"Certainly, why not!"

"We shall have two shots each; just in case, each of us will put a letter in his pocket blaming himself for his own death."

"Now, that I don't quite agree with," Bazarov said. "It smacks a bit of the French novel and doesn't sound plausible."

"Perhaps. But you will concede that it will not be very pleasant to be suspected of murder?"

"I agree. But there is a way of avoiding that sad contingency. We have no seconds, but we can have a witness."

"Who exactly, may I ask?"

"Why, Pyotr."

"What Pyotr?"

"Your brother's valet. He's a man who enjoys the advantages of a modern education and will play his part with all due *comme il faut*."

"I believe you are jesting, my dear sir."

"Not at all. If you consider my suggestion, you will find it sensible and simple. Murder will out, but I undertake to prepare Pyotr for the occasion and bring him to the field of battle."

"You still persist in jesting," Pavel Petrovich said, getting up from his chair. "But after the kind willingness you have shown, I have no right to complain. And so, everything is arranged. By the way, have you pistols?"

"How would I have pistols, Pavel Petrovich? I'm not a soldier."

"In that case I offer you mine. You can rest assured that I haven't used them for five years."

Pavel Petrovich picked up his cane.

"Till our pleasant meeting tomorrow, my dear sir," Bazarov said, seeing his visitor out.

Pavel Petrovich took his departure, while Bazarov stood before the closed door after Pavel Petrovich had gone, then suddenly exclaimed, "Well, I never! How very fine and how stupid! What a farce we've played! Like a couple of trained dogs dancing on their hind legs. But I couldn't very well refuse him; he might have hit me, and then. . . ." (Bazarov paled at the very thought; all his pride rose up in arms.) "I'd have had to throttle him then like a kitten." He went back to his microscope, but his heart had been stirred and the calm that was necessary for observations had vanished. "He saw us today," he thought. "But could he have got himself so worked up on his brother's account? What a fuss to make over a kiss. There's something else behind it. Bah! Why, I believe he's in love with her himself! Of course he is; it's as clear as daylight. What a holy mess! A bad situation," he decided at length, "whichever way you look at it. In the first place I run a risk, and in any case I'll have to leave; and there's Arkady . . . and that lamb Nikolai Petrovich. A bad situation!"

The day passed somehow in a peculiarly quiet and listless fashion. Fenichka might have been nonexistent; she sat in her room like a mouse in its hole. Nikolai Petrovich looked worried; it had been reported to him that his wheat had developed brant, and he had been counting particularly on that crop. Pavel Petrovich oppressed everybody, even Prokofich, with his icy courtesy. Bazarov began a letter to his father, then tore it up and threw it under the table. "If I die," he thought, "they'll hear about it; but I'm not going to die. I'll be around for a long time yet." He told Pyotr to come and see him the next morning at daybreak on important business—Pyotr thought that he wanted to take him to St. Petersburg. Bazarov went to bed late, and was tortured all night by troubled dreams. Odintsova visited his dreams; she was his mother too, and a kitten with black whiskers followed about, and that kitten was Fenichka. Pavel Petrovich appeared in the shape of a big forest, with which he had to fight a duel.

Pyotr woke him at four o'clock; he dressed quickly and went out with him.

The morning was bright and fresh; fleecy cloudlets stood in the pale azure of the sky; dew lay on the leaves and grasses and gleamed like silver on the spiders' webs; the dark moist earth still seemed to retain the rosy traces of sunrise; the song of the larks poured down from the skies. Bazarov reached the copse, and sat down in the shade on the fringe of the woods. Only then did he disclose to Pyotr the service that was required of him. The educated valet was frightened out of his wits; but Bazarov set his fears at rest by assuring him that all he had to do was to stand at a distance and watch, and that he bore no responsibility whatsoever. "Just think," he added, "what an important part you're destined to play!" Pyotr spread his hands, stared down at his feet, and leaned against a birch tree, his face sickly green.

The road from Maryino skirted the woods; a light dust lay upon it, untouched by wheel or foot since yesterday. Bazarov looked down the road despite himself, plucked and nibbled blades of grass, and kept on saying to himself, "What folly!" The chill morning air made him shiver once or twice. Pyotr glanced at him mournfully, but Bazarov merely smiled—he was not scared.

There was a sound of hoofs on the road. A peasant appeared from behind the trees. He was driving two hobbled horses before him, and in passing Bazarov, he looked at him rather oddly without taking off his cap, which struck Pyotr as an ill omen. "This man is up early too," Bazarov thought, "but at least for a purpose. While we ... ?"

"I think he's coming," Pyotr whispered.

Bazarov looked up and saw Pavel Petrovich. Attired in a light checked jacket and snow-white trousers, he was striding swiftly down the road, carrying under his arm a case wrapped up in a green cloth.

"Excuse me, I am afraid I have kept you waiting," he

said, bowing first to Bazarov, then to Pyotr, giving him his due as something in the nature of a second. "I did not want to wake my valet."

"That's all right," Bazarov answered. "We've only just arrived ourselves."

"Ah! All the better!" Pavel Petrovich looked round. "Nobody in sight, nobody will interfere. Shall we begin?"

"Let's begin."

"I presume you require no further explanations?"

"No."

"Would you like to load?" Pavel Petrovich asked, drawing the pistols from the case.

"No, load them yourself, and I'll measure off the distance. My legs are longer," Bazarov added with a humorous smile. "One, two, three . . ."

"Yevgeny Vasilich!" Pyotr barely managed to stammer (he shook like an aspen leaf). "Do what you like, but I'll step aside."

"Four, five . . . Step aside, old chap; you can even stand behind a tree and stop up your ears, but don't shut your eyes. If anybody drops, run and pick him up . . . six, seven, eight . . ." Bazarov stopped. "Will that do," he asked, turning to Pavel Petrovich, "or shall I throw in another couple of paces?"

"As you wish," the other retorted, pushing home a second bullet.

"Well, let's throw in another two paces." Bazarov traced a line on the ground with the toe of his boot. "Here's the barrier. By the way, how many paces do we have to take from the barrier? That's an important point too. We didn't discuss it yesterday."

"Ten paces I should say," replied Pavel Petrovich, offering Bazarov the pistols. "Will you be so good as to choose?"

"I will. But come, Pavel Petrovich, don't you agree that our duel is ridiculous to the point of absurdity? Just take a look at our second's face."

"You still wish to treat the matter as a joke," Pavel Petrovich replied. "I do not deny that our duel is peculiar, but I consider it my duty to warn you that I intend to fight in earnest. *A bon entendeur, salut!*"

"Oh, I haven't the slightest doubt we are determined to annihilate each other; but why not have a laugh and combine *utile dulci?* So there we are: my Latin to your French."

"I'm going to fight in earnest," Pavel Petrovich repeated and took up his position. Bazarov in turn counted off ten paces from the barrier and stopped.

"Are you ready?" Pavel Petrovich asked.

"Quite."

"We can close in."

Bazarov moved forward slowly, and Pavel Petrovich advanced on him, his left hand thrust into his pocket and his right steadily raising the muzzle of his pistol. "He's aiming straight at my nose," thought Bazarov, "and how carefully he's squinting, the bounder! This is an unpleasant sensation though; I'll keep my eye on his watch chain." Something whizzed sharply close to Bazarov's ear, followed by an instantaneous report. "I've heard it, so I suppose I'm all right," the thought flashed through his mind. He took another step and pulled the trigger without taking aim.

Pavel Petrovich gave a slight start and clutched his thigh. Blood trickled down his white trousers.

Bazarov threw his pistol down and approached his adversary.

"Are you wounded?" he asked.

"You had the right to call me to the barrier," said Pavel Petrovich. "It's nothing. According to the conditions each of us has another shot."

"Sorry, we'll have to leave that for another time," Bazarov said, supporting Pavel Petrovich, who had begun to grow pale. "Now I am no longer a dueler, but a doctor, and I must examine your wound. Pyotr! Come here! Where are you hiding?"

"It's nothing . . . I don't need any help," Pavel Petrovich said slowly, "and . . . we must . . . again . . ." He wanted to tug at his moustache, but his hand dropped nervelessly. His eyes rolled up and he lost consciousness.

"Good Lord! A fainting fit! Imagine that!" exclaimed Bazarov, lowering Pavel Petrovich on to the grass. "Let's see what it's all about!" He pulled out a handkerchief, wiped away the blood, and felt around the wound. "The bone is intact," he muttered, "superficial flesh wound, bullet's gone clean through, one muscle *vastus externus* slightly affected. Fit to dance a jig in three weeks! Imagine, fainting! These nervous types are really something . . . And look at that tender skin."

"Is he killed, sir?" Pyotr spluttered behind him, his voice trembling.

Bazarov turned round.

"Go and get some water man. Quickly! He'll outlive both of us."

But the model servant did not seem to understand what had been said to him, for he did not budge. Pavel Petrovich slowly opened his eyes. "He's going to die!" Pyotr quavered and began crossing himself.

"You're right. . . . What a stupid face!" the wounded man murmured with a wan smile.

"Go and fetch the confounded water!" Bazarov shouted.

"There's no need to. It was a momentary *vertige*. Help me up. That's better. . . . This scratch merely has to be bandaged and I'll be able to walk home, or the carriage could be sent out for me. The duel, if you like, will not be resumed. You have acted nobly . . . today, today, mind you."

"There's no need to rake up the past," Bazarov answered. "As for the future, there's no need to worry about that either, because I intend to slip away at once. Now let me tie your leg up; your wound is not dangerous, but still it's advisable to stem the blood. But first let us restore this mortal to his senses."

Bazarov shook Pyotr by the collar and sent him for the carriage.

"Mind you don't scare my brother," Pavel Petrovich admonished him. "Don't you dare tell him anything."

Pyotr ran off. While he was gone for the carriage the adversaries sat on the ground in silence. Pavel Petrovich tried to avoid looking at Bazarov; he had no wish to make up with him; he was ashamed of his arrogance and his failure, ashamed of the whole business he had stirred up, though he realized that it could not have ended more satisfactorily. "At any rate, he won't be hanging around here any more," he comforted himself. "That's one good thing." The silence was becoming oppressive and awkward. Both felt ill at ease. Each realized that the other understood him perfectly. Between friends this is a pleasant awareness, but between foes an extremely unpleasant one, particularly when there is no way to clear things up or to part company.

"I didn't tie your leg up too tight, did I?" Bazarov asked at length.

"No, it's all right, it's splendid," replied Pavel Petrovich, adding after a little pause, "My brother won't be deceived; he'll have to be told that we argued about politics."

"Very good," Bazarov said. "You can say I scoffed at all the Anglomaniacs."

"Splendid. What do you suppose that man thinks of us?" resumed Pavel Petrovich, pointing to the peasant who had driven the hobbled horses past Bazarov a few minutes before the duel, and who now, coming back down the road, pulled himself together and doffed his cap at the sight of the "gentlefolk."

"Who knows!" Bazarov said. "Probably he doesn't think anything. The Russian peasant is the mysterious stranger Mrs. Radcliffe used to talk so much about. You can't make him out. He can't even make himself out."

"So that's what you think!" Pavel Petrovich began, then suddenly exclaimed, "Look what that idiot of yours, Pyotr, has gone and done! There's my brother coming!"

Bazarov turned and saw a pale-faced Nikolai Petrovich sitting in the carriage. He jumped out before the vehicle stopped and rushed up to his brother.

"What does it all mean?" he cried in an agitated voice; "Yevgeny Vasilich, what is the matter?"

"It's all right," Pavel Petrovich answered. "They shouldn't

have bothered you. Mr. Bazarov and I have had a little quarrel, and I'm a little the worse for it."

"What is it all about, for God's sake?"

"Well, if you want to know, Mr. Bazarov passed some disparaging remarks on Sir Robert Peel. I hasten to add that it was all my fault, and Mr. Bazarov behaved splendidly. I challenged him."

"But you're bleeding!"

"Did you think I had water in my veins? But this blood-letting is good for me. Isn't that so, doctor? Help me get into the carriage, brother, and don't look so glum. I'll be all right tomorrow. There, that's fine. Go on, coachman."

Nikolai Petrovich followed behind the carriage; Bazarov brought up the rear.

"I must ask you to attend my brother, until another doctor is brought down from town," Nikolai Petrovich said to him.

Bazarov inclined his head.

An hour later Pavel Petrovich was lying in bed with his leg skillfully dressed. The whole house was in an uproar: Fenichka swooned; Nikolai Petrovich furtively wrung his hands; while Pavel Petrovich laughed and joked, especially with Bazarov. Pavel Petrovich put on a fine cambric shirt, a spruce morning jacket and a fez. He would not allow the blinds to be lowered and complained, in a droll way, at the necessity of abstaining from food.

During the night, however, his temperature rose, and his head ached. A doctor arrived from town. (Nikolai Petrovich had disregarded his brother's protests, and Bazarov himself had insisted on it; he sat in his room all day long, yellow and grim, and dropped in to see the patient for very brief visits; once or twice he had encountered Fenichka, who recoiled from him in horror.) The new doctor recommended cool drinks, and confirmed Bazarov's assurance that there was absolutely no danger. Nikolai Petrovich told him that his brother had accidentally wounded himself, to which the doctor had replied, "Hm!" but on receiving twenty-five rubles in silver, had added, "Surprising—these things do happen, you know!"

Nobody in the house undressed or went to bed. Every now and then, Nikolai Petrovich tiptoed into his brother's room and tiptoed out again. The patient dropped into a heavy slumber, groaned a little, said to him in French, *"Couchez-vous"* and asked for a drink. Nikolai Petrovich once made Fenichka take him a glass of lemonade; Pavel Petrovich gazed at her fixedly and drained the glass. Towards morning the fever rose somewhat and the patient became slightly delirious. At first Pavel Petrovich uttered incoherent words; then he suddenly opened his eyes, and seeing his brother bending solicitously over him, he murmured:

"Don't you think, Nikolai, that Fenichka looks a bit like Nelly?"

"What Nelly, Pavel?"

"Imagine you asking. The Princess R—. Especially the upper part of her face. *C'est de la même famille.*"

Nikolai Petrovich said nothing, but he wondered at the tenacity with which old feelings clung to a man.

"That's when they crop up," he thought.

"Oh, how I love that empty creature!" Pavel Petrovich moaned, clasping his hands behind his head in anguish. "No insolent lout will dare touch her, not while I . . ." he babbled a minute later.

Nikolai Petrovich merely sighed; he never suspected to whom those words applied.

The next day, at about eight in the morning, Bazarov came in to see him. He had packed his luggage and released all his frogs, insects and birds.

"You have come to say good-bye?" Nikolai Petrovich said, rising to meet him.

"Yes, sir."

"I understand you, and entirely approve of you. My poor brother was to blame of course—and he's been punished for it. He told me himself he had placed you in a position that gave you no other option. I do believe that you weren't able to avoid this duel which . . . which to a certain extent was due merely to the constant antagonism of your mutual views." (Nikolai Petrovich got mixed up in his speech.) "My brother is a man of the old school, quick-tempered and stubborn. . . . Thank God it ended the way it did. I have taken all the necessary precautions to hush the matter up."

"I'll leave you my address, in case there's any trouble," Bazarov said casually.

"I hope there won't be, Yevgeny Vasilich. I'm very sorry that your sojourn in my house has . . . has ended the way it has. I'm all the more grieved since Arkady . . ."

"I'll probably be seeing him," interposed Bazarov; who always chafed at every kind of "explanation" and "demonstration." "If not, please give him my regards and please accept my regrets."

"And please accept mine . . ." Nikolai Petrovich began with a bow. Bazarov, however, had left without waiting for the end of his little speech.

On learning that Bazarov was going away, Pavel Petrovich expressed a wish to see him, and shook hands with him. But Bazarov remained as cold as ice; he realized that Pavel Petrovich was trying to be magnanimous. He did not manage to take leave of Fenichka: he only exchanged a look with her through the window. He thought she looked sad. "She'll go under, I'm afraid," he said to himself. "Well, let's hope she'll pull through somehow!" Pyotr broke down entirely and wept on his shoulder, until Bazarov sobered him with a remark about "closing the floodgates," while Dunyasha fled to the wood, to hide her agitation. The cause of all this misery climbed into the cart, lit a cigar, and when, at a bend in the road three versts down, the Kirsanov farmstead with its new house unfolded for the last time before his gaze, he merely spat. Muttering "Damned squirarchy!" he drew his coat closer about him.

Pavel Petrovich soon felt better, but he was kept in bed for about a week. He endured what he called his *captivity* patiently, but fussed a good deal over his toilet and demanded frequent perfumings of the room. Nikolai Petrovich read him magazines; Fenichka waited upon him as before, bringing him his broth, lemonade, soft-boiled eggs and tea; but she was

seized by a secret terror every time she entered his room.
Pavel Petrovich's unexpected conduct had frightened the
whole household, and her more than anyone else. Prokofich
alone was undisturbed and talked about gentlemen in his day
who had damaged each other too, but then it had been between real gentlemen. As for such miscreants as these, they
would simply have ordered them to be flogged in the stables
for their impudence.

Fenichka scarcely had any pricks of conscience, but sometimes she thought about the real cause of the quarrel and it
worried her. And Pavel Petrovich looked at her so queerly . . .
she could feel his gaze upon her even when she had her back
to him. She grew thin from constant anxiety, and, as could
be expected, even more charming.

One day—it was in the morning—Pavel Petrovich was
feeling well and moved from his bed to the sofa, and Nikolai
Petrovich, having inquired about his health, went to visit
the threshing floor. Fenichka brought in a cup of tea, and,
setting it down on the table, she was about to leave. Pavel
Petrovich detained her.

"Why are you in such a hurry, Fedosya Nikolayevna?" he
began. "Have you anything to do?"

"No sir. . . . But I must pour the tea."

"Dunyasha will do that without you. Keep a sick man
company a little. I want to speak to you by the way."

Fenichka sat down on the edge of an armchair.

"Look here," Pavel Petrovich said, pulling at his mustache.
"I have long wanted to ask you. . . . You seem to be afraid
of me."

"I, sir?"

"Yes, you. You never look at me. One would think your
conscience was not clear."

Fenichka reddened, but turned her eyes to Pavel Petrovich.
Her heart fluttered because he looked at her so strangely.

"Your conscience is clear, isn't it?" he demanded.

"Why shouldn't it be?" she whispered.

"Who knows! Whom have you wronged, I wonder. Me?
That's improbable. Somebody else in the house? That, too,

is unlikely. My brother perhaps? But you love him, don't you?"

"I do."

"With all your heart and soul?"

"I love Nikolai Petrovich dearly."

"Do you? Look at me, Fenichka." (He used that name for the first time.) "You know, it's a great sin to lie!"

"I'm not lying, Pavel Petrovich. How could I not love Nikolai Petrovich? I wouldn't care to live if I didn't!"

"And you would not give him up for anybody?"

"For whom would I give him up?"

"One never knows! Why, for that gentleman, say, who has just left."

Fenichka stood up: "My God, why do you torment me, Pavel Petrovich? What have I done to you? How can you say a thing like that?"

"Fenichka," Pavel Petrovich said in a melancholy voice, "I saw it, you know. . . ."

"Saw what, sir?"

"Out there . . . in the arbor."

Fenichka crimsoned to the roots of her hair.

"But it wasn't my fault!" she said with an effort.

Pavel Petrovich sat up.

"Not your fault? Not in the least?"

"Nikolai Petrovich is the only man in the world I love and I'll love him as long as I live," Fenichka blurted out with sudden vehemence, and sobs rose in her throat. "As for what you saw, I'll swear on the Day of Judgment that it was not my fault, and it would be better for me to die now than to be suspected of such a thing—such a sin towards my bene-factor, Nikolai Petrovich. . . ."

Here her voice broke, and at the same instant she became aware that Pavel Petrovich had seized her hand and was squeezing it. She looked at him dumbfounded. His face had turned pale, his eyes glistened, and, what was most astonishing, a heavy solitary tear rolled down his cheek.

"Fenichka," he said in a strange whisper, "love my brother, love him! He's such a kind, good man! Don't betray him for anybody in the world—don't listen to anybody! Just think,

what can be more terrible than to love and not be loved!
Don't ever forsake my poor Nikolai!"

Fenichka's eyes had dried up and her fear had passed—
so great was her astonishment. But then . . . Pavel Petrovich
himself pressed her hand to his lips, and clung to it without
kissing it, merely sighing fitfully from time to time. . . .

"Goodness gracious!" she thought. "I wonder if he isn't
going to have a fit?"

At that moment all the memories of a ruined life had
flooded in upon him.

The staircase creaked under a quick step. . . . He pushed
her away and fell back on his pillow. The door opened—and
in came Nikolai Petrovich, looking gay, fresh and pink. Mitya,
as fresh and pink as his father, clad in a single undershirt,
leaped and wriggled on his chest, his bare little toes catching
in the big buttons of the country-made coat.

Fenichka ran to him impulsively, and, flinging her arms
around him and her son, nestled her head against his shoulder.
Nikolai Petrovich marveled: his coy bashful Fenichka had
never shown him signs of affection in the presence of a third
person.

"What is the matter with you?" he said, and glancing at
his brother, transferred Mitya to her arms. "You are not feeling worse, are you?" he asked, coming up to Pavel Petrovich.

The latter buried his face in a cambric handkerchief. "No
. . . nothing . . . I'm all right. . . . On the contrary, I feel
much better."

"You shouldn't have been in such a hurry to move to the
sofa. Where are you going?" Nikolai Petrovich added, turning
to Fenichka, but she had already closed the door behind
her. "I wanted to show you the baby. He misses his uncle.
What made her carry him off? What is the matter with you,
though? Has anything happened here between you?"

"Brother!" Pavel Petrovich said solemnly.

Nikolai Petrovich started. He was awestruck, he could not
explain why.

"Brother," Pavel Petrovich repeated, "give me your word
that you will carry out my request."

"What request? What do you want to say?"

"It's very important; all the happiness of your life, I believe, depends upon it. I have been thinking a good deal lately about what I am going to tell you. . . . Brother, fulfill your obligation, the obligation of an honest and upright man. Put a stop to temptation and the bad example you are setting —you, the best of men!"

"What do you mean, Pavel?"

"Marry Fenichka. . . . She loves you; she is the mother of your child."

Nikolai Petrovich stepped back and flung up his arms.

"And you say that, Pavel? You, whom I always considered a determined opponent of such marriages! You say that! Why, don't you know that it was only out of respect for you that I did not do what you rightly call my duty!"

"You were wrong to have respected me in that case," Pavel Petrovich said with a mournful smile. "I'm beginning to think Bazarov was right when he accused me of being an aristocrat. No, dear brother, it's time we stopped putting on airs and thinking about society. We are old and humble folk; it's time we discarded the hollow vanities. Aye, let us start doing our duty, as you say; and I shouldn't wonder if it brought us happiness too."

Nikolai Petrovich embraced his brother.

"You have opened my eyes completely!" he cried. "Haven't I always said that you were the kindest and cleverest man in the world. And now I see you are as sensible as you are generous."

"Easy, easy," Pavel Petrovich interrupted him, "don't jar the leg of your sensible brother who, at the age of nearly fifty, fought a duel like a junior ensign. And so this matter is settled: Fenichka will be my . . . sister-in-law."

"Dear Pavel! But what will Arkady say?"

"Arkady? Why, he'll be jubilant! Marriage is not one of his principles, but then his sense of equality will be flattered. No, really, what's this idea of caste *au dix-neuvième siècle?*"

"Ah, Pavel, Pavel! Let me kiss you again. Don't be afraid, I'll be careful."

The brothers embraced.

"What about announcing your decision to her now?" Pavel Petrovich said.

"What's the hurry?" Nikolai Petrovich answered. "Why, did you discuss it with her?"

"Discuss it with her? *Quelle idée!*"

"Well, that's fine. First of all get well. This won't run away from us. This wants thinking over carefully. . . ."

"But you have decided, haven't you?"

"Of course I have, and I thank you from the bottom of my heart. I'll leave you now! You must have a rest; this excitement is no good for you. . . . But we'll talk it over again. Go to sleep, dear, and God grant you good health!"

"Why is he thanking me?" Pavel Petrovich thought when he was left by himself. "As if it didn't depend upon him! As for me, as soon as he marries I'll go off somewhere far away, to Dresden or Florence, and live there until I give up the ghost."

Pavel Petrovich dabbed his forehead with Eau de Cologne and shut his eyes. In the bright light of day his handsome emaciated head lay on the white pillow like the head of a corpse. . . . He was indeed a living corpse.

25

IN the garden at Nikolskoye, Katya and Arkady were sitting on a grassy bank in the shade of a tall ash; at their feet lay Fifi, her long body gracefully curved in what sportsmen call "the hare stance." Both Katya and Arkady were silent; he was holding a half-opened book in his hands while she was picking the remaining crumbs of white bread from a basket and throwing them to a small family of sparrows which were hopping and chirruping at her feet, with the timorous audacity of their kind. A gentle breeze stirred among the ash leaves, throwing shifting patches of pale gold sunshine on the shaded path and Fifi's tawny back; Arkady and Katya were enclosed in deep shadow, and occasionally a strip of brilliance blazed up in her hair. Neither spoke, but their very silence, the way they sat side by side, breathed a trustful intimacy. Each seemed to be unaware of his neighbor, yet secretly glad of his nearness. Their faces, too, had changed since last we saw them: Arkady looked calmer, Katya more animated, bolder.

"Don't you think that the Russian word for ash tree is very apt?" Arkady said. "No other tree stands out in the air so lightly and clearly."*

Katya looked up and murmured "yes," and Arkady thought: "She does not rebuke me for talking *pretty*."

"I don't like Heine," Katya said, indicating the book in Arkady's hands with her eyes, "either when he laughs or when he cries. I like him when he is wistful."

"And I like him when he laughs," Arkady observed.

* The Russian for "ash tree" is *yasen*, which is a derivative of *yasny—clear*, *bright*.—Tr.

"There speak the old traces of your satiric bent. . . ." ("Old traces!" thought Arkady; "If only Bazarov could have heard it.") "You wait, we shall convert you."

"Who will convert me? You?"

"Who? My sister! Porfiry Platonich, with whom you no longer quarrel; Auntie, whom you accompanied to church the other day."

"I couldn't very well refuse, could I? As to Anna Sergeyevna, she agreed with Yevgeny on many points, you remember."

"My sister was under his influence then, as you were."

"As I was! Why, have you noticed that I've escaped his influence?"

Katya was silent.

"I know, you never did like him," Arkady resumed.

"I am in no position to judge him."

"Do you know what, Katerina Sergeyevna? Every time I hear you say that, I don't believe it. There isn't a person any one of us could not judge! It's just an excuse."

"Well then, if you want to know—I wouldn't exactly say that I don't like him, but I feel that he's a stranger to me and I am a stranger to him . . . and so are you."

"How is that?"

"How shall I put it. . . . He's predatory, while we are tame."

"And am I tame too?"

Katya nodded.

Arkady scratched his ear.

"Katerina Sergeyevna, that is really offensive."

"Why, would you like to be predatory?"

"Predatory—no; but strong, energetic."

"It's not a thing you can want. . . . Now your friend—he doesn't want it, but he has it."

"Hm! So you think he had a big influence on Anna Sergeyevna?"

"Yes. But nobody can get the better of her for long," Katya added in a low voice.

"What makes you think so?"

"She's very proud . . . no, not that . . . she puts great store by her independence."

"Who doesn't?" Arkady said, and in the same instant it flashed upon him: "Of what use is it?"

"Of what use is it?" also passed through Katya's mind. Young people who see each other often on a friendly footing constantly think the same thoughts.

Arkady smiled and, moving slightly closer to Katya, said in a whisper: "Confess that you are a little afraid of her."

"Of whom?"

"Of *her*," Arkady repeated meaningly.

"What about you?" Katya countered.

"I am too. Notice, I said *too*."

Katya wagged a forefinger at him.

"That surprises me," she went on. "You were never so much in my sister's good graces as you are now—much more so than during your first visit."

"Is that so?"

"Didn't you notice it? Aren't you glad?"

Arkady pondered.

"In what way could I have won Anna Sergeyevna's approval? It's not really because of your mother's letters that I brought her, is it?"

"It's that, and other reasons as well, which I won't tell you."

"Why not?"

"I won't."

"Oh, I know—you're very obstinate."

"I am."

"And observant."

Katya threw him a sidelong glance.

"Does that make you angry? What are you thinking of?"

"I was thinking, where did you get such keen powers of observation. You are so timid, so mistrustful, you shun everybody. . . ."

"I have lived by myself a good deal; it makes you think. But do I shun everybody?"

Arkady threw her a grateful glance.

"Well," he went on, "people in your position, I mean with

your wealth, rarely possess that gift. Truth doesn't reach them any more easily than it does kings."

"But I am not rich."

Arkady was taken aback and did not at once grasp her meaning. "Indeed, the estate's her sister's!" then dawned on him. The thought was not an unpleasant one.

"How nicely you said that!" he murmured.

"Why?"

"You said it nicely, simply, without shame or affection. By the way, I should imagine that the feelings of a person who knows and admits that he is poor have a peculiar touch of vanity about them."

"I never experienced anything of the kind, thanks to my sister; I just mentioned my position because it happened to come up."

"Yes, I know. But confess that you have a little of that vanity I've just been speaking about."

"For example?"

"For example, you wouldn't—pardon the question—you wouldn't marry a rich man, would you?"

"If I loved him very much . . . No, even then, I don't think I would."

"Ah! You see!" exclaimed Arkady, adding after a pause, "Why wouldn't you marry him?"

"Because there's a song about the lowly bride . . ."

"Perhaps it's because you want to dominate, or . . ."

"Oh, no! What for? On the contrary, I am ready to submit; it's only inequality that is unbearable. I can understand a person submitting and yet retaining her self-respect; that's happiness. But a life of subordination. . . . No, I've had enough of that."

"Had enough of that," Arkady echoed. "Yes, yes," he went on, "you have your sister's blood in your veins. You're just as independent as she is; only you are more reticent. You would never, I'm sure, declare your feelings first, no matter how strong and sacred they were. . . ."

"How could it be otherwise?" Katya said.

"You are equally clever; you have as much character as she has, if not more."

"Don't compare me to my sister, please," Katya broke in hastily. "You place me at too great a disadvantage. You seem to have forgotten that my sister is beautiful and clever and . . . you of all people, Arkady Nikolaich, should not be saying such things, and with a serious face too."

"What do you mean by 'you of all people,' and what makes you think I'm joking?"

"Of course you're joking."

"Do you think so? What if I'm convinced of what I'm saying? What if I believe that I haven't expressed myself forcefully enough?"

"I don't understand you."

"Really? Well, now I see that I've been praising your powers of observation too highly."

"What do you mean?"

Arkady made no reply and turned away, while Katya hunted for more crumbs in the basket and threw them to the sparrows. But the sweep of her hand was too vigorous, and they flew away without taking a peck.

"Katerina Sergeyevna," Arkady said suddenly. "I suppose it's all the same to you, but I want you to know that I don't prefer your sister or anybody else in the world to you."

He got up and walked quickly away, as though frightened by his own outburst.

Katya dropped both her hands, together with the basket, on her lap, and with head bent, looked long after Arkady's retreating figure. A blush slowly kindled in her cheeks. Her lips, however, were unsmiling, and her dark eyes expressed bewilderment and a feeling of something else—something to which she could not yet give a name.

"You're alone?" Anna Sergeyevna's voice sounded nearby. "I thought you went into the garden with Arkady."

Katya's eyes travelled slowly to her sister (elegantly, even exquisitely dressed, she stood in the pathway and tickled Fifi's ears with the tip of her open parasol) and she answered as slowly: "Yes, I'm alone."

"So I see," the former retorted with a little laugh. "He's gone to his room, I suppose?"

"Yes."

"Have you been reading together?"

"Yes."

Anna Sergeyevna took Katya by the chin and raised her head.

"You haven't quarrelled, I hope?"

"No," Katya said and gently removed her sister's hand.

"How solemn you sound! I thought I'd find him here and offer to take a walk with him. He's been after me all the time about it. They've brought a pair of shoes for you from town. Go and try them on. I noticed yesterday that yours were quite worn out. Generally you don't pay enough attention to yourself, and you have such charming little feet! Your hands are lovely too . . . though a bit too large. You must make the most of your feet. But there, you have no coquetry in you at all."

Anna Sergeyevna proceeded down the path with a faint swish of her beautiful gown. Katya rose to her feet and, taking Heine with her, went away too—but not to try on the shoes.

"Charming little feet," she was thinking as she slowly and lightly ascended the sun-baked stone steps of the verandah. "Charming little feet, you say. . . . Well, he'll be at them."

She felt disconcerted and took the rest of the steps at a run.

As Arkady walked down the passage to his room, the butler overtook him and announced that Mr. Bazarov was waiting for him there.

"Yevgeny!" Arkady muttered, with a feeling of dismay. "Has he been here long?"

"Just arrived, sir, and asked not to be announced to Anna Sergeyevna, but to be led straight up to your room."

"I wonder if anything is wrong at home?" Arkady thought, and, racing up the stairs, he pulled open the door. Bazarov's appearance instantly reassured him, though a more practised eye would have perceived the signs of an inner perturbation in the thin, energetic figure of the unexpected visitor.

A dusty coat flung over his shoulders and a cap on his head, he was seated on the windowsill. He did not get up even when Arkady flung his arms around his neck, with noisy exclamations.

"This is a surprise! What brings you here?" Arkady repeated over and over again, bustling about with the air of a man who believes himself pleased and wants to show it. "Everything is all right at home, I hope, everybody is well?"

"Everything's all right, but everybody is not well," Bazarov said. "Stop chattering. Send for a drink of *kvass* and sit down and listen to what I'm going to tell you in a few, but, I hope, pithy words."

Arkady calmed down, and Bazarov told him about his duel with Pavel Petrovich. Arkady was startled and even distressed, but he deemed it wiser not to show it. He merely asked whether his uncle's wound was really not dangerous, and being told that it was quite an interesting one—though not from the medical standpoint—he smiled wryly, although his heart was filled with a nameless horror and shame. Bazarov seemed to understand what was passing in his mind.

"Yes, Arkady," he said, "that's what comes of living with feudal lords. You'll become a feudal lord yourself, before you know it, and take part in knightly tournaments. Well, I decided to wing my way home," Bazarov wound up his story, "and on the way dropped in here to . . . tell you all about it, I would say, if I didn't think it silly to tell a useless lie. No, I dropped in here—damned if I know why! You see, it's a good thing for a man to seize himself by his top knot now and then and pull himself up like a radish out of its bed. That's what I did recently. . . . But I wanted to have another look at what I had parted with—the bed I grew in."

"I hope these words don't apply to me," Arkady said excitedly. "I hope you don't think of parting with *me*."

Bazarov gave him a close, almost piercing look.

"Will that distress you so much? I think *you* have already parted with me. You're so clean, fresh as a daisy . . . you must be getting along splendidly with Anna Sergeyevna."

"What do you mean—getting along?"

"Why, didn't you come down from town for her sake, little duckling? By the way, how are the Sunday schools getting along. Aren't you in love with her? Or have things come to the point where you think you should put on a modest front?"

"Yevgeny, you know I've always been frank with you; I assure you, I swear to God, that you are mistaken."

"Hm! A new word," Bazarov observed in an undertone. "There's no need to get excited, it doesn't matter to me at all. A romanticist would say, 'I feel that we have reached the parting of the ways,' but I say simply that we are fed up with each other."

"Yevgeny. . . ."

"My dear boy, there's no harm in that. Think of the things people get fed up with in this world. And now, what about saying good-bye? Since I've been here I have a nasty kind of feeling, as though I've been wading through Gogol's letters to the Governor of Kaluga's lady. By the way, I ordered the horses not to be unharnessed."

"Oh come, you can't do that!"

"Why not?"

"I say nothing about myself, but it will be extremely impolite to Anna Sergeyevna, who will certainly be wanting to see you."

"That's where you're mistaken."

"On the contrary, I believe I'm right," Arkady retorted. "What's the use of pretending? If it comes to that, didn't you come down here because of her?"

"That may be so, but still you're mistaken."

Arkady, however, was right, Anna Sergeyevna wanted to see Bazarov and sent him an invitation through the butler. Bazarov changed his clothes before going to see her; he had packed his new suit so that it could be easily reached.

Odintsova received him not in the room where he had so suddenly made love to her, but in the drawing room. She graciously proffered him her fingertips, but her face wore a tense look.

"Anna Sergeyevna," Bazarov hastened to say, "first of all

I want to reassure you. You now see a mortal who has long since come to his senses and hopes that his folly has been forgotten. I am going away for a long time, and I think you will understand that though I am not a soft creature, it would be a most unpleasant thing for me to carry away the thought that you remember me with loathing."

Anna Sergeyevna drew a deep breath like a person who has climbed a high hill, and her face broke into a smile. She extended her hand again to Bazarov and responded to the pressure of his own.

"Let bygones be bygones," she said, "all the more since, honestly speaking, I sinned too, if not by coquetry, then in some other way. There—let's be friends as of old. It was only a dream, wasn't it? And who remembers dreams?"

"Who indeed? And then love . . . love is nothing but an affectation."

"Really? I'm awfully glad to hear it."

Thus did Anna Sergeyevna express herself, and thus did Bazarov express himself. Both thought they were speaking the truth; but was there the truth, the whole truth, in what they said? They did not know themselves, nor certainly does the author. But they fell to conversing as though they fully believed each other.

Among other things Anna Sergeyevna asked Bazarov how he had spent his time at the Kirsanovs'. He was on the point of telling her about his duel with Pavel Petrovich, but was checked by the thought that she might believe he was posing, and he answered that he had been working all the time.

"And I was in the doldrums at first," Anna Sergeyevna said. "God knows why. I even thought of going abroad; can you imagine? Then it passed. Your friend Arkady Nikolaich arrived, and I fell into the old rut again, into my real role."

"What role is that, may I ask?"

"The role of aunt, chaperone, mother—call it what you will. By the way, formerly I couldn't quite understand your close friendship with Arkady Nikolaich, you know. I used to think him rather insignificant. But I've come to know him better now, and find that he's clever. . . . The main thing, he's young, young. . . . Not like you and me, Yevgeny Vasilich."

"Is he still shy of you?" Bazarov asked.

"Why, was he . . . " Anna Sergeyevna broke off, then added, after a moment's reflection, "He's become more trustful now. He talks to me. He used to avoid me altogether. True, I never sought his company. Katya and he are great friends."

Bazarov felt annoyed. "Everlasting women's wiles!" he thought.

"You say he avoided you," he said with a cold sneer, "but it was probably no secret to you that he was in love with you?"

"What? He too . . .?" Anna Sergeyevna let fall unguardedly.

"He too," Bazarov repeated with a humble bow. "Do you mean to say you didn't know it and that this is news to you?"

Anna Sergeyevna dropped her eyes. "You are mistaken, Yevgeny Vasilich."

"I don't think so. But perhaps I should not have mentioned it." "That will teach you to be artful," he added to himself.

"Why not? But I think here again you attach too much importance to a momentary impression. I am beginning to think that you are prone to exaggeration."

"Let's not discuss it, Anna Sergeyevna."

"Why not?" she retorted, and forthwith changed the subject. She felt ill at ease with Bazarov after all, although she had told him, and had persuaded herself, that everything was forgotten. While chatting with him in the most casual way, even while joking with him, she yet felt vaguely nervous. Thus do passengers at sea chat and laugh unconcernedly, for all the world as if they were on *terra firma*, yet at the slightest hitch or the slightest sign of anything untoward happening their faces instantly betray a peculiar alarm, testifying to a constant sense of imminent danger.

Anna Sergeyevna's talk with Bazarov did not last long. She became lost in thought, replied absent-mindedly and finally suggested going into the sitting room, where they found the princess and Katya. "And where's Arkady Nikolaich?" the hostess asked. When she learned that he had not shown up for more than an hour, she sent for him. It took some time to find him: he had taken himself off to the depths of the garden, and with chin propped on his clasped hands was sunk in thought. They were profound and grave, those thoughts of his, but not despondent. He knew that Anna Sergeyevna was sitting alone with Bazarov, yet he felt no pangs of jealousy as he used to. On the contrary, his face had a soft light upon it; a look of wonder, of gladness, and resolve.

26

THE late Odintsov had disliked innovations, but
tolerated "some play of refined taste," a consequence of which
was the erection in his garden, between the hothouse and
the pond, of a structure resembling a Greek portico, built of
Russian bricks. The rear blank wall of this portico, or gallery,
contained six niches for statues which Odintsov had intended
to import from abroad. These statues were to represent
Solitude, Silence, Meditation, Melancholy, Modesty and
Sentiment. One of these, the Goddess of Silence, with a finger
on her lips, had been delivered and set in its place, but the
same day the household urchins had broken the nose off;
though a local plasterer had undertaken to fix up a new nose
"twice as good as the old one," Odintsov had had the statue
removed. A place was found for it in a corner of the threshing shed, and there it had stood for many years striking
superstitious terror into the hearts of the peasant women.
The front part of the portico had long been overgrown with
brushwood: only the capitals of the columns were visible
above the dense foliage. Inside the portico it was cool, even
at noon. Anna Sergeyevna had shunned the place ever since
she had seen a grass snake there, but Katya often came
to sit on a large stone seat built in one of the niches. Here,
in the cool shade, she would sit and read, work, or give herself up to that sensation of utter peace which is no doubt
familiar to everyone, and the charm of which consists in a
barely conscious, quiet awareness of the sweeping wave of
life surging ceaselessly both around and within us.
The day after Bazarov's arrival Katya was sitting on her

favorite seat, with Arkady once more beside her. He had persuaded her to come with him to "the portico."

It was about an hour before lunchtime; the dewy morning had turned to sultry day. Arkady's face preserved the expression of the day before; Katya looked worried. Her sister had called her to her study soon after breakfast, and after having stroked and caressed her—a thing that always frightened Katya somewhat—had advised her to be more discreet with Arkady and, in particular to avoid secluded talks with him, which, allegedly, had been noticed by her aunt and the whole household. The evening before Anna Sergeyevna had been out of sorts, and Katya herself had felt uneasy, as though conscious of some guilt. While yielding to Arkady's request, she promised herself that this would be the last time.

"Katerina Sergeyevna," he began with a sort of bashful sangfroid, "ever since I've had the happiness of living with you under one roof, I've discussed many things with you, but there is one—er . . . matter of great importance to me I haven't yet touched on. You passed a remark yesterday about my having been converted here," he went on, seeking and at the same time avoiding Katya's questioning gaze. "As a matter of fact I have changed a good deal, and you know that better than anybody—you, to whom I really owe this change."

"I? Me?" Katya said.

"I am no longer the bumptious boy who first came here," Arkady went on. "After all, I'm going on twenty-four. I still want to be useful; I want to devote all my efforts to the service of truth, but I no longer seek my ideals where I sought them before. I find that . . . they are much nearer. Until now I did not know myself; I set myself tasks that were beyond my strength. My eyes have recently been opened, owing to a certain feeling. . . . I'm not expressing myself quite clearly, but I hope you'll understand me. . . ."

Katya did not say anything, but she no longer looked at Arkady.

"I believe," he resumed in a more agitated voice, while a finch in the birch tree overhead blithely sang its song, "I believe it's the duty of every honest man to be entirely frank with those . . . with those people who . . . in short, with those who are near to him, and therefore I . . . I intend . . ."

Here Arkady's eloquence failed him; he faltered, floundered and was obliged to make a pause. Katya kept her eyes cast down. She did not seem to understand what he was driving at and appeared to be waiting for something.

"I suppose that I will surprise you," Arkady began, nerving himself once more to the task, "all the more since this feeling applies to a certain extent . . . to a certain extent, mind you—to you. Yesterday, you remember, you reproached me for not being serious enough," Arkady went on with the air of a man who has stumbled into a quagmire, feels that he is sinking deeper at every step, yet presses on in the hope of quickly getting clear. "That reproach is frequently pointed . . . falls on . . . young men even when they have ceased to deserve it. If I had more self-assurance . . ." ("Why don't you help me out, for God's sake!" Arkady was thinking frantically, but Katya still did not turn her head.) "If only I dared to hope . . ."

"If only I could be sure of what you say," fell the clear voice of Anna Sergeyevna.

The words died on Arkady's lips, and Katya turned pale. Anna Sergeyevna was walking along the path accompanied by Bazarov. Katya and Arkady could not see them, but they heard every word, the rustling of a gown, their very breathing. They took several steps and came to a standstill, as though deliberately, right in front of the portico.

"There, you see," Anna Sergeyevna went on, "we're both wrong; neither of us is in the first flush of youth, especially. We have seen something of life, we are tired; we are both— why beat about the bush?—clever. At first we became interested in one another. Curiosity was stirred . . . and then . . ."

"And then I fizzled out," Bazarov threw in.

"You know that was not the cause of our drifting apart. But be that as it may, we did not need each other. That's the point; we had too much—how shall I put it—too much in common. We did not grasp it immediately. Arkady, on the other hand . . ."

"Do you need him?" Bazarov asked.

"Oh come, Yevgeny Vasilich. You say he has taken a fancy to me, and I've always had the feeling that he likes me. I know I'm old enough to be his aunt, but I won't conceal from you that he is beginning to occupy my thoughts. There's a peculiar charm in this young, fresh feeling. . . ."

"The word *fascination* is more commonly used in such cases," Bazarov interrupted her and his voice, though calm, had a note of suppressed bitterness in it. "Arkady was as close as wax with me yesterday and said nothing about you or your sister. . . . That's an important symptom."

"He's like a brother to Katya," Anna Sergeyevna said, "and that's what I like in him, though perhaps I ought not to allow such intimacy between them."

"Is that the voice of . . . a sister?" Bazarov drawled. "Of course . . . but why are we standing. Let's walk on. What an odd conversation we are having—don't you think so? I would never have thought I would be speaking to you in this way. You know I am afraid of you . . . and yet I trust you, because you are really very kind."

"To begin with, I'm not at all kind; and secondly I don't mean anything to you any more, and you tell me that I am kind. . . . It's like placing a wreath of flowers on a dead man's head."

"Yevgeny Vasilich, we have no power . . ." she had begun, but a gust of wind, rustling amid the leaves, carried her words away.

"But then you are free," Bazarov said after a pause. The rest was indistinguishable. The footsteps retreated . . . silence fell.

Arkady turned to Katya. She had not changed her position, only her head was bent lower.

"Katerina Sergeyevna," his voice shook and he clenched his hands, "I love you for ever and for good. I love nobody but you. That is what I have been wanting to tell you, to know your mind, and ask you for your hand, because I am not rich and feel I'm prepared to sacrifice everything. . . . You don't answer? You don't believe me? You think I am speaking lightly? But recall the last few days! Couldn't you have seen that everything else—I assure you—everything else, all that, has long vanished without a trace? Look at me, say something. . . . I love . . . I love you. . . . Believe me!"

Katya looked at him with moist shining eyes, and after a long hesitation, she murmured, with the shadow of a smile, "Yes."

Arkady leapt from his seat. "Yes! You said, 'Yes,' Katerina Sergeyevna! What does it mean? Does it mean that I love you, or that you believe me? . . . Or . . . or . . . I dare not utter it. . . ."

"Yes," Katya repeated, and this time he understood her. He seized her large beautiful hands and, breathless with rapture, pressed them to his heart. He could scarcely stand on his feet and kept repeating, "Katya, Katya . . ." while she began to cry openly and ingenuously, laughing softly at her own tears. He who has not seen such tears in the eyes of his beloved, who has never thrilled to the gratitude and shame of it, has never known how happy mortal man can be on this earth.

Early next morning, Anna Sergeyevna sent for Bazarov and, with a forced laugh, handed him a folded sheet of notepaper. It was a letter from Arkady, in which he asked for her sister's hand.

Bazarov ran his eye over the letter and checked an impulse to betray the feeling of malicious glee that suddenly welled up in him.

"So that's it," he said, "and you, no earlier than yesterday, I believe, thought that he entertained a brotherly love for Katerina Sergeyevna. What do you intend to do now?"

"What would *you* advise?" Anna Sergeyevna asked, still laughing.

"Well," replied Bazarov, also with a laugh, although he no more felt like laughing than she did, "I think you should give the young people your blessing. The match is a good one in all respects. Kirsanov is fairly well off, he's the only son, and his father's a decent fellow—he won't oppose it."

Odintsova took a turn about the room. Her face changed from red to white.

"You think so?" she said. "Ah well! I see no objections. . . . I'm glad for Katya's sake . . . and for Arkady Nikolaich's, too. Of course, I'll wait for his father's answer. I'll send him home. It turns out after all that I was right yesterday when I told you we were both getting old. How is it I didn't notice anything? That's what surprises me!"

Anna Sergeyevna laughed again and instantly turned away.

"Young people today are too clever altogether," Bazarov remarked, laughing too. "Good-bye," he went on after a slight pause. "I hope you'll see the matter through to a happy ending; I'll look on from a distance and rejoice."

Odintsova turned to him quickly.

"Why, are you going? Why shouldn't you stay *now?* Do stay . . . it's thrilling to talk to you . . . like walking on the brink of a precipice. At first it's a bit terrifying, then somehow you pluck up courage. Do stay."

"Thanks for the invitation, Anna Sergeyevna, and for your flattering opinion of my conversational gifts. But I've been moving too long in alien spheres as it is. Flying fish can stay in the air for a certain time, but back into the water they must soon flop. Please allow me to flop back into my element."

Odintsova studied him. His pale face twitched with a bitter smile. "That man loved me!" she thought, and suddenly felt sorry for him. She stretched out her hand to him in sympathy.

But he understood her.

"No!" he said, falling back a step. "I'm a poor man, but I have never yet accepted alms. Good-bye, madam, and keep well."

"I'm sure that this is not the last we'll be seeing of each other," Anna Sergeyevna said with an involuntary gesture. "Anything can happen in this world," Bazarov answered, bowed, and went out.

"So you've decided to build a nest?" he was saying to Arkady the same day, squatting in front of the suitcase he was packing. "Well, not a bad idea. But why were you so sly about it? I expected you to sail on an entirely different tack. Or perhaps you were taken unawares yourself?"

"As a matter of fact, I didn't expect it at the time I left you," replied Arkady. "But why are you fencing with yourself, saying 'it's a good idea.' I know your views on marriage."

"Ah, my dear friend!" Bazarov said, "the way you talk! Don't you see what I'm doing: there's an empty space in my suitcase and I'm filling it up with hay. It's the same with the suitcase of life: fill it up with whatever you like so long as there is no void. Don't take offense, please. You probably remember the opinion I always had of Katerina Sergeyevna. Some girls pass as clever only because they sigh cleverly, but yours will hold her own, and gain a hold on you too, I vow— but that's as it should be." He slammed the lid down and stood up. "And now I repeat to you at parting—it's no use fooling ourselves. We are parting for good, and you realize that yourself. You have acted wisely. You are not made for our bitter, crabbed, lonely life; you haven't the daring or the fury. You have only the audacity and the ardor of youth. That's no good for our job. You gentlemen of the nobility can't work up more than a noble humility or a noble indignation, and that's not worth a rap. You don't fight, for instance— yet you think you are heroes—whereas we hanker for a fight. Why, our dust would eat your eyes out, our dirt would besmirch you. Besides, you do not come up to us; you admire yourselves, and you like to wallow in self-reproach. We're tired of all that; we want something new! We have others to break! You're a decent chap, but after all you're a softy, a chip off a liberal gentleman's block—*et voilà tout*, as my father would say."

"You're saying good-bye to me for good, Yevgeny," Arkady said sadly, "and you have no other words to say to me?"

Bazarov scratched the back of his head.

"I have, Arkady, I have other words too, but I won't say them, because that would mean being romantic, mushy. You

go on and get married. Feather your little nest and multiply—
the more 'kiddies' the better. They'll be fine fellows if only
because they come into the world at the right time—not like
you and me. Aha, I see the horses are ready! Time to go!
I've taken leave of everybody. . . . Well? Let's embrace, what
d'you say?"

Arkady flung himself on the neck of his former preceptor
and friend, tears gushing from his eyes.

"Ah, youth, youth!" Bazarov said calmly. "But I rely on
Katerina Sergeyevna. You'll see how soon she'll console you!"

"Good-bye, old chap!" he said to Arkady, after having
climbed into the cart, and pointing to a pair of jackdaws
perched side by side on the stable roof, he added, "There's
an object lesson for you!"

"What does that mean?" asked Arkady.

"What? Are you that bad in natural history or have you
forgotten that the jackdaw is the most respectable of domestic
birds? Follow his example! . . . Good-bye, signor!"

The cart creaked and rolled away.

Bazarov had spoken the truth. Talking that evening to
Katya, Arkady completely forgot his preceptor. He was already beginning to fall under her influence. Katya felt it
and was not surprised. He was to go to Maryino the next day
to talk the matter over with Nikolai Petrovich. Anna Sergeyevna did not want to put any restraint on the young
people, and if she did not leave them alone together for too
long it was merely for the sake of propriety. She magnani-
mously kept the princess out of their way. The news of the
forthcoming marriage had reduced that lady to a tearful
frenzy. At first Anna Sergeyevna had feared that the sight
of their happiness would be rather painful to her, but it
turned out the other way: the sight not only did not distress
her, she found it entertaining, even touching. It both pleased
and saddened her. "It seems Bazarov was right," she mused.
"Curiosity, nothing but curiosity, and a love of ease, and
selfishness. . . ."

"Children!" she said aloud, "is love an affectation?"

But neither Katya nor Arkady understood her. They were shy of her; the conversation they had involuntarily over-heard stuck fast in their minds. Anna Sergeyevna, however, soon set them at ease. She had no difficulty in doing so, for her own mind was at ease.

27

THE old Bazarovs were the more delighted by their son's sudden return since they had not been expecting him. Arina Vlasyevna ran about the house in such a flutter of excitement that Vasily Ivanich likened her to a "grouse hen": indeed, her bobtailed little jacket gave her a birdlike appearance. As for himself, all he did was to grunt and nibble the amber tip of his pipe, and gripping his neck with his hands, he kept twisting his head as though testing to see whether it was properly screwed on; then he would suddenly open his mouth wide and laugh soundlessly.

"I've come to stay for six whole weeks, old chap," Bazarov told him, "and I want to do some work, so please don't disturb me."

"You'll forget what I look like, that's how much I'll disturb you!" retorted Vasily Ivanich.

And he was as good as his word. Having reinstalled his son in his study he all but hid himself and restrained his wife from too exuberant a display of affection. "My dear," he said to her, "the last time Yevgeny was here we annoyed him a little with our attentions. We'll have to be wiser now." Arina Vlasyevna agreed with her husband, but gained little by it, for she saw her son only at mealtimes now and was afraid to talk to him at all. "Yevgeny dear!" she would say, and before he could look around, she was fumbling with her reticule strings and stammering, "Nothing, nothing, I was just . . ." and then she would go to Vasily Ivanich, and, propping her cheek up in her hand, would say, "How could we find out, dear, what Yevgeny would like for dinner today—cabbage soup or borsch?" "But why didn't you ask him yourself?" "I didn't want to bother him!"

Bazarov however, soon stopped shutting himself up. His burst of activity petered out, to be followed by dreary boredom and a vague restlessness. There was a strange lassitude in all his movements, and even his gait, usually firm and impetuously confident, underwent a change. He no longer took his solitary walks and began to seek company. He took his tea in the parlor, prowled about the garden with Vasily Ivanich and smoked silently with him. Once he asked after Father Alexei. The change gladdened Vasily Ivanich at first, but his joy was short-lived. "Yevgeny worries me," he complained in private to his wife. "It's not as if he was displeased or angry. That wouldn't be so bad. He's distressed, and he's miserable. That's the worst of it. Never says a word. I'd rather he scolded us. He is getting thinner and I don't like his complexion at all."

"God above us!" whispered the old lady; "I'd put a holy amulet on his neck, but I don't suppose he'd let me."

Vasily Ivanich very tactfully tried to sound him out once or twice about his work, his health and Arkady. But Bazarov answered him in a reluctant, offhand way, and noticing one day that his father was trying to worm something out of him, he said with annoyance, "Why do you walk around me on tiptoe? It's worse than before."

"There, there, I didn't mean anything!" poor Vasily Ivanich put in hastily.

His political hints were no more successful. He once broached the subject of progress and the imminent emancipation of the peasantry, in the hope of rousing his son's interest, but the latter remarked indifferently, "I was passing down by the fence yesterday and heard the peasant boys yelling a current ditty: *I'm sick with love for you, sweetheart,* instead of one of the good old songs. There's progress for you."

Sometimes Bazarov would take a walk through the village and, in his usual bantering way, enter into conversation with one of the peasants. "Well," he would say to him, "trot out your views on life, old man; you're said to have in you all the power and future of Russia; you're to start a new era in history; you're going to give us a real language and real laws!" The man would either say nothing or come out with something like this: "Aye, that we can . . . now, ye see, the point is . . . our position's like this."

"You just explain to me what this *mir* of yours is?"* said Bazarov one day, interrupting the peasant. "Isn't it the *mir* that rests on three fishes?"

"It's the earth, sir, that be standing on three fishes," the man explained in a benign, patriarchal, singsong voice. "Our *mir*, to be sure, is under the masters' will, seeing that you're our fathers, in a manner o' speaking. An' the stricter the master the better the muzhik likes it."

After listening to an oration of this kind Bazarov once contemptuously shrugged his shoulders and turned away, leaving the peasant to shuffle off.

"What 'ave ye been talking about?" a dour-faced middle-aged peasant asked his fellow villager from the doorstep of his hut. "About tax arrears?"

"Tax arrears, no!" replied the first peasant, with no trace of the patriarchal singsong in his voice, which now sounded disdainfully grim. "He just wanted to jabber, that's all. He's a gent. What does he understand?"

"Aye, what does he understand!" the other muzhik echoed, and wagging their heads and adjusting their sashes they fell to discussing their own affairs. Alas! Bazarov of the contemptuously shrugging shoulders, Bazarov who knew how to speak to the peasants (so he had boasted while arguing with Pavel Petrovich), Bazarov, with all his self-assurance, never suspected that to the peasants he was something of a fool.

However, he found an occupation for himself at last. Once, in his presence, Vasily Ivanich was dressing a peasant's injured foot, but the old doctor's hands shook and he could not manage the bandages. His son helped him, and hence-

---

* The Russian word *mir* has a double meaning: *village community* and *world.—Tr.*

forth began to take a hand in his practice, though he continued to poke fun both at the remedies he himself advised and at his father, who promptly made use of them. Bazarov's jibes, however, did not put Vasily Ivanich out in the least; they even amused him. Holding his greasy dressing gown together across his stomach with two fingers and puffing at his pipe, he listened delightedly to his son's disparaging comments, and the more malicious they were the more heartily did the happy father laugh, revealing every one of his blackened teeth. He even repeated Bazarov's inane or senseless extravagances, and for several days, for instance, went about reiterating, without rhyme or reason, "Oh, worse than useless," simply because his son had used that expression on learning that he attended matins. "Thank God, he's cheered up a bit!" he whispered to his wife. "He made short work of me today; it was simply great!" The thought that he had such an assistant delighted him and filled him with pride. "Yes, my dear," he would say to a peasant woman clad in a man's drab overcoat and a Russian peasant headdress, while he handed her a bottle of Goulard's extract or a jar of henbane ointment, "you ought to thank your lucky star, my good woman, that my son happens to be staying with me. You're being treated by the latest scientific methods. Do you realize that? The Emperor of the French, Napoleon, hasn't a better doctor." And the woman, who had come complaining of "having the racks" (the meaning of which words, by the way, she didn't know herself), would bow and fish out from her bosom the doctor's fee—four eggs wrapped up in the corner of a towel.

Once Bazarov even extracted a tooth for a passing haberdashery peddler, and though it was just an ordinary tooth as teeth go, Vasily Ivanich kept it as a curiosity and showed it to Father Alexei, repeating ceaselessly:

"You just look at those roots! The strength Yevgeny has! That peddler fellow was simply hoisted out of his seat. Why, I don't think an oak could have stood it."

"Remarkable!" Father Alexei observed at length, not knowing what to say or how to shake off the ecstatic old man.

One day a peasant from a nearby village brought his brother, who was ill with typhus, to Vasily Ivanich. The poor fellow lay dying, face downwards on a bundle of hay. His body was covered with dark blotches and he had been unconscious for some time. Vasily Ivanich expressed his regret that it had not occurred to anybody to seek medical aid before and declared that there was no hope. Indeed, by the time the peasant reached home, his brother had died in the cart.

Three days later Bazarov came into his father's room and asked whether he had some lunar caustic.

"I have. Who do you want it for?"

"I need it . . . to cauterize a cut."

"Who for?"

"For myself."

"Yourself? What for? What cut? Where is it?"

"Here, on my finger. I went to the village today, you know, the one they brought that typhus peasant from. They decided to make a post-mortem for some reason or other, and I hadn't had any practice of that kind for some time."

"Well?"

"Well, so I asked the local doctor to let me do it. Well, I cut my finger."

Vasily Ivanich suddenly turned pale, and without uttering a word, rushed into his study and reappeared immediately with a stick of lunar caustic in his hand. Bazarov was about to take it and go.

"For God's sake, let me do it myself," Vasily Ivanich muttered.

Bazarov smiled ironically.

"You're a greedy one for a bit of practice!"

"Don't joke, please. Show me your finger. It's not much of a cut. Does it hurt?"

"Press harder, don't be afraid."

Vasily Ivanich stopped.

"Don't you think we'd better sear it with an iron, Yevgeny?"

"That should have been done before; as a matter of fact,

even the lunar caustic is useless now. If I've been infected, it's too late already."

"Too late . . ." Vasily Ivanich could barely utter the words.

"I should think so! More than four hours have passed."

Vasily Ivanich cauterized the cut again.

"Didn't the district doctor have any lunar caustic?"

"No."

"How could that be, my God! A doctor—and not to have such an essential thing!"

"You should have seen what his lancets looked like," Bazarov said and walked out.

All that evening and the next day Vasily Ivanich invented all possible excuses for going into his son's room, and though he did not mention a word about the cut and even tried to talk about everything else under the sun, he peered so intently into his eyes and watched him so anxiously that Bazarov lost his patience and threatened to go away. Vasily Ivanich promised that he would stop fretting, the more so since Arina Vlasyevna, from whom he had of course concealed everything, had also begun to worry him about why he did not sleep and what had come over him. He kept this up for two whole days, though he did not at all like the look of his son, whom he stealthily watched. On the third day at dinner, however, he could contain himself no longer. Bazarov sat with his eyes downcast and did not touch his food.

"Why don't you eat? The food's very tasty, I think."

"I don't eat because I don't want to."

"Have you lost your appetite? How's your head?" he added timidly. "Does it ache?"

"It does. Why shouldn't it?"

Arina Vlasyevna sat up, all ears.

"Don't be angry, Yevgeny, please," Vasily Ivanich went on, "but won't you let me feel your pulse?"

Bazarov got up.

"I can tell you without feeling my pulse that I have a high temperature."

"Have you had chills too?"

"Yes. I'll go and lie down; send me some lime-flower tea. Probably caught a cold."

"No wonder I heard you coughing last night," Arina Vlasyevna said.

"Caught a cold," Bazarov repeated and left the room.

Arina Vlasyevna busied herself brewing lime tea, and Vasily Ivanich went into the next room and clutched his hair in speechless anguish.

Bazarov remained in bed that day, and spent the night in a heavy half-waking slumber. At one o'clock in the morning he opened his eyes with an effort, and seeing the pale face of his father, bending over him, illuminated by the dim light of the icon lamp, he told him to go away. The old man obeyed, but returned immediately on tiptoe and, standing half-hidden behind the bookcase door, watched his son with an unshifting gaze. Arina Vlasyevna was up too, and kept peeping through the half-open door to see "how darling Yevgeny was breathing," and take a look at Vasily Ivanich. All she could see, however, was his bent motionless back, but even that made her feel easier. In the morning Bazarov attempted to get up. He became dizzy and his nose began to bleed, so he went back to bed. Vasily Ivanich tended him silently. Arina Vlasyevna came in and asked how he was feeling. He answered, "Better," and turned his face to the wall. Vasily Ivanich waved both his hands at his wife; she bit her lip so as not to cry, and went out. Everything in the house suddenly seemed to go dark; everybody wore a long face. A strange hush descended upon everything. A noisy cock in the farmyard was carried off to the village, wondering at this summary treatment. Bazarov continued to lie with his face to the wall. Vasily Ivanich tried asking him various questions, but they tired Bazarov, and the old man sat in his armchair without stirring, cracking his fingers now and then. He went out into the garden for a few moments, stood there like a stone image, as if petrified with unutterable amazement (his face these days generally wore a look of permanent amazement) and returned again to his son, trying to avoid his wife's anxious questioning. At last she clutched his arm and whispered in a convulsed, almost menacing voice, "What's the matter with him?" At that he pulled himself together and forced himself to smile by way of reply, but to his horror, he began to laugh instead. He had sent for a doctor in the morning. He thought it necessary to tell his son about it, for fear of making him angry.

Bazarov suddenly turned over on the sofa, stared dully at his father and asked for a drink.

Vasily Ivanich gave him some water and took the opportunity to touch his forehead. He had a high fever.

"I'm hooked, old chap," Bazarov began in a slow hoarse voice. "I'm infected, and in a few days you'll be burying me."

Vasily Ivanich staggered as if someone had hit him in the legs.

"Yevgeny!" he stammered, "what are you talking about? God bless you! You've caught a chill. . . ."

"Come, come," Bazarov broke in unhurriedly. "Fancy a doctor saying that. All the symptoms of blood poisoning, you know it yourself."

"Where are symptoms . . . of blood poisoning, Yevgeny? The things you say!"

"And what's this?" Bazarov said, and turning back his shirt sleeve he showed his father the sinister red patches that had broken out on his body.

Vasily Ivanich started and went cold with horror.

"What of it," he brought out at last, "what if . . . even if it is anything. . . ."

"*Pyaemia*," his son prompted.

"Er, yes . . . anything epidemic. . . ."

"*Pyaemia*," Bazarov repeated grimly and distinctly. "Have you forgotten your notebooks?"

"Yes, yes, all right, have it your way. . . . We'll pull you through all the same!"

"Not likely. But that's not the point. I didn't expect to die so soon; that's a stroke of bad luck. You and Mother should now make the best of your strong religious feelings; here you have an opportunity of putting it to the test." He drank some more water. "And I want to ask you to do one thing for me . . . while my head is still my own. Tomorrow or the day after, my brain will hand in its resignation, you know. I'm not sure even now whether I'm talking sense. While I was lying here I seemed to see red hounds chasing around me, and you came to a point over me, as though I were a woodcock. I feel kind of drunk. Can you follow me?"

"Why, you're speaking quite normally, Yevgeny."

"All the better; you told me you've sent for a doctor. . . . That's your bit of fun . . . now, do me a favor too. Send a messenger . . ."

"To Arkady Nikolaich?" the old man broke in.

"Who's Arkady Nikolaich?" Bazarov murmured half-musingly. "Oh, that fledgling! No, don't bother him, he's become a jackdaw now. Don't worry, it's not delirium yet. Send a messenger to Odintsova, Anna Sergeyevna, she has an estate near here. . . . Do you know her?" Vasily Ivanich nodded. "Tell her that Yevgeny, that is Bazarov, sends his regards and wants her to know that he is dying. Will you do that?"

"I will. . . . But you are not going to die, Yevgeny, it's impossible. . . . Now, think for yourself. . . . Would it be fair?"

"I don't know about that, but see that you send a messenger."

"I'll send a man right away and write her a note myself."

"No, what for? Just tell her that I send my regards, nothing else. Now I'll go back to my hounds. Funny! I try to bring my thoughts round to the idea of death, but nothing comes of it. All I see is a smudge . . . and nothing more."

He turned heavily to the wall once more; and Vasily Ivanich left the study, and dragging himself to his wife's bedroom, he dropped down on his knees before the holy images.

"Pray, Arina, pray!" he moaned. "Our son is dying."

The doctor arrived—the same practitioner who had failed Bazarov with the lunar caustic—and after examining the patient, advised the wait-and-see method of treatment, with several added words about the possibility of recovery.

"Have you ever seen people in my condition who don't go

off to Elysium?" Bazarov asked, and suddenly gripping the leg of a heavy table standing near the sofa, he shook it and shifted it from its place.

"All the strength is still there," he said, "yet I must die! . . . An old man, at least, has had time to grow out of the habit of living, but I. . . . Try to negate death after that. It negates you and that's all there is to it! Who is crying?" he added after a while. "Mother? Poor Mother! Whom will she now feed her marvelous borsch to? And you, too, Vasily Ivanich, have turned on the waterworks, I see? Well, if Christianity doesn't help, be a philosopher, or a stoic! You boasted of being a philosopher, didn't you?"

"What a philosopher I am!" wailed Vasily Ivanich, the tears streaming down his cheeks.

Bazarov grew worse hour by hour; the disease was progressing rapidly, as is frequently the case in surgical blood poisoning. He had not yet lost consciousness and understood what was being said; he was still fighting.

"I don't want to rave," he whispered, clenching his fists, "what nonsense!" Then he would say, "Come on, subtract ten from eight, what is the result?" Vasily Ivanich went about like one insane, suggesting one remedy after another, and kept covering his son's feet. "Cold wrappings . . . an emetic . . . mustard poultices to the stomach . . . blood-letting," he muttered over and over again. The doctor, whom he implored to stay, nodded assent to everything he said, and gave the sick man lemonade, while for himself he would request now a pipe, now "a warming stimulant," by which he meant vodka. Arina Vlasyevna sat on a low seat by the door and only went out now and again to pray. Some days ago a hand mirror had slipped out of her fingers and broken, and she always held that to be a bad omen. Anfisushka could not find words to comfort her. Timofeich rode off to Odintsova.

Bazarov had a bad night. He ran a high fever. Toward morning he felt slightly better. He asked Arina Vlasyevna to comb his hair, kissed her hand, and took one or two sips of tea. Vasily Ivanich brightened up a little.

"Thank God!" he kept on saying. "The crisis has come . . . the crisis has passed."

"Nonsense!" Bazarov said. "What's in a word! You hit on a word, say 'crisis' and you're comforted. Surprising how people still believe in words. Tell a man, for example, that he's a fool without beating him and he'll be miserable; call him a clever fellow without giving him any money and he'll be tickled."

This little speech of Bazarov's, which was reminiscent of his old "quips," delighted Vasily Ivanich.

"Bravo! Well said!" he cried, making as though he were clasping his hands.

Bazarov smiled sadly.

"Well then, what do you think," he said, "has the crisis come or passed?"

"All I see is that you're better, that's the main thing," said Vasily Ivanich.

"Very well, rejoice—that's always a good thing. Did you send to her?"

"Yes, of course."

The change for the better did not last long. The patient suffered a relapse. Vasily Ivanich sat by Bazarov's bedside. Something more than ordinary anguish seemed to be preying on the old man's mind. He tried several times to speak but could not.

"Yevgeny!" he brought out at last. "My son, my dearest, my darling boy!"

The unusual appeal had its effect on Bazarov. He turned his head slightly, and with an obvious effort to shake off his torpor, he said, "What is it, my dear father?"

"Yevgeny," Vasily Ivanich went on and dropped on his knees before Bazarov, though the latter had not opened his eyes and could not see him. "Yevgeny, you're better now; please God you'll get well now; but take this opportunity, for your mother's sake and mine—do your Christian duty! It's terrible that I have to tell you this; but it would be more terrible . . . it's for ever, Yevgeny . . . just think what it means. . . ."

The old man's voice broke, and a queer look crept into his son's face, though he still lay with his eyes shut.

"I don't object, if that can comfort you," he murmured at last. "But I don't think you need hurry yet. You say yourself I'm better."

"You are, Yevgeny, you are; but who knows, it's all God's will, and if you'd perform this duty. . . ."

"No, I'll wait," Bazarov interrupted. "I agree with you that the crisis has set in. If we're mistaken, well!—even an unconscious man can receive the last sacrament."

"But, Yevgeny dear. . . ."

"I'll wait. And now I want to sleep. Don't disturb me."

And he laid his head back in its former position.

The old man got up, sat down in the armchair, and taking hold of his chin, began biting his fingers. . . .

The sound of a carriage-spring, a sound which is so noticeable in the quiet of the country, suddenly struck his ear. Ever nearer and nearer rumbled the light wheels; one could now hear the snorting of the horses. . . . Vasily Ivanich darted to the window. A two-seater drawn by a team of four horses swept into his yard. Without stopping to think what this might mean, he rushed out onto the porch on a sudden impulse of unreasoning joy. A liveried footman opened the carriage door and a lady in a black veil and a black mantle stepped out.

"I am Odintsova," she said. "Is Yevgeny Vasilich still alive? Are you his father? I have brought a doctor with me."

"My good angel!" Vasily Ivanich cried, and seizing her hand he pressed it convulsively to his lips, while the doctor accompanying her, a bespectacled little man with a German face, was descending leisurely from the carriage. "He's alive, my Yevgeny's still alive, and now he'll be saved! Wife! Wife! An angel from heaven has come to us. . . !"

"What is it, good God!" stammered the old lady, running out of the parlor, and in a state of utter bewilderment she threw herself at Anna Sergeyevna's feet and began frantically kissing the hem of her gown.

"Oh, please, what are you doing!" Anna Sergeyevna kept saying, but Arina Vlasyevna was deaf to her protests, and Vasily Ivanich kept repeating, "Angel! Angel!"

"Wo ist der Kranke? Ver iss der patient?" the doctor said not without some indignation.

Vasily Ivanich caught himself.

"Here, this way please, *wertester Herr Kollege,"* he added, remembering old times.

"Ah!" the German uttered with a sour grin.

Vasily Ivanich led him into the study.

"A doctor from Anna Sergeyevna Odintsova," he said, bending down to his son's ear. "And she's here too."

Bazarov instantly opened his eyes. "What did you say?"

"I said, Anna Sergeyevna Odintsova is here and has brought you a doctor, this gentleman here."

Bazarov's eyes travelled round the room.

"She's here . . . I want to see her."

"You'll see her, Yevgeny; let us first have a talk with the doctor. I'll tell him your case history since Sidor Sidorich" (that was the name of the district practitioner) "has left, and we'll hold a little consultation."

Bazarov glanced at the German. "Well, do it quickly, but don't speak Latin. I know what *jam moritur* means."

"Der Herr scheint des Deutschen mächtig zu sein," said this new disciple of Aesculapius, turning to Vasily Ivanich.

"Ich . . . habe. . . . Better speak Russian," the old man said.

"Ach! So, so, verr goot. . . ."

And the consultation began.

Half an hour later Anna Sergeyevna, accompanied by Vasily Ivanich, entered the sickroom. The doctor had already told her in a whisper that there was no hope for the patient's recovery.

She glanced at Bazarov . . . and stopped dead in the doorway, struck at once by the flushed and ashy face, with its dull eyes fixed upon her. She was frightened with a chill, harrowing terror, and the thought that she would have felt differently had she loved him flashed through her mind.

"Thanks," he said with an effort. "I didn't expect it. It was kind of you. So we meet again, as you promised."

"Anna Sergeyevna was so good . . ." Vasily Ivanich began.

"Father, leave us alone. Anna Sergeyevna, do you mind? I believe that now. . . ."

He indicated his prostrate helpless body with a motion of his head.

Vasily Ivanich left the room.

"There, thanks," Bazarov repeated. "This is a royal favor. They say royalty visit the dying too."

"Yevgeny Vasilich, I hope. . . ."

"Heigh-ho! Anna Sergeyevna, let's speak the truth. It's all up with me. I've been caught in the wheel. So there was no sense in thinking about the future. Death is an old story, but its always new to everyone. I've managed to keep my courage up so far . . . and then the coma will set in, and then phewt!" He made a feeble gesture. "Well, what shall I tell you. . . . That I loved you? There was no sense in that before, still less now. Love is a form and my own form is decomposing. Let me tell you rather how lovely you are! There you stand, so beautiful. . . ."

Anna Sergeyevna shuddered involuntarily.

"Never mind, don't worry . . . sit down there. . . . Don't come near me. My disease is contagious, you know."

Anna Sergeyevna swiftly crossed the room and sat down in an armchair near the sofa on which Bazarov lay.

"How kind!" he whispered. "Ah, how near, and how young, fresh and pure . . . in this hideous room! Well, farewell! Live long—that's best of all—and make the most of things while there is time. Just look at the revolting sight—a half-crushed worm, but still showing off. I used to think I'd kick up a lot of dust yet. Who said die? There's plenty to be done. Why, I feel like a giant! Now the giant's chief anxiety is how to die decently, though nobody cares a straw. . . . All the same, I won't wag my tail."

Bazarov fell silent and began fumbling for the glass. Anna

Sergeyevna gave him a drink without taking off her glove, hardly daring to breathe.

"You will forget me," he resumed. "The dead are no company for the living. My father will tell you, no doubt, what a man Russia is losing. . . . that's nonsense; but don't disillusion the old man. We all live in a fool's paradise, you know. And be kind to Mother. You won't find such people if you search your world high and low . . . Russia needs me. . . . No, apparently she doesn't. Who is needed? The cobbler is needed; the tailor, the butcher . . . he sells meat . . . the butcher. . . . Look here, I'm getting mixed up. . . . There's a forest here. . . ."

Bazarov put his hand to his forehead.

Anna Sergeyevna leaned over towards him.

"Yevgeny Vasilich, I'm here. . . ."

He instantly took his hand away and raised himself on his elbow.

"Farewell," he said with sudden force and his eyes lit up with a last gleam. "Farewell. . . . Listen. . . . I didn't kiss you that time, you know . . . Breathe on the dying lamp, let it go out. . . ."

Anna Sergeyevna put her lips to his brow.

"That's all!" he murmured and sank back on his pillow. "Now . . . darkness. . . ."

Anna Sergeyevna quietly left the room.

"Well?" Vasily Ivanich asked her in a whisper.

"He's fallen asleep," she replied in a voice that was barely audible.

Bazarov was to wake no more. In the evening he fell into a coma and the next day he died. Father Alexei performed the religious rites over him. During the ceremony of extreme unction, when the consecrated oil was applied to his chest, one eye opened and it seemed as though, at the sight of the priest in his vestments, the fumes of incense rising from the censer and the candles in front of the icons, something akin to a shudder of horror flitted across the livid face of the dying man. When at length he breathed his last, and the whole house resounded with cries of lamentation, Vasily

Ivanich was seized with a sudden frenzy. "I said I would murmur at it," he shouted hoarsely, his face distorted and aflame, shaking his fist in the air as though defying somebody, "and I will murmur, I will!" But Arina Vlasyevna, all in tears, clung to his neck, and both dropped to their knees on the floor. "And there they knelt," Anfisushka afterwards related in the servants' hall, "side by side, with drooping heads, like two poor lambs at noontide. . . ."

But the heat of noon passes, then comes evening and night, bringing a return to the peaceful haven where sweetly sleep the tired and weary. . . .

28

SIX months had passed. White winter had come with the hush of its bitter cloudless frosts, its heavy blanket of crunching snow, the warm-tinted rime on the trees, pale emerald skies, wreaths of smoke over the chimneys, clouds of steam eddying from quickly opened doors, fresh frost-nipped faces and the hurried trot of chilled horses. A January day was drawing to a close; the cold breath of evening gripped the still air in an icy clutch and the blood-red glow of sunset swiftly faded. The lights went up in the Maryino home; Prokofich, in a black frock coat and white gloves was, with unusual solemnity, setting the table for seven. A week before in the little parish church a double wedding had taken place unostentatiously and almost without witnesses—that of Arkady and Katya, and of Nikolai Petrovich and Fenichka—and on this day Nikolai Petrovich was giving a farewell dinner in honor of his brother, who was leaving for Moscow on business. Anna Sergeyevna had gone to Moscow, too, immediately after the wedding. She had generously endowed the young newlyweds.

Exactly at three o'clock everyone sat down to the table. Mitya was given a place there too; he now had a nurse in a brocaded cap. Pavel Petrovich was seated between Katya and Fenichka; the "husbands" sat next to their wives. Our friends had changed of late: they all seemed to be better-looking and more grown-up. Pavel Petrovich alone had grown thinner, but this gave an added touch of elegance and the grand seigneur manner to his expressive features. Fenichka, too, had changed. In a fresh silk gown, with a broad velvet headdress and a gold chain round her neck, she sat respectfully immobile, respectful both to herself and to everything around her, and smiled with an air that seemed to say: "Please excuse me, it's not my fault." Everybody else was smiling too, and also looking apologetic about it. All felt a bit awkward and a bit sad, but really very happy. Everybody waited on everybody else with amusing courtesy, as though all had agreed to play an innocent comedy. Katya was the calmest of all. She looked trustingly about her, and one could tell that she had become as dear to Nikolai Petrovich as his own daughter. Toward the end of the dinner he got up, and lifting his glass, turned to Pavel Petrovich.

"You are leaving us . . . you are leaving us, dear brother," he began, "but of course, not for long; still, I want to tell you that I . . . that we . . . how I . . . how we. . . . That's the trouble, speech-making is not in my line! Arkady, say something."

"No, Dad, not *ex tempore*."

"And do you think I can! Oh, well, brother, let me just embrace you and wish you all the very best, and come back to us quickly!"

Pavel Petrovich kissed everybody, including, naturally, Mitya; and in addition he kissed Fenichka's hand, which she had not yet learned to proffer properly, and, quaffing his replenished glass, uttered with a deep sigh, "Good luck to you, my friends! *Farewell!*" This English word passed unnoticed, but everybody was touched.

"To the memory of Bazarov," Katya whispered into her husband's ear, and clinked glasses with him. Arkady responded by squeezing her hand. He did not venture, however, to propose this toast aloud.

This would seem to be the end. But perhaps some reader is curious to know what the other characters of our story are doing at the present time, at this particular moment. We are ready to gratify him.

Anna Sergeyevna recently married, not for love but by conviction, one of Russia's future public men, a very clever lawyer of sound common sense, firm will and remarkable rhetoric—a man still young, good-natured and cold as ice.

They get on extremely well together, and may eventually come to know happiness, perhaps love—who can tell? The Princess X— died, and was forgotten on the very day of her death. The Kirsanovs, father and son, have settled down at Maryino. Things are beginning to look up with them. Arkady has become a keen farmer, and the farm is yielding a fairly large income. Nikolai Petrovich has become a *mirovoi posrednik** and works with might and main; he is constantly touring his district, and making long speeches (he nurtures a belief that the muzhiks should be "made to listen to reason," meaning reduced to a state of stupefaction by constantly drumming into them one and the same thing) though, frankly speaking, he does not quite satisfy either the educated nobility who hold forth turgidly or mournfully, as the case may be, on *emancipation* (with a nasal pronunciation) or the uneducated nobility who badly curse "that damned *'muncipation.*" He is too mild for either. Katerina Sergeyevna has given birth to a son Nikolai, and Mitya is already spry of foot and active of tongue. Fenichka—Fedosya Nikolayevna— adores nobody so much, after her husband and Mitya, as her daughter-in-law, and when the latter sits down to play the piano, she could listen to her all day long. In passing, a word about Pyotr. He has become utterly benumbed with stupidity and self-importance, and has refined his pronunciation to the point of unintelligibility. He has married, too, and received an appreciable dowry with his bride, the daughter of an urban market gardener who had turned down two good suitors be- cause they possessed no watches, whereas Pyotr had a watch and a pair of patent leather shoes besides.

On the Brühl Terrace in Dresden, between two and four in the afternoon, the fashionable promenade hour, you may meet a man of about fifty, quite grey and to all appearances suffering from gout, but still handsome, elegantly dressed, and with that peculiar grace that is acquired only through long contact with the higher circles of society. This is Pavel Petrovich. He left Moscow to go abroad for the sake of his

* Arbiter of the peace, or arbitrator, a post introduced in Russia after the emancipation of the peasantry for settling differences between peasants and landlord.—*Tr.*

health and took up his abode in Dresden, where he associates for the most part with Englishmen and Russian visitors. With the Englishmen he bears himself simply, almost modestly, but with a sense of dignity. They find him somewhat boring, but respect in him the *perfect gentleman*. With the Russians he is more casual, gives rein to his spleen, cracks jokes at his own expense and theirs, but it is all done with a charming manner of inoffensive insouciance. He holds Pan-Slavist views, which, as everyone knows, are considered *très distingué* in high society. He reads nothing Russian, but he has on his desk a silver ashtray in the shape of a muzhik's bast sandal. He is much run after by our tourists. Matvei Ilyich Kolyazin, who is *in the temporary opposition*, paid a majestic call on him on his way to the Bohemian waters. The natives for their part, of whom he sees very little, stand in almost reverent awe of him. Nobody can book a ticket for the court choir or the theatre as easily and quickly as *der Herr Baron von Kirsanoff*. He still tries, to the best of his ability, to do good; he still makes a slight stir—wasn't he once a society lion?—but life to him is a burden, a heavier burden than he himself suspects. One need only glance at him in the Russian church, where he stands apart, leaning motionless against the wall, lost long in thought, in tight-lipped bitter silence; suddenly he collects himself and begins to make the sign of the cross with an almost imperceptible motion of his hand.

Kukshina, too, is living abroad. She is now in Heidelberg, and is no longer studying natural science, but architecture, in which she claims to have discovered new laws. She still hobnobs with the students, especially with young Russian physicists and chemists, of whom Heidelberg is full, and who astonish the naïve German professors first by their very sober view of things, as well as by their utter inertness and sheer laziness. With two or three such chemists, who are unable to distinguish oxygen from nitrogen, but are chock-full of negation and self-respect, and with the great Yelisevich, Sitnikov, also aspiring to greatness, whiles away the tedious hours in St. Petersburg, where, he assures us, he is carrying on Bazarov's "cause." Rumor has it that he recently received a thrashing, but he paid it back: in a mean little paragraph squeezed into a mean little journal he insinuated that his assailant was a coward. He calls that irony. His father bullies him as of old, and his wife considers him a ninny . . . and a man of letters.

There is a small country graveyard in a remote corner of Russia. Like nearly all our graveyards, it presents a sorry sight. The ditches around it are covered with a rank overgrowth; the drab wooden crosses have pitched forward and are rotting under their once painted roofs; the tombstones have all shifted, as though someone were pushing them from below; two or three starveling trees hardly afford a meager shade; sheep wander freely over the graves. But there is one grave that no man touches and no beast tramples. Only birds alight thereon and sing there at dawn. It is surrounded by an iron railing, and two fir trees have been planted at each end. In this grave lies Yevgeny Bazarov. Here, from the nearby village, often comes a decrepit old couple—husband and wife. Supporting each other, they plod on with weary footsteps. They come to the enclosure, fall down upon their knees and cry long and bitterly, and long do they gaze at the mute tombstone under which their son lies. They exchange a brief word, dust the stone and set straight a branch of a fir tree, then pray once more and are unable to tear themselves away from this spot, where they seem to be nearer to their son and to the memories of him. . . . Can it be that their prayers and their tears are fruitless? Can it be that love, sacred devoted love, is not all powerful? Nay! However passionate, however sinning and rebellious the heart that lies buried in the grave, the flowers that grow on it gaze at you serenely with their innocent eyes. It is not of eternal peace alone they speak to us, of that great peace of "impassive" nature; they speak to us, too, of eternal reconciliation and of the life everlasting. . . .

ABOUT THE EDITOR:

Neal Burroughs, Russian teacher, translator and adapter is an American, born in 1921 in New York City. His mother, on securing a position as English language editor and radio broadcaster in Moscow, U.S.S.R., took her young son, then aged seven, with her. Mr. Burroughs spent his childhood in suburban Moscow boarding schools where he pursued his elementary and junior high school education. He matriculated at Moscow University in 1941. The war came that year and young Burroughs, though he volunteered for service in the army, was instructed to continue with his education. When the University, as a precautionary measure, was moved to Ashkhabad in the Turkmenian S.S.R. and then to Sverdlovsk, beyond the Urals, the American student went along. The University returned to the capital in 1943 still listing Burroughs among its undergraduates. He returned to his native United States in 1946.

For the last several years Neal Burroughs has been busy teaching and translating from the Russian. He was consultant on the Russian sources to Mildred Stock, who wrote "Ira Aldridge, The Negro Tragedian" (Macmillan). He evaluated the stories in Mikhail Sholokov's "Tales of the Don" (Knopf).